Praise for
Real Wifeys: On the Grind

"Marking her solo debut with this new series launch, Mink . . . gives Kaeyla a snappy and profane voice laced with sarcasm. She's a charismatic woman, both vulnerable and tough. Female readers will love her, but men may want to check their own woman's purse for Taser wires. Load your shelves with multiple copies."

—*Library Journal*

"A gritty new urban series with a down-and-dirty intensity that's heartbreaking."

—*Publishers Weekly*

"The story line has an interesting flow that demonstrates Meesha's natural literary flair as she captivates the reader within the realms of her spellbinding plots."

—Urban Reviews

"Main character Goldie from *Real Wifeys: On the Grind* is unforgettable, shocking, and filled with sassiness. But there's something to be learned from the notorious wifey. Bravo!"

—Cydney Rax, author of *Brothers & Wives*

"A never-a-dull-moment, real-life ride. Strap on your seat belt. Meesha Mink goes sexy and deep!"

—Pynk, bestselling author of *Sixty-Nine*

"*Real Wifeys: On the Grind* is a five-star page-turner that you will not want to put down. A must read, must recommend, and must review."

—Coast 2 Coast Readers

Praise for
Desperate Hoodwives

"A can't-miss new series."

—*Essence*

"Let's just say this sassy, sexy, streetwise story could kick some butt over on Wisteria Lane." (Listed as Required Reading)

—*New York Post*

"The authors hold back little in this cautionary tale dripping with sex, vice, and yearning."

—*Publishers Weekly*

"A wonderfully written story with colorful characters that will keep you flipping the pages—I loved it."

—K'wan, *Essence* bestselling author

"Move over Wisteria Lane. Drama and scandal have permanently moved to Bentley Manor. *Desperate Hoodwives* is a wonderfully written novel that is sassy, smart, and unadulterated!"

—Danielle Santiago, *Essence* bestselling author

"A sexy tale that will keep you gasping as you turn the pages . . ."

—Miasha, *Essence* bestselling author

Praise for
Shameless Hoodwives

"*Shameless Hoodwives* by Meesha Mink and De'Nesha Diamond is listed as one of the magazine's TOP 10 Summer Sizzlers!"

—*Essence*

REAL WIFEYS

Get Money

AN URBAN TALE

MEESHA MINK

A Touchstone Book
Published by Simon & Schuster
New York London Toronto Sydney New Delhi

Touchstone
A Division of Simon & Schuster, Inc.
1230 Avenue of the Americas
New York, NY 10020

First Touchstone trade paperback edition January 2012

TOUCHSTONE and colophon are registered trademarks of Simon & Schuster,
Inc.

For information about special discounts for bulk purchases,
please contact Simon & Schuster Special Sales at 1-866-506-1949 or
business@simonandschuster.com.

The Simon & Schuster Speakers Bureau can bring authors to your live event. For
more information or to book an event contact the Simon & Schuster Speakers
Bureau at 1-866-248-3049 or visit our website at www.simonspeakers.com.

Designed by Akasha Archer

Manufactured in the United States of America

10   9   8   7   6   5   4   3   2   1

Library of Congress Cataloging-in-Publication Data
Mink, Meesha.
    Real wifeys: get money: an urban tale / Meesha Mink.—1st Touchstone trade
paperback ed.
        p. cm.
    1. African American women—Fiction.   2. Inner cities—Fiction.   3. Newark
(N.J.)—Fiction.   I. Title.
    PS3552.R8945R37 2012
    813'.54—dc23   2011029109

ISBN 978-1-4516-4082-3
ISBN 978-1-4516-4083-0 (ebook)

For all the little ghetto girls who have dreams. Be it writing, singing, dancing, excelling at academics or athletics. Remember to . . . Believe. Achieve. Receive.

Wifey: (n.) a girlfriend, usually live-in, who does all the work of a wife without being legally married.

Prologue

*L*oyalty is *everything* to me.

I'm *that* chick. The one who is the good friend. The good listener. The one to have a friend's back. The type of woman to hold secrets. The one to fight for a friend. To drive the getaway car. To help hide the gun, the body, and provide an alibi. That's me.

But see, that ride-or-die mess doesn't get you anywhere but shocked as hell when you find out your friend ain't checking or repping for you the same way. That she ain't shit and will never be shit. That the whole time her phony-as-a-three-dollar-bill ass been hiding the knife that she would plunge in your back. In my back. I still couldn't believe that shit.

I made money for her.

I helped her get her grind together.

I recruited new chicks to dance for her.

I defended her when the other dancers talked shit behind her back.

I called that no-good, blonde-haired, mixed-breed bitch a friend.

But no more. No *mas*. Fuck that.

I hated that bitch with a passion. I hated everything about her, from the way she looked to the way she moved. I hated that she walked this earth. I hated that she *thought* she was the best thing God ever created—on some real conceited-type shit—but she's absolutely mistaken. See, after her, God made me. And I'm a bad bitch too. A beautiful, curvy, dark-skinned chick who refused to let a redbone make me feel less than. Fuck *that*.

And if it's the last thing I do on this earth, I'm going to make her pay. She will have a mirror moment when she asks her tri-fling self: "Why did I fuck a good friend over? Why did I do that shit?" She's going to regret the day she stabbed me in the back by spreading her legs to my man. I hope the dick was worth it to her, because it just brought her a fucking enemy.

And I know to *really* get at her, I have to be about this paper. I need to get this money. I'll give it to the bitch. She's making that money on some real rags-to-riches shit. I don't have a choice but to get where she's at. See, I learned in college that water seeks its own level, and I know to reach where she at—to really get at her the way I want—I have to step it up.

I can't rely on *his* money, *his* fame, *his* nothing. Not no more. I have to get my own. It's time to get money and then get my revenge. I got plenty of time to get straight. See, revenge is best served up cold, and that bitch will never see me coming.

This. Is. War.

Ready

Three Months Earlier

From the moment I laid eyes on Make$ at Club Infinity that night, something about that dude just drew me in. He was a Newark, New Jersey–based rapper on the rise whose first album had went gold on the wings of his platinum-selling hit single "Get Like Me." But what got me wasn't just his celebrity, or the fact that I recognized him from his video in mad rotation on MTV and BET, or his hit record, or being on the cover of magazines, or even his spot posted up in the VIP section of the club that night. Not even the fact that he sent one of his security guards to invite me past the velvet rope to take a spot next to him. I'm not gone lie and say I didn't feel extra special with all those disappointed chicks eyeing and vying to be me in that moment. But even that wasn't what *drew* me in to him. It was a vibe or some shit between us when he took off those shades and looked me in my eyes. I was so gone. Instantly. Right in the club like in that old Usher song. For me, it felt like love at first sight in the club.

Even though I was a stripper when we met, I wasn't a ho—far from it. But when he asked me to leave with him—to be with him—it made me think he felt that craziness between us too. And I went. I took that nigga's hand, forgetting about my girls Goldie and Missy that I came to the club with, forgetting that I didn't know him or anyone in his huge entourage, forgetting that what I thought was taking a chance on love might've been taking a chance on my safety. He asked. I accepted. My first rapper. My first one-night stand. And to me, my first real shot at love.

That was seven months ago and *everything* about that nigga had me straight fucked up from the jump. All the emotions I had wrapped up in him—emotions I thought would fade—was stronger than ever. I was in love. Deeply. Just twenty-four and wide open.

But . . .

That meant all the power was in his hands. Thing was, I straight up didn't know if all the love I gave was equal to the love I was getting from him. There were plenty of times that shit seemed unbalanced as hell. Unfair. Fucked up. See, being the one in a relationship to love the most means you're the one to get hurt the most too.

A pang crossed my chest that burned with the fire of a bullet's graze as I watched everything and nothing outside the window of Fornos of Spain restaurant down in the neck on Ferry Street in Newark.

"Luscious . . . Luscious?"

I shifted my jet-black eyes from looking out at the crowded streets to the face of my friend—and ex-boss—Kaeyla Dennis. "Huh?" I said, thinking as always that her nickname of Goldie suited her, with her honey complexion and eyes combined with shoulder-length hair highlighted with natural blond streaks that screamed her ass was only half-black.

Goldie arched a brow as she eyed me. "What the hell you braining on?" she asked, her East Coast accent even heavier than mine.

My years at Rutgers University—before I dropped out—had cleaned my shit up just a little bit.

"I was just wondering what Make$'s ass was up to on that road," I admitted, picking up my wine goblet to take a sip and feeling the many layers of my lip gloss damn near glue my bottom lip to the glass.

Goldie shook her head, her glossy hair pulled back into a tight asymmetrical reverse French braid that I was already planning to copy. She was the type of chick that made any woman in her company want to elevate their game because she stayed on point. What woman would want to look like a lame-ass loser, like she was doing them a favor even being in their company?

"If you had stayed on top of your own grind and made your own fuckin' money, you wouldn't have time to try and stay on top of some dude out there livin' life while you sittin' home waitin' on him," Goldie said, before picking up her vibrating BlackBerry.

Goldie stayed handling her B.I.

Truth be told, I looked up to the bossy bitch. She wasn't playing about her grind. I'd heard her story about that old married man embarrassing her in front of his wife and everybody living in King Court projects when his ass got caught with Goldie. She went from wifey with a dream of marriage to falling the fuck off. *Hard.*

But she crawled back on her feet. She went from being a waitress at a twenty-four-hour diner to stripping at Club Naughty on Hawthorne Avenue. From my janky-ass spot as a daytime stripper, I saw her rise to being the headliner of the entire cub. And when she realized Slick Rick, the owner—and her lover—wasn't cutting her in on a big enough slice of the profits she kicked his ass—big donkey dick and all—to the curb and opened her own strip club in her little-ass two-bedroom apartment.

Chick was bold as hell for that shit.

I guess me and Missy was shot the fuck out too since we were the first two strippers to become "Goldie's Girls." Between doing them weekend shows in her apartment and then Goldie hiring us out for private shows and parties and shit, the three of us all made serious money.

I can't front: Goldie taught me shit to make *sure* we made money. Hell, she schooled all of us on taking our shows beyond straight tits-and-ass shakes. We put on shows. Created fantasies. Fucked niggas' heads up. Made them better lovers to their women because they was dreaming about us the whole time.

Goldie was running the pole game in the tristate area and the streets knew it.

That's why our asses got robbed at gunpoint last month during one of our shows. And to really make shit fucked up, besides robbing everybody in the apartment, they pulled a *Let's Do it Again* move and made us all strip before they hauled ass.

That was one of the craziest nights of my life . . . and the last time I stripped. Missy was still doing private shows for Goldie.

Me? I was off the pole. Once me and Make$ got serious he put pressure on me to quit stripping. I tried like hell to sneak and do it, but no haps. He started accusing me of messing around on him on them nights I told him I left but I really snuck and went right to shake all my tits and ass in men's faces. I knew I had to dead that shit . . . especially when word hit the street about the robbery.

Besides, I got tired of lying to him about it, and Goldie got tired of me missing shows. It was him or the pole. So I chose my man over my money.

"So you wouldn't dead that shit for a man willing to take care of you and give you a better life?" I asked, feeling a little defensive because Goldie's opinion really mattered to me. Even after I stopped working for her we remained friends.

Goldie leaned back in her chair as she laughed a little—kinda sarcastic and shit. "I been there and it got me nowhere but with my ass wet and my face cracked when his wife made him choose," she said. "Choosing a man would have me still getting fucked *and* fucked over by Rick. That's nothing."

The waitress came and refilled our glasses. I took that moment to send Make$ a text:

LOVE U. HAVE A GOOD SHOW. XOXOXO

Goldie rolled her eyes as she watched me. "That nigga got

you sprung," she teased, smiling even though her eyes were filled with pity for me.

I hated when Make$ was touring. I wasn't crazy. My man was in the middle of groupie central. Straight pussy patrol. But being onstage was how he made his money—shit, *our* money—and I didn't want to knock his hustle. Still, all the wondering about just what his ass was up to when he was out of my sight had me feeling like I was losing my mind sometimes.

I sat my BlackBerry on the table next to the python Gucci hobo Make$ surprised me with just last week. It was just material shit and I'd take one hundred percent of his heart over all the shit he laced me with.

Not that being the wifey of a hip-hop star didn't mean enjoying a nice shopping spree or being able to open my walk-in closet and pick out clothes that would make most chicks salivate. But there's shit in the world more important than the latest red-bottom heels or designer labels. Still, it was a nice surprise. To me it was more about the gesture than the actual gift. It could've been a single rose and I would've smelled it every day and tried to water it and cut the stem to give it as much life as I could. And even when it died, I would press the rose in my memory book and keep it for the rest of my life.

Like I said, I loved that ninja.

Bzzz . . . Bzzz . . . Bzzz . . .

I looked down at my vibrating BlackBerry. I couldn't lie. I felt mad disappointed that it wasn't my man, my heart, my love, Make$, calling.

Not really in the mood to yap it up with my cousin Eve, I let the phone go to voice mail. That chick was all about her three G's: gambling, gossiping, and going shopping. I was enjoying my wine-and-dine with Goldie, and even if I wasn't, sitting on the phone talking about how much she won at bingo, cute clothes, or rumors about this one and that one was irrelevant to me.

Not like my heart.

That was mad important.

"So there's no one you would risk it all for?" I asked.

Goldie pushed back her chair and crossed her legs in the distressed denims she wore with a pair of navy suede heels that perfectly matched the color of the jean. I didn't need to see the bottoms to know they were red-lacquered. "Honestly, I was really feelin' this dude I was in business with, a dude named Has. Fine motherfucka. Dreads. Tall. Dark. Swagger. Nigga was on ten for real. *But* . . . I'm glad I followed my head and not my clit, because a few months later that nigga got caught up in a Fed raid and I'm not the prison-wifey type, you know? Writing letters, putting pussy on lock, sending care packages, and putting my hard-earned money on his books and shit? Nah, I'll pass."

She picked up her cell phone and scrolled through it with her thumb before she pushed the BlackBerry across the table at me. I turned it around and looked down at the photo of a dude with long, neat and slender dreads. The picture wasn't that clear, but there was no denying that this tall man posted up outside a corner store was hella fine. I pushed the BlackBerry back at her.

"It's blurry 'cause I snuck and took a picture of him when he wasn't looking and he moved," she said, looking down at the picture. The look she made, twisting up her mouth and waving her hand to fan herself, made me laugh.

"But . . . I still think about what if," she admitted, picking up the billfold our waitress sat on the table. "I just know that nigga can do a serious fuckdown. He walk like he gotta keep his thighs open 'cause his dick swinging. You know? One of them dangerous dicks."

Their waitress smiled as she began to clear our plates.

Goldie winked up at her as she slid a folded fifty-dollar bill into the woman's lean hand. "That's your tip. I don't care what they say—you don't split your shit," she said with a "so there" look.

I gathered up my bag, keys, and BlackBerry as the waitress

thanked Goldie. She always tipped heavy—probably remembering her days on her feet at Dino's.

"Did Make$ talk to you about Goldie's Girls dancing for him?" Goldie asked, sliding on a pair of oversize shades as we left the restaurant.

My steps faltered and I flashed back to my birthday party last month. I'd walked outside to find Goldie and Make$ talking alone. That shit had fucked with my head and had me feeling some kind of way for a sec, like "What's up with *this* shit?" I couldn't help it: Goldie was the type of chick you imagined every man wanted.

I questioned Make$ later that night but he got me straight that a redbone, half-breed chick like Goldie wasn't his type. He liked that deep chocolate he found all over me. And that night I fucked and sucked him extra hard just in case he forgot the quality of pussy he had at home.

"When did that go down?" I asked as we strutted in our stilettos to our cars. A spring breeze pressed our clothes against our bodies and these two white guys—probably Portuguese— took in the free show.

We both deactivated our alarms. *Boo-doop.* Hers a convertible cherry-red Lexus, and I was whipping Make$'s shiny black Jaguar XF while he was out of town.

Goldie tossed her oversize clutch onto the passenger seat before looking at me over her shoulder, her shades still in place and shielding her eyes. "His management heard about the shows and didn't even realize that me and Make$ met through you," she said with ease. "He made an offer and the money was too good to turn down. Fuck that."

I nodded like I understood even though my mind was racing as I opened the door to the Jag. "Good thing I quit working for you, huh?" I said. "I don't think Make$ want his girl up onstage like that."

Goldie shrugged. "You good?" she asked, still looking at me.

I knew damn well she wasn't checking if I was full from my meal of garlic shrimp and yellow rice. Before I could answer her truthfully I had to do a little gut check for myself. Did I want my friends to dance for my man? Dancing onstage wasn't stripping but I knew damn well Make$'s manager, Chill Will, wasn't hiring Goldie and the crew because they could dougie they ass off.

I had to remember that Goldie didn't want Make$. I couldn't even see them together, plus she could be my eyes and have my back to make sure my man wasn't on a straight pussy mission when he was away. "I'm real good," I assured her, feeling my worries drift away.

Goldie nodded before she slid into her Lexus and drove away with a brief toot of her horn.

It wasn't until I was behind the wheel of the Jag sitting at one of the million lights along the stretch of the Ironbound section that it hit me. Make$ didn't even bother to ask me if I wanted my friends dancing for him or to answer my text. . . .

A horn blared behind me and I cut my eyes to the rearview mirror to see some big dude in an SUV behind me. I shifted my eyes back ahead to the green traffic light before I pulled off, deciding he wasn't worth me even flipping his swollen-neck ass the bird.

Besides, wasn't no need taking my mess and stress out on some nondescript Negro. Wasn't his fault that there was anything I'd rather do than drive to our two-bedroom apartment in the Twelve50 luxury apartments. Wasn't his fault that there wasn't shit waiting for me but another lonely-ass night.

The towering streetlights lining the downtown Newark street flickered on as the sun faded. The sidewalks were filled with people finishing up their shopping and rushing to their cars or waiting at corner bus stops for whatever bus got them closer to home. Newark was a smaller version of New York with just as big a heart.

As I drove the Jag into the parking garage next door to the

regal-looking high-rise we called home, I picked up my Black-
Berry and called Make$'s phone again, knowing even as I dialed
his number that I was wasting my time.

"I'm somewhere making money. No time to talk. Get at me."

"Terrence, this Luscious," I began, meaning to use his given
name to make sure he knew I was testy as hell as I climbed out
of the car with my bag in my hand and popped the trunk. I
grabbed the glossy shopping bags from my mini shopping spree
at my favorite boutique in Montclair. Soon the five-inch heels of
my sandals clicked against the hard concrete as I left the parking
structure.

I made my way into the lofty apartment building with the
phone pressed to my face with the same urgency I felt to hear
from him. "Yo, I haven't talked to you all day. This shit is damn
bananas. You know? I can see not answering when you practicing or performing, but that shit is not all day, Terrence, so why
you playing? Why you keep acting fucked up and shady when
you touring—"

As I noticed the concierge stare openly in my face from his
spot behind a large wooden station in the middle of the grand
lobby, I bit back the rest of my words and gave him a polite
smile. The Twelve50 was a long way from the apartments in the
other wards across the city—in more than just distance. It was a
stylish building for young up-and-coming professionals in downtown Newark. Our neighbors were young attorneys, business-
men, and local politicians. I knew I couldn't put my nigger on in
front of these bougie folks. I pressed a glossy thumbnail to the
PDA to end the call. Hell with it. I was just parroting the other
twenty messages I left since Goldie and I parted ways at the restaurant. I felt like a fiend chasing a fix.

Wishing I was there. Feeling out of control. Thinking all
kinds of crazy shit.

Truth be told, sometimes it felt like I was losing my mind
worrying about what he was up to. I loved that nigga. We was a

team out there. I had his back and there wasn't a damn thing I wouldn't—or hadn't—done for or to him. Nothing.

I just didn't know if he was holding me down with the same ferocity . . . or loyalty.

"Welcome home, Miss Jordan."

I pushed my sixteen-inch jet-black weave behind my ear as I nodded my head in greeting at the uniformed concierge and kept moving across the polished floors to the elevator lobby. It was hard to ignore the sophisticated beauty of the décor. Twelve50 wasn't shit like the Pavilion over on Martin Luther King Boulevard, where I had a shitty studio apartment that was smaller than Goldie's living room in the low-rise projects where we used to strip on the weekends.

The Twelve50 had a twenty-four-hour doorman and concierge service, a state-of-the-art health club with locker rooms and saunas, a six-lane bowling alley, an indoor basketball court, and an entertainment room complete with flat-screen televisions.

Not bad for Newark. Not bad at all.

Now I wasn't crazy. I knew the building wasn't touching the high life of those luxury apartments on New York's Upper East Side. Far from it. Our rent was twenty-five hundred, not twenty-five thousand. Still . . . I was happy to leave that studio apartment on MLK behind when we moved in two weeks ago.

As soon as I walked into our spacious apartment I immediately felt at home. The interior designer we hired took Make$'s need for dark leather and my love of soft neutrals to create a spot for us that was stylish and comfortable. I kicked off my heels and padded barefoot from the foyer. I stopped just long enough in the gourmet kitchen to set my hobo on the granite countertop and to pour a goblet of premium moscato before moving into the living room. The row of windows offered up views of the cityscape. Being on the thirty-first floor had us looking down at the city that raised us.

Humph, he moved me up like George did Weezie, but as

beautiful as our apartment was, the loneliness I felt? There wasn't a damn thing pretty about that.

I let out this pitiful-ass sigh into my glass, feeling sick and tired of my damn self.

Brrrnnnggg . . . Brrrnnnggg . . . Brrrnnnggg . . .

I took another sip of my wine and looked over my shoulder at the ringing cordless phone. Setting the goblet on the windowsill, I made my way across the hardwood floors to pick it up. It was the doorman.

"Yes."

"Uhm . . . Ms. Peaches and guests are here," he said.

I rolled my eyes heavenward. "Okay, thank you," I said, even as a fire fueled by irritation burned my stomach.

Peaches and them was Make$'s mother and two sisters. *All* of them bitches had issues that kept them hopping on my last damn nerve. Lonely as I was, them hood hos was company I could do without.

"Shit," I swore, fighting the urge to block the front door with our sectional.

Instead I rushed around the apartment and grabbed up my purse and any random bills or personal items we had lying around, including Make$'s stash of weed, coke, and pills from the huge wooden box on the oversize ottoman in the center of the living room. As far as I knew, Peaches smoked weed and got fucked up on the regular, but our apartment was not going to be her cop spot. I carried everything into our bedroom and set it on the middle of the bed, not taking time to notice the plush linen and décor—more of the stylish work of our designer out of Maplewood.

I locked the door—and double-checked that it was a hundred percent secured—before I headed back to the living room just as someone banged on the door like they was the police enforcing a damn search warrant.

"You better not be in there fucking some other dude in my

son's crib," Peaches yelled through the door before going at it with her fist again as she laughed like the straight-up fool she was.

Bam-bam-bam.

She probably was scaring the hell out my neighbors on the floor. They already side-eyed me and Make$ like we were not be trusted.

"Dumb bitch," I muttered under my breath before I put on a big fake-ass grin and opened the door with my keys still in my hand.

My eyes widened at the sight of Make$'s mother. It was amazing that after seven months this crazy bitch could still shock me with her ways. "What's up, Peaches?" I said, fighting hard not to stare at her petite four-foot frame in skintight jeans and a flashy gold strapless bra underneath a black sheer tank with thigh-high suede boots that it was entirely too hot for.

"Whaddup," she said, heading past me and straight for the kitchen.

Looking like a fucking dancehall reject or some shit. There was many things Peaches' ass was wrong for—like having Make$ when she was just thirteen—but the top two errors was her thinking she had style and class. Coming from me—a college dropout, ex-stripper, without job the first—that was saying just how low the chick could go.

His twenty-year-old twin sisters, Heaven and Earth, strolled in next, smelling of too much knock-off perfume and dressed from head to toe in matching Baby Phat like their ass owned stock in the company. One was on her cell phone, motioning with her neck and finger like the bitch was having a seizure.

"Girl, I told him if he wanted me to do *that* to him and for me to let him do *that* to me then it was going to take more than a trip to Dr. Jays and some appetizers from Applebee's! What-what?" she said, before turning to high-five her twin like she just gave an uplifting speech instead of revealing she was a trick. And a cheap trick at that.

I sighed on the inside as I pushed the door closed, wishing they was on the other side. This bullshit right here could turn into an all-night affair of me entertaining they ass—at my cost. In their eyes this was Make$'s house, and if they felt like chilling, enjoying the 3-D flat-screen and all the other luxuries, then in the words of Sheree from *Real Housewives of Atlanta*: "Who gone check them, boo?"

I eyed them already kicking off they rubber-bottomed, pleather shoes. "What y'all doing on this side of town—"

The door wouldn't close and I turned with a frown. But that shit dropped from my face quick as hell at the sight of Make$ standing there with a big grin on his thin face, his usual toothpick in the corner of his mouth. My eyes took this nigga—*my* nigga—all in as I smiled like a cat getting stroked.

He was about thirty shades lighter than me—all light-bright fine and shit—but his tat addiction had him covered all on his neck, arms, and chest. He was just my height and slender, and I loved to see him naked and grinding above all my thickness.

As I stepped into his arms, removed his shades, and kissed him like I hadn't seen his little sexy ass in months instead of days, I thoroughly blocked out the sight of his entourage piled up in the hallway behind him or his mother clapping and carrying on about tricking me. I didn't give a fuck about none of that or none of them as I gently sucked his tongue into my mouth, tasting his liquor, weed, and cigarettes.

My man was home and it was water for my thirst.

His hands came down to grab my thighs before moving up under my skirt to grab my ass in the silk thong I wore. I felt his dick get hard against my stomach as my clit tingled.

"Put her dress down, I don't need to see all that black ass," Peaches said with attitude from behind us.

"Fuck them," he whispered into my mouth, reaching down to grab my hand. "Come give me my pussy."

I licked my lips and pressed my face against his shoulder as he led me to our bedroom. It had been like this since our first night. When it was on, it didn't matter where, and we didn't give a fuck about nobody. Fuck it, enjoy the show, you know?

"Y'all so fucking nasty," Peaches called behind us, just seconds before the front door shut and the sounds of more voices and loud music suddenly filled the air.

Bump her. I was about to fuck the hell out of her son.

Make$ pressed my back against the closed door and tore the top of my dress. He lifted up his diamond pendant of the world and unscrewed it to dust my nipples with the cocaine hidden inside of it. I didn't give a fuck that he just ruined a four-hundred-dollar dress. I felt a thrill as my nipples went numb from the powder. He circled one nipple with his tongue before sucking it between his moist lips. My pussy just got wetter. The nigga's tongue game was *bananas* and better than his dick game. He sucked. I fucked. We balanced each other to make sure our ish wasn't bullshit. You know?

"Yes. Yes," I moaned, arching my back as I pressed my hands to the back of his head as he snorted more of the coke off my chest.

"Huh, baby. Get on this shit with me," Make$ said, the coke already making his tongue sound thick in his mouth.

I opened my eyes to look at him as he sucked the tip of his finger and then dipped it inside the world like it was a mini bowl of Fun Dip or some shit. He pressed the coated finger to my mouth.

I didn't like him getting high, and when he wasn't on that powder I always talked to him about slowing down. But when he offered me some of his world I took it. He said getting high together while we fucked gave him something to look forward to if he was going to stop doing it all together.

"I love the hell out of you, Make$," I whispered to him before I unrolled my tongue and licked the coke from his finger. I made sure not to hit a lot of it. I wasn't trying to get hooked, and the shit just made me feel nervous. I didn't like it and I damn sure didn't plan to love it.

Make$ reached one hand down behind me and turned the knob. He lifted his head and looked at me. "It's locked," he said with a little smirk of his lips.

"You know how your mama go," I said, looking at him through lids heavy with wanting his dick inside of me.

He laughed and nodded. "Good looking out, baby," he said, before kissing my lips again.

I turned in the small space between his body and the door, wiggling my ass against his hard dick as I tried to make room to unlock the door.

"Man, fuck it," he said, his lips pressed against my shoulder.

The sound of his belt and pants dropping soon filled the air along with the noise of his crew partying it up in our living room. He brought one hand around to finger my wet and swollen clit in circles that made me cry out against the door. He backed away from me. I looked over my shoulder as he fell back against the wall of the hallway, his dick hard and hanging from his body. "Back that ass up on this dick, girl," Make$ said, closing the diamond pendant.

"Sit on the floor," I told him, pulling off my thong and hitching my torn dress up around my hips. "I wanna ride that dick, baby."

Make$ dropped to the floor and I squatted to ease my pussy down onto his dick. He sucked away at my exposed titties as I worked my hips, bringing my clit against the base of his dick. His shit wasn't itty-bitty but it wasn't nowhere near an eleven-inch beast. But we were straight. Like I said. He sucked. I fucked. I always came faster when I got on top.

"You know I had to come home and celebrate with my wifey," Make$ said, leaning his head back against the wall.

Needing the feel of his hot mouth and tongue on my nipples to push me over the edge to a nut, I guided his mouth right back to my jiggling breasts as I enjoyed the feel of my clit being stroked.

"Celebrate what?" I finally asked, panting for breath as I felt the pressure building deep in my pussy.

"We booked for shows all summer long and I got a meeting with Platinum Records in the morning," he said, before grabbing my breasts and licking away at both nipples at once.

I fucked him harder even as disappointment nipped at me.

Not even free-falling through a high intensified by an explosive nut could erase that a major deal moving him over to Platinum Records meant him going back into the studio to work on his sophomore release. More money. More fame. More lonely nights . . . for me.

Two Months Later

I felt like a celebrity my damn self as I walked inside Club Infinity in New York with my cousin Eve and our friend Michel right behind me. The three of us were looking, smelling, and feeling good. Eve and Michel were my friends and my distractions when Make$ was away. And most nights that we went out, we headed straight for Club Infinity, one of the hottest spots on the East Coast. Celebs rolled through like nothing. The biggest names hosted parties.

The line was damn near around the corner, but when we walked straight up to the door it was on my own steam and not because my cousin Mali was working security, like the first time I brought Missy and Goldie there. Being the wifey of Make$ had its privileges, and we were led straight to a VIP booth upstairs, with the neon lights flashing against our bodies.

Once we was set up with drinks, we settled back against the leather booth circling the area. It was hard not to have a ball at Club Infinity. I picked up the flute of champagne Michel handed me before I stood up on my spiked peep-toe platforms and walked over to the glass wall surrounding our VIP area. I moved my hips to the bass-driven music as I looked down at the crowd below us. Nothing but a good time. A damn good time.

I wished Make$ was there with me and not in Miami doing yet another show. He hadn't lied—the amount of shows he did was increasing. His summer was fully booked, and I overheard him and his manager saying how adding Goldie and the girls to the shows was the reason. I forced myself not to think about the ow they were putting on. I'd never been to one of the shows, and I made sure not to watch any videos of them on the Internet. I had enough of my own tits and ass to see.

I knew how some of the bitches working with Goldie rolled. Coko and Ming was two freaky lesbo bitches who stayed fucked up and fucking—especially for some money. Goldie didn't know about they side-hustle but I did. They used to laugh about double-teaming some dude in bed and doing whatever it took to make him hit high notes like a woman.

I hated that I pictured them and Make$ fucking.

I felt anger and jealousy eat me up inside at the thought of that bullshit. I quizzed Make$ nonstop about his time on the road but what was he gonna say, "Yeah, I smash on the regular out on tour?" Please. It was bad enough when I had to worry about groupies and shit, but now my man *took* pussy with him on the road. He had plenty of money to burn, and that was right up Coko and Ming's freaky alley. And to top all that drama? I hated that Goldie and them got to see my man perform. She got to travel with him and be up on the stage with him in those bright lights.

Me? My ass been ordered to stay behind. Stay home. Hold him down while he worked and have the pussy ready when he got home to play.

I stayed on Make$'s ass to catch him slipping on me with some other bitch. And I did whatever I had to. Snooping. Sniffing. Questioning. Fucking and sucking. Whatever I thought it took to not feel that crazy panic at the thought of him fucking around on me. Falling in love with another bitch. Leaving me.

I closed my eyes and took a deep swallow of the champagne.

My only consolation? Goldie was my eyes and ears on that motherfucka. So far so good.

"Where ya man at now, Luscious?"

I looked over at my cousin Eve as she walked up to stand beside me, looking tall and thin and cute with her short jet-black pixie cut. Her pink strapless dress was short and her gold heels were high.

"Miami," I told her, leaning over to say it into her ear over the blaring music.

She raised a brow in question. "Ain't no way I could have my man touring and whoring while I sit at home. Fuck that shit."

I gave her a wink and a smile that everything was cool. Nothing but a motherfucking lie.

Eve was my cousin on my mother's side, but she wasn't the type of chick to share your business with. It wasn't that she didn't have my back; she just was immature as hell. We was the same age physically but definitely not mentally. Cool as we were, the chick couldn't hold water, so I fed her with a long spoon and kept her from stirring too deep in my shit with her Maury-like dramatics. She was cool to party with but a definite no-go on anything serious.

Humph. Eve always had some bum-beat niggas around her. She didn't believe in boyfriends and kept plenty of "friends." I never dipped and told her what to do with her life—even when she caught one of her "friends" sucking a dude's dick.

Because I didn't tell her what to do with her heart and pussy . . . she wasn't going to tell me what to do with mine.

Michel stepped up on the other side of me in a black sequin romper and smelling heavily of some flowery perfume that I knew was sprayed everywhere. Wide-set decorated smoky eyes that any tanned Jersey shore chick would die for were locked on topless dancers doing sultry acrobatics from metal poles suspended from the ceilings.

"Those fake titties defying gravity like a motherfucker," I said, cutting my eyes up to Michel, who towered over my five-foot-seven-inch frame with damn near four more inches.

"Yes, honey, and the show is even making me want to let my dick swing," *he* said, his voice soft and effeminate—but Michel, aka Michael, was all man. He took drag to a whole 'nother level.

We'd been friends since I moved into my first apartment, and he was the only person I let do my hair and makeup. Bootleg unlicensed stylist or not, Michel was self-taught *and* the shit . . . and he knew it.

We all laughed as he squatted his long and shapely legs as if his dick would miraculously slip from the tape securing it in the crack of his ass and make a shadow on the floor. Apart from his family and his lovers, we were the only ones who knew he wasn't one hundred percent woman. He tucked his dick. That's *his* business.

Michel was the perfect tranny for those brothas wanting to enjoy the tricks and treats of a man but wanting their lover deep undercover as a woman. He would've stumped the whole Maury audience on one of those "Man or Woman" shows. And the bitch had a gaydar that was out of this world.

He already assured me that Make$ was straight. *Yes, I asked.*

Michel was also good for a teaching a bitch how to suck a dick proper. Fuck that. Who knew a dick better than a man?

Thanks to him and the afternoon we spent practicing with a dildo, I could make a nigga nut in a minute or less—one of the reasons I had Make$'s head gone from my brain game that first night. *Swallow it. Gargle it. Ow!*

"Yo, Luscious, ain't that your mother-in-law?" Eve asked, pointing over the rail toward the bar.

I looked down where she pointed and talk about being disappointed. I felt that shit all in my guts. Seeing Peaches in her five shades of red fucked my night up. Seeing the bartender sit a bottle of Patrón in front of her *really* wrecked my shit. One, Peaches couldn't handle her liquor and two, I knew that shit went right on Make$'s tab . . . and the night was still early.

"Dayuuum. I see that bitch more than I see my own parents," I said, drawing it out as I stomped my foot. No, I didn't give a damn how childish that was.

Michel and Eve laughed at the expression on my face.

Wasn't a damn thing funny about a future mother-in-law who was just fifteen years older than me but acted twenty years immature.

I just thanked God Peaches and her crew didn't spot me in the club, because she would've lamped in VIP with us all night and invited them pigeons flocking behind her. Nothing.

"I guess the chick with her think she Nicki Minaj with that ratty-ass pink and blonde hairdo?" Eve asked.

Michel's brow lifted. "Got that quick weave looking like a lost weave," he said, lifting a hand to smooth his own shoulder-length auburn lace-front wig.

I couldn't do or say shit *but* laugh.

Deciding to ignore Peaches, I turned and grabbed the bottle from the bucket of ice to refill our glasses. And we had a ball . . . especially when "Moment for Life" came on. It had dropped more than a year ago but that was my theme song in my head.

"I wish that I could have this moment for life . . . " we sang together, dancing around the VIP area.

As I closed my eyes, pressed one hand to my chest and raised the other to the ceiling, I thought about making it through my struggles . . .

My parents cutting me off when I dropped out of college . . .

Stripping to survive and pay my bills . . .

Not stripping good enough to get off that dead-ass day shift . . .

Struggling to afford to pay the rent on my shitty apartment . . .

Eating Oodles of Noodles and Dollar Store canned goods damn near three times a day . . . every *motherfucking* day . . .

Wearing the same jeans three times a week with different cheap-ass shirts because I put paying my bills before clothes shopping . . .

All the faces I done shook my ass in . . . all the sweaty hands on my body . . . all the funky breath in my face, and all the laps I grinded on . . .

The chance we took on our lives and our safety stripping in Goldie's apartment right up until the night we were robbed at gunpoint . . .

But all of that was behind me. I made it.

"I wish that I could have this moment for life . . ."

Now, at this moment in time in my life, things were so different . . . so much better . . . not everything but most things. I was happy for that. I said the lyrics harder and sang the chorus louder.

Things were a little better between my parents and me.

No more stripping.

A better apartment and a better lifestyle.

More clothes and shoes and things than I could ever dream about.

Money to burn . . . and with Make$'s career blowing up, that meant even more money to burn.

Being in love.

And then maybe marriage and babies. My own family.

Shit, my life was good. I was blessed. I was thankful for all the good and just praying for the end of the not-so-good.

"Oh shit, Luscious, look. Oh my God! *Look!*" Eve screamed, gripping my arm like she had claws.

I opened my eyes and looked where Eve pointed just in time to see Peaches get backhanded across the face by a heavy-set chick who looked like she was in less of a mood for Peaches' bullshit than me.

"Let us pray, Lord Jesus," Michel said, shaking his head. "This *ain't* looking good."

I knew some dumb shit would pop off.

I watched over the rim of my glass as the big girl yoked Peaches' little petite ass up by her throat and shook her like a rag doll. *That's gotta hurt.*

Nicki Façade tried to jump on Big Girl's back but just got shook off like a fly. Peaches' other friend didn't even fuck with it and disappeared into the crowd.

"She better sit her ass down before the last of them tracks get snatched," Michel said.

The shit was funny but I knew he was serious as hell . . . and so was the big girl.

"Luscious," Eve said, her tone all disapproving and shit.

"What?" I asked, making sure to sound extra blasé because I *really* didn't give a fuck.

There was a crowd starting to circle the drama.

Big Girl drew back her arm and landed her fist dead in Peaches' mouth. Blood squirted out like crazy while Peaches' little body was lifted off her feet as she fell back into the crowd. Everybody in the circle leaned back with nasty frowns on their faces.

I released a breath that was maxed out with aggravation. Like I said, I knew something was gonna pop off, and I should've hauled ass when Eve first pointed Peaches out to me. I pushed my flute into Eve's hand and stepped out of my shoes to kick over at her too. I was down the stairs and through the crowd in no time. I had to make myself ignore my pretty feet sticking to God knows what on the tiled floor. *Ugh!*

Much as Peaches pissed me off, I couldn't stand there and watch Make$'s mama get her ass beat—no matter how much she probably deserved it. Or how badly I wished it was me delivering the smackdown.

"Yo, Peaches, you all right?" I asked, squatting down beside where the crowd let her land on the floor. My stomach turned at the blood running down her chin.

"What the fuck you think?" she snapped before wiping her mouth with the back of her hand.

I barely heard her over the music. Peaches' scuffle had barely made a blip on the radar of Club Infinity. Except for those in the immediate area, the party was still going strong.

Suddenly the neon lights flashing across Peaches' face disappeared. The hairs on the back of my neck stood on end.

"I ain't scared of you, you Precious-looking bitch," Peaches yelled over my shoulder, bloody spit landing against my skin as I helped her to her feet.

"Oh, you want some more?" a deep voice that was more masculine than Michel's asked.

I felt like slapping Peaches my damn self. Instead I turned around and held my hands up. *This big bitch does look like Precious for real, though*, I thought, before I took a deep breath and swung, catching her off guard. Three quick punches. They landed between her eyes, sending her head back.

"Damn right, Luscious," Peaches yelled from behind me.

I straight blocked *her* the fuck out and dashed around that big bitch to kick the back of her leg hard as hell before she got her shit together. She dropped to her knees and I pushed against her back with both my hands to knock her ass down the rest of the way.

A big bitch like that, about two hundred and seventy pounds? Shit, I *had* to fight dirty. Fuck the dumb shit.

Peaches started doing the dougie just as the house lights came on and the music faded away. Somebody had dropped the dime to management about the fight . . . and my ass was glad. *Shee-it!!*

"Oh my God, she peed on herself," someone hollered.

I looked down at the floor and sure enough a puddle of pee spread across the floor from between the big girl's thighs.

My mouth fell open in shock as she jumped up to her feet and squared up in her own pee with her dukes up like she was really ready to straight whup my ass. *Oh shit!* My eyes got big as shit and I wished like hell I had Goldie's taser, because I would shoot her one to her neck and drop her.

I could tell she was embarrassed by the fists to her dome *and* wetting her damn self.

I saw my damn studded shoe flying through the air. My heart ached as that motherfucker missed her and landed in the puddle. I looked up and Eve shrugged apologetically with just one shoe under her arm.

Oh hell no. Who wanted a pissy Louboutin?

She swung. I ducked.

I can't even lie: I was glad when security came rushing over and got between us before she could really put in work on my ass.

I motioned to Michel and Eve that it was time to go as they "escorted" Precious, Peaches, and me right through the crowd and out the door to the street. Those waiting in line to get in was glad for the show. Hella embarrassing.

I couldn't do shit but shake my head as I stood in the street in my bare damn feet. I came out to party, have a little fun with my friends, and try not to fixate on what the fuck my man was doing. Getting lumped the fuck up because of some of his mama's shit wasn't in my plans at all.

"Damn, stripper Barbie, I ain't know you had it in you," Peaches said, lighting a blunt she pulled out her bra.

That's because God has kept me from fucking you up, that's why, I thought. "What was y'all fighting over?" I asked, glad to see Eve and Michel finally leave the club. I took my purse from her and reached inside for the little gel flats I usually put on after the club.

"That big bitch stepped on my toe and I told her Precious, Magilla Gorilla, Fat Albert, Al Roker, and Biggie-looking ass to get *off* my fucking toe!" Peaches jerked her thumb over her shoulder at the girl walking up the street with her friends. "Shit, did I lie?"

When Eve tried to hand me my shoes—both of them—I eyed her like she was crazy. "You can throw *them* pissy motherfuckers in the trash," I said, dead serious.

Michel raked his slender fingers through his hair. "I know that's right," he agreed.

Eve looked back at me like I was crazy. "Fucking Louboutins? *I'll* rock these pissy motherfuckers then."

I shrugged. I wasn't the type of chick to waste money, but I didn't want to drag nobody else's piss and possible germs in Make$'s car or our apartment. Nothing.

"Oh *heeeeeeellll* no," Peaches said, stepping up next to Eve and pulling a plastic grocery bag from her purse. "Put them Loubies right in this bag, beanpole."

I rolled my eyes, even as I wondered who in they right mind carried grocery bags balled up in they pocketbook. Why? Who? When? Why? How?

"You not gone waste my son's money, Miss Chocoliscious," she snapped. "And I'm gone tell Terrence that's how you living. I told him he need to let me handle his money while he gone. You ain't had job the first since you fell off the stripper pole and you just wasting money like you Keyshia Cole, Mary J. Blige, or some shit. Fuck you and fuck what you thinking, baby boo. You wait 'til I talk to him."

"Girl, you right, Peaches," Nikki Façade cosigned, digging under her loose tracks to scratch her scalp.

Eve and Michel and I shared a long look. I knew they had to be thinking what I was thinking. I just fought a bitch for her ass and she flipped the script on me in a heartbeat.

I wasn't worrying about fucking up my cash flow. Peaches was on a strict allowance outside of the house he bought her, and there was no way he was trusting her crazy ass with his money. Hell, I barely had a lot of access to it.

Still, that bitch was dirty. I should've left her laid the fuck out on the floor, but hindsight is always clearer.

Dumb bitch.

*   *   *

Since Make$ was out of town, Michel and Eve spent the night with me. A couple of bottles of moscato and retelling about our club escapade kept my mind occupied, but as soon as I set them up in the guest room and made my way to our master suite I felt all my loneliness again. That shit was starting to fit me like a second skin.

Sometimes it felt like it was suffocating me.

Most bitches would spend his money, enjoy his whip, lamp in the nice crib, and find a jump-off for a little phone conversation and sexual stimulation on *their* terms. But no other nigga did it for me. I didn't want nobody but Make$. A couple of his friends—like his childhood friend and fellow rapper Tek-9, had even tried me on the sneak tip, but I played like I couldn't read between the lines. Besides, I couldn't even picture myself chilling with—and definitely not sexing—another dude.

My mama always taught me that a woman can't do the shit a man do. Our bodies are built different, and trying to handle two or three dicks in steady rotation would fuck up a woman's reputation *and* her pussy walls.

I picked up my cell phone from the bed, hating myself for checking to see if the ringer was off and I missed his call or text. I felt disappointment before I even confirmed that there wasn't shit wrong with my phone but there was a lot wrong with my relationship—at least when he was on the road. When he was home we were straight.

We spent a lot of time together. Whenever he had an event I was right there on the red carpet with him chinning and grinning. Award shows. Premieres. Vacations. Shopping sprees. But also plenty of romantic surprises and hearing "I love you." That ninja was straight on point . . . until he got out of my eyesight.

I called his phone and it went straight to voice mail. I didn't bother leaving a message. He would eventually call me back and have his excuse ready. I'd heard them all:

"I turned the ringer down by mistake."

"I couldn't hear the ringer over the loud music."

"I was sleeping. I didn't hear it."

"You know I don't like to be interrupted when I'm in the studio."

"I texted you . . . didn't you get it?"

I sat up in bed and reached for the pack of Newports I kept in the top drawer of my nightstand. Visions of him eating the pussy of some random bitch ate me up inside as I leaned back against the leather-padded headboard and lit the cigarette. I only smoked when I was stressed the fuck out.

I dialed Goldie's cell phone. I hated to call her this late, but my desire to talk to Make$ outweighed any doubts or concerns I had.

My heart was racing as I listened to Goldie's phone ring in my ear.

"Whaddup, Luscious?"

I exhaled a stream of smoke, filling the air with the smell of Newports. "I hate to call you so late, but I been calling my so-called man's phone and that motherfucka ain't answering," I said, hating how hard my heart was pumping. Hating it even more how desperate I felt.

"After the show, I left him and his crew at the venue. Maybe he's in his suite wasted. They was drinkin' and smokin' like crazy."

I tucked my phone between my ear and shoulder as I tapped the ashes into the palm of my hand. "Would you go check his room for me? I don't know why he ain't let me go with him."

The line stayed quiet and that made me go all stiff and shit. I frowned. "Yo, Goldie, go check and see if he in his room . . . motherfuckin' alone," I said, climbing out of bed to dump my ashes into the commode in our adjoining all-white master bath.

I dumped the cigarette too, the taste of it making me nauseous. The embers went out with a hiss. I didn't even inhale.

"Luscious, I'm in my bed. Just keep trying his phone."

I paused on my way back to the bed and looked down at my phone like "You ain't *that* tired." I would have hopped up out of bed and did a bed check on her man if she asked me. Who cared if it was 2 a.m.? "I tried the other girls but they at some club," I told her. Meaning? *There's no one to do it but you, Goldie, so stop playing.*

"If I see him before we fly out I'll tell him you was looking for him. A'ight then. Night."

Click.

It wasn't Goldie's responsibility to keep up with my man, but damn. The letdown and the hang-up. That shit felt like "Bitch, fuck you."

Bzzz.

My phone vibrated in my hand and Make$'s face filled the screen. My heart pounded. "Hey baby," I said, feeling the pleasure in my heart that he called even as my doubts fucked with my head.

"We just left the after-party. I wanted to call you before I went to bed. Tired as fuck, you know. This touring kicking my ass but I gotta hustle until I sign that new deal with a big advance, you know?"

I nodded but to keep it one hundred, I really didn't *know.* Make$ made a good enough living, and we lived well but nothing over the top. He had more than enough to slow the fuck up some. "I know," I lied, focusing on hearing any noises in his background to peep if what he told me was the truth.

I heard the television and I relaxed a little bit. I pictured him sitting on the edge of the bed, no shirt, just boxers, jewelry still on.

Make$ yawned. "I know I'm away a lot but when I get back next week we're going on a trip. Wherever you want," he promised.

Now this the shit. Make$'s word was good like money. I

knew that all I had to do was point to a spot on the map and we would be there just like he said. I knew we would go shopping for the trip and we would spend the entire time together. He would focus on us and make it known that what we had—what we was building—was important.

It was like there was two of him, Terrence the boyfriend who was so completely on point when we were together and Make$ the public persona on the road. But I was no secret in the industry: I was on his arms at parties, premieres, and red-carpet events. He never denied me in interviews.

As soon as he went on tour his slick ass started acting shady.

"Hey, Luscious, I love your chocolate ass, a'ight," he said, his voice deep and rough. "That's on some real shit. I know you miss me. I miss you too, but I gotta make this money. You know more than anybody the load I'm carrying on my shoulders. The people relying on me. Yo, the only thing I know for sure is you love me and I know you got my back. Ya heard me?"

I nodded as I licked my lips. "I love you too, baby," I reassured him.

"I'm tired. I'll call you when I get up, a'ight?"

I nodded again and then remembered he couldn't see me. "A'ight."

The call disconnected and I was left in the middle of the battle of Terrence vs. Make$.

That two-sided shit of his was a complete mind-fuck.

3

One Month Later

The sound of loud talking and laughter woke me from my sleep. I popped one eye open with the rest of my face pressed deep into lavender-scented pillows. I felt like shit. Worse than shit. Head was pounding. My body felt like a truck rolled over it ten times. My eyes were too puffy and heavy to open.

Last night we got fucked up and this morning I felt completely fucked over.

Make$ and I stayed up all night, drinking, smoking, and talking. The morning after was never as much fun as the night before.

I stretched my body against the bed before I kicked off the covers and hopped out of bed. Like always when my man was home for more than a day our bedroom was fucked up. Clothes and sneakers were everywhere. Shopping bags still yet to be unpacked were stacked in a corner by the window. A dirty plate with remnants of whatever he ate last night and cigarette ends sat on the floor. The underwear and socks he stepped out of still sat on the floor in front of the bathroom door.

Shit. This mess had my damn name written all over it. That ninja didn't even try to clean up behind himself. He made it clear those were part of my duties as his wifey. And from the noises coming from the living room, he had his bullshit as entourage in there making more of a fucking disaster zone for me to fight.

Fuck this shit.

Yes, Make$ took damn good care of me, but I wasn't his

maid. When he moved me on up, I thought I'd get treated more like Weezie than fucking Florence. The fuck?

Clearing my throat, I stretched before I kicked a stack of glossy photos his publicist sent over for him to autograph. I was passing the mirror on the way to the bathroom when I did a double take at my reflection. White crusted spots were on my stomach and breasts.

Make$'s nut.

I smiled. It looked like glaze on a chocolate donut, with my smooth, dark-skinned complexion. Last night I sucked that dick so good and then just before he nutted, I jacked him off and let his cum rain down on me. Fuck it. What I won't do another bitch will. I'm simply not having that.

I took a quick shower and made a half-ass attempt at cleaning our bedroom. There really was no need until his ass went back on the road because that nigga was comfortable in mess. With a chick like Peaches as his mother, that's all his ass probably was used to.

Dressed in a pair of sweats and a baby tee, I padded barefoot out the bedroom and down the hall. The smell of weed knocked me in the face, and the air just below the ceiling was filled with silver haze. The living room was packed like a club. Niggas was everywhere, and Make$ sat on the leather ottoman in the middle of them knuckleheads.

"Whaddup, y'all," I said, opening the double-sided fridge to grab a bottle of water.

"Whaddup," they all said in unison, their eyes locked on the flat-screen on the wall.

Make$ turned to eye me, his shades and jewelry already in place. I knew he was checking to see what I had on. Usually I strolled my thick chocolate ass around in thongs or boy shorts with a baby tee. Pussy and nipples pressed against the material and meant to turn him the fuck on.

I made a playful face at him before I blew him a kiss.

He lowered his shades to look over them and wink at me.

"Yo, here come the best part," his friend Tank said, pointing at the screen with one of his juicy fingers, looking like a fat and greasy Biggie reject. That nigga's head was so gone, I didn't fuck with him too much. I didn't trust his mind-set. *At all*.

I looked at the TV, being nosy, and frowned at the grainy image of me getting hauled out of Club Infinity last month. Some motherfucker with a cell phone videotaped it and loaded that shit up on WorldStarHipHop. "Why you watching this old shit?" I asked, coming out of the kitchen to sit next to Make$ on the ottoman. I slid my hand against his slender thigh. I could feel the tip of his dick in the sleep pants he still had on.

"I never saw it," he said. "My moms said to watch it before I watch the next vid."

"Next video?" I asked, lost like a motherfucker.

"Yup." He raised the remote to load the next DVD.

I jumped back a little bit as Peaches' face filled the screen. She looked like Make$ with a short blonde wig on. She was standing in the middle of some nondescript street by herself, blazing on a blunt like her shit was medicinal and not illegal. *Now what?* I thought.

"Hey baby. What's poppin'? I know you're not one to fuck with and that's because ya mama ain't one to play with either. I refuse to be disrespected. I don't take no shit and I raised you not to take no motherfuckin' bullshit either. Ya heard me? Now watch how yo mama made sure this bitch wished she didn't bust my fucking lip in the club. Lights. Camera. Action. Whooop-whoooooooop!"

Peaches took a big drag off her blunt and blew a thick stream of smoke directly into the camera.

My stomach got tight as fuck as the screen went black before it came back on inside an abandoned apartment that looked too grimy for rats and roaches to even fuck with. The windows were boarded. There was graffiti on the walls and discarded crack pipes and dope bags on the floors.

I jumped back when two figures dressed all in back with ski masks on filled the screen before the camera dipped down to take in a body lying in the middle of the dirty matted rug. A big body. Like Big Girl from the fight at the club.

No, the fuck that ain't . . .

One of the figures that could have been women or skinny dudes nudged the body with a black boot.

She cried out in pain.

They said nothing as they began punching and kicking her again. And again. And again.

My stomach clenched.

The fellas littered around the apartment all laughed.

But there wasn't shit funny.

I looked at Make$ and he was quiet. His shades were in place, but his mouth was a thin line. The muscle in his jaw was flexing in and out. He sat still as a fucking statue. Was he pissed off?

I knew that seeing the video of his mother getting knocked the fuck out had been embarrassing for him. That shit was the talk of gossip blogs and radio stations for weeks. But was he in on this retaliation shit? And why tape it?

I didn't say shit as I shifted my eyes back to the screen.

One of the figures bent down to box the woman in her face. Kick her. Spit on her. Degrade her. She curled into a ball to protect herself from some of the blows.

The camera zoomed in on her face. It was bloody and swollen. One of her eyes was closed shut and already purplish. Her lip was busted. A gash on her forehead was down to the white meat. I didn't recognize her.

What the fuck?

I felt my stomach hurl at this bullshit. I made to stand up but Make$'s hand shot out to grab my wrist tight as hell and pull me back down.

When one of them picked up a broken broom handle and snatched the skirt she wore up to probe between her legs, I tried to snatch the remote from Make$'s hand. "Turn that bullshit off."

He moved the remote out of my reach. "Chill, Luscious."

The screen went black before Peaches' crazy ass filled the screen again. "Bitch thought she could swerve on me in the club and that shit was a done dada? Nothing."

She started laughing crazy as hell.

I snatched my fucking hand away and ran the fuck out of there, pushing some random motherfucker out of my way. Whoever it was hollered out in surprise. Fuck 'em. I slammed our bedroom door so hard I knew everyone on that floor felt the vibrations.

Peaches was crazy. What I was just taking a guess at before, I now knew for sure. That little bitch was out of her fucking mind.

"What's your problem?"

I turned away from where I stood at the window and eyed Make$ walking into our bedroom with the DVD in his hand. "You knew about that shit?" I asked, watching the disc as my heart pounded.

"Nah," he said.

I eyed him. Was this fucker lying? Was he as crazy as his mama? "That shit was so over the top and unnecessary," I snapped, running my hands through my jet-black weave. "Your mama started a fucking fight and lost. I already fought the bitch. Everything was handled. That shit was dead. You know what I'm saying? So what the fuck is *that* shit?"

"Yo," Make$ roared, making a fist that he shook at his side as the veins in his neck strained beneath the cover of his tattoos. "I will handle it, Luscious."

"Handle what? Ya mama out here wilding out, acting crazy, talking stupid—"

"Yo, don't disrespect my mother!" Make$ shouted, pointing

his finger at me like he was ready to storm across the room and slap me up.

My eyes got hard. He could fuck with it if he chose, but then the choice was mine whether to let him get away with it. Love or no love. Being my financial security blanket or not. My father never laid a hand on me—not even to spank me—and I'd be damned if *any* other man used me as his punching bag. There wasn't a motherfucker alive who would touch me and walk away the same.

I was as serious as a heart attack.

"Why don't you tell your mother to stop disrespecting herself, calling up radio stations and giving interviews about random dumb shit," I snapped, waving my hand at him dismissively. "So you cosigning that bullshit? Huh? You okay with chancing your career? Huh? You wanna go to jail for that shit that she fucking *taped*? Huh, Terrence? Huh?" I asked him, my voice hard and my eyes blazing. "Y'all better get up off that motherfucking Soprano-Godfather-Scarface-gangbanging mind-set! Fuck y'all think this is?"

"A'ight, Luscious," Make$ said, sounding aggravated. "I'll take care of it."

I came across the room, damn near slipping on the pile of photos. I kicked at them in frustration, sending some flying up into the air to float down around us. "Take care of what? What exactly did she leave you to clean up?" I asked, my hands whizzing across the air. "Where is that girl? What's going to keep her from going to the police? Who was the people in there whipping her ass? Who taped it? Is that the only copy? Why—"

Make$ flung the DVD across the room and it sliced into our custom-painted walls. "Shut the fuck up! Damn! You fuckin' five-oh or some shit? What the fuck? I *said* I would handle it."

I left well enough alone and just released a heavy-ass breath that was filled with aggravation. I wanted so badly to tell this Negro that his mother and/or his crew would be his downfall.

Fuck it, though. That nigga was hardheaded as hell, so why waste my breath?

When Make$ turned to leave the room he was already unscrewing his pendant of the world. Getting fucked up wasn't going to change shit. Everything he cherished in that small world of his was nothing but an escape. A fucking cop-out. A reason not to deal with the real world. I couldn't stand that shit. It was a sign of weakness that I didn't want to see in him.

I looked up and caught sight of myself in the mirror, thinking of the times I did coke with him because I didn't want to disappoint him. It was a sign of weakness that I couldn't stand seeing in myself.

I turned away from the reflection.

Funny thing was, it wasn't the sight of my own image and shame that fucked with me. An image of that girl beaten and laid up in some abandoned house flashed.

Where was she?

How was she?

I sat on the windowsill and looked down at the triangle-shaped Military Park. I didn't know shit about its history or all the statues but I knew there was many times in the months since we moved here that I would sit in the window and look out at the park and find some peace. I grew up in Newark, and nothing about the small park ever stood out to me as a kid. And now I lived in a upscale apartment building overlooking it.

I should be mad happy.

Not hoping that some girl I fought in the club—to defend my man's mother—wasn't in a hospital bed or grave.

It was shit like this that made my parents side-eye my relationship with Make$. The only thing my daddy hated more than me stripping was having Make$ in my life. My father hated hip-hop and especially hated Make$'s use of profanity and half-naked women in his videos and photo shoots.

We all went to dinner when I first introduced him to my parents and they couldn't wait to call me to their house the next day to beat me over the head about his tattoos, his chain-smoking, his ever-present shades. His everything. So now I just kept them separated, because no one was going to change. When I did fuck with a family function, I didn't bring Make$, and he didn't mind one damn bit.

They didn't even know the half about Make$, and if they did, shit would only get worse. If my parents knew I use to ride with Make$ when he was in the dope game, they would probably kidnap me away from him. Thankfully, he stopped all that hustling and focused on his music. Still, all of that mess plus the nights I cried myself to sleep because I was so lonely and worried that my man was fucking around on me? My parents would flip.

I closed my eyes and drew my legs up to my chest, resting my forehead on top of my knees. I wished things could be different with my parents. My family.

It had been months since I been to their house, and we all lived right within the limits of the city of Newark. They were in Weequahic, a working middle-class neighborhood of single-family homes. But our disagreements over the way I chose to live my life kept plenty of distance between us. The nurse and college professor didn't dream of raising a college dropout turned stripper turned live-in wifey of a rapper. (Kanye they would swallow up, but Make$, with his tats, open love of weed, and jail record? They wasn't cosigning that at all.)

But I felt their disapproval way before I climbed my ass on the pole. I was never their perfect angel. By the time I went to college and got some freedom to do what I wanted, whenever I wanted, I went crazy. I did everything I thought they wouldn't want me to do and it made it all even more fun. Partying. Smoking weed. Drinking. Fucking. No church on Sundays. No curfews. No rules. No disapproving looks.

Life was *bananas* back then *and* secret as hell, until my grades got sent home. My parents wanted to know just what I was up to since my grades wasn't up to shit. But I was too far gone by then. Freedom was everything to me and there was no turning back.

That was the beginning of the end of my relationship with my parents. Now it was all about quick phone calls over visits and dropping gifts off on the holidays. The less time we all spent together the better.

Bzzzzzz . . . Bzzzzzz . . . Bzzzzzz . . .

I looked over at my BlackBerry vibrating on my nightstand. *Fuck it.* I didn't feel like talking. In that moment I was feeling too much like my parents were right about the world I chose to live in. I used to laugh off their claims of danger, thinking they was just being hypersensitive middle-class black folks who didn't understand that a lot of hip-hop was about upholding an image more than anything.

But that DVD was fucking with me. There was no excuse for that girl to get jumped like that. No excuse.

Bzzzzzz . . . Bzzzzzz . . . Bzzzzzz . . .

Pushing up off the windowsill, I walked over to the bed to pick up my cell phone. I frowned at the number before I answered. "Hello?"

"Miss Jordan?"

I rolled my eyes, feeling irritated as hell. "Yes?" I said, just short of snapping.

As the words filled my ear, I went from feeling weak at the knees to being strengthened by anger. "Oh hell no."

My heart pounded.

I felt nauseous.

I felt like crying.

I was fucked up. Fucked all the way up.

I dropped the phone. I was shaking all over like I couldn't control myself as I stormed out of the bedroom and came marching down the hall like I was going to war.

The sight of Make$ and his motherfucking mooching-ass

minions howling with laughter without a care in the world just kicked shit up a hundred notches for me. Wasn't a bit of pause on this shit.

I pushed niggas out my way hard as fuck, ignoring their shouts of surprise, grabbed the remote from Make$'s hand, and flung that motherfucker dead into the center of the flat-screen on the wall. The silence in the room came with a quickness.

Make$ jumped to his feet. "Fuck wrong with you, Luscious?" he spat, stepping up to press his face close to mine. Nose to nose. Angry eyes locked. Both chests heaving.

Fuck it. It was on.

"Get the fuck out!" I yelled at the top of my voice, giving him one last hard stare before I turned and pushed past these openmouthed, shell-shocked motherfuckers to throw the front door wide open.

"Yo, Make$, man, what's up with your girl?" someone asked, with way too much attitude.

I paused and calmly nodded my head as I walked back toward our bedroom like I didn't have a care in the world. "I got nine motherfucking reasons why this living room better be cleared out when I get back," I said, easy as hell. No worries. Make$'s nine-millimeter was in my name anyway.

We'll see if these heads get a little less hard when the barrel of a gun is pressed to them.

Yes, I was that serious.

"Yo, let me handle this little dustup real quick. I'll get with y'all later."

I turned and stood, hands on curvy hips, as they all filed out the apartment. As soon as the door shut behind them I stalked over to Make$ with long strides and arms already swinging. "You no-good, lying son of a bitch," I spat, landing two blows to his chest that caused him to stumble his skinny ass backward.

"Bitch, what the fuck wrong with you?" he roared, stepping forward to grab at my throat.

"Get your fucking hands off me," I said in this hard voice filled with all the emotions getting at me in that moment. I pushed him away from me and he stumbled again. I snatched up one of the glasses sitting on the end table and flung it at his ass.

He ducked.

It bounced off the window.

"I trusted you, motherfucker, and now you and one of your nasty little side-fucks gave me a fucking STD," I told him in a voice that was a small whisper that was filled with all these big-ass emotions. PAIN. ANGER. HURT. HATRED.

"An STD? That's some bullshit, Luscious," Make$ said, holding out his hands to block anything I might fling across the room at his ass.

Tears filled my eyes, but I fought the urge to crumble to the floor and have a good cry. Fuck that shit. I started picking up random shit and tossing it at that cheating bastard, hoping I knocked him the fuck out.

The remote.

CRASH.

His new diamond and platinum watch.

BOOM.

"Luscious!"

A box of blunt cigars landed against his cheek.

"Stop it, Luscious!"

The CD cover they used to snort powder whizzed across the room.

"Why you tearin' up the fucking house?!"

"Because my doctor just told me I got trich, bitch."

A old takeout container filled with chicken bones and remnants of fried rice landed against his chest.

I looked around for something else to throw and Make$ came storming across the room, wrapping his arms around mine and locking me tight against his body. The little fucker was thin but strong. *Shit.*

We both stumbled, lost our balance, and fell backward. My head caught the corner of the glass buffet table against the wall. The table tipped forward and crashed down on us. He pushed it off.

"Luscious, baby, you all right?" he asked.

I cried out, closing my eyes with a wince as I felt the warm oozing of blood against my scalp. Even as the pain throbbed, I fought his hands off me, not able to stand his touch. "You lying motherfucker," I screamed, tears burring my vision and pain searing my heart.

I clawed him like a cat with nothing to lose.

My fingernails dug into the skin of Make$'s face and he cried out.

That shit wasn't nothing against the pain I was feeling. Fuck the gash on my head and the blood I felt running down my neck. This nigga right here broke my heart. My world felt like everything was crashing around me. It felt out-of-body. I *wished* it was unreal. But this was the realest shit ever.

There was no denying a nasty-ass STD, and there wasn't but one way I could get it. In my twenty-four years I had *never* even had a fucking yeast infection. Ugh!

"Luscious, that's a fucking lie," he said again.

I eyed him hard before I pointed my finger against his forehead. "No, you the lie, motherfucker. You the no-good, cheating, disease-spreading trick master. Motherfucker," I said with emphasis, swatting them stupid-ass shades off his face.

He slapped my hand away.

Whap.

"A'ight, Luscious, keep your hands to your fuckin' self before you get hurt," he said.

I laughed, bitter as hell. So bitter. "What you gone do, whup my ass? Huh? Huh? Nigga please. Try me, nigga," I said, claiming my anger and letting it fuel me because the pain of his betrayal and his disrespect would destroy me if I didn't.

"You ain't even had enough decency to strap up with them dirty birds you out there fucking 'cause you a Mr. Jay-Z wannabe, fucking Lil Wayne 2.0 bitch." I fought the urge to straight box that nigga in his face. "Huh, you excited them bitches want you for your money and your name that you raw-dogging bitches? That's how you out there? That's how you handling your B.I. Negro? Huh? That's how you handling . . . *me*?"

I broke. Tears filled my eyes as I looked at him. I patted my chest, the diamond jewelry he gave me flashing from my hand and wrist. That shit meant nothing. "That's the respect you got for me? For *this*?" I asked, waving my hand around our apartment. Our home.

Right then, in that moment, I wanted nothing but a kiss on the forehead from my father or to bury my head in my mother's lap to make me feel better. It's funny how grown and independent you think you are until something fucks your world right up and nothing can straighten you out like Mommy and Daddy.

Make$ reached for me. I stepped back from him, shaking my head, my lips twisted downward. "Nah. You want them bitches? Have them, Terrence. Oh, no no no. I'm sorry. You're Make$. Right?" I gave him a nasty once-over with my eyes that I knew were filled with the pain I couldn't fight off.

"Luscious, you know I ain't fucking nobody. If I have something I must've had it before we starting going together," Make$ said, his eyes all over my face.

I turned from him, not at all buying the bullshit he wanted to sell me.

"Oh shit, you bleeding," he said. "It's blood everywhere."

I felt him step up behind where I stood with my arms crossed over my chest. "Don't fucking touch me," I told him, my voice *hard*.

"Man, Luscious, it's blood all down your shirt and in your hair. You must've busted your fucking head open on that table," Make$ said, his voice filled with concern.

FUCK HIM.

I turned and pushed past him to get to our bedroom. When I came back the gun was in my hand and pointed at him. I'd never really held the gun except to move it, but it felt good. My finger resting lightly on the trigger felt natural. "Get the fuck out," I said, picturing him fucking some other bitch. And then me. And then another bitch. And then me.

Make$'s eyes got big as shit as he held up his hands. "Yo, Luscious, shit ain't even that serious. Put the fucking gun down," he said, trying to sound calm.

There wasn't shit calming about a cheating man and an STD.

He stepped closer to me.

I extended my arm and tightened my grip on the gun as I turned it sideways. "Who you fucking, *Ter-rence*? Huh?" I asked, a tear that wasn't near as lonely as I felt racing down my cheek.

"Man, Luscious, if I gave you—"

I made a dum-dum face. "If? *If*? Nigga, ain't no ifs about it. You trying to say it's me that gave you this shit?"

"Man, I love you, Luscious, and you know this. I give you everything I have and I promised you more," Make$ said, holding his hands up like I was robbing him. He was the one who stole my heart and then broke it.

I shook my head and bit my lip. The gun felt heavy in my hands, so I locked my elbow tighter. "I'm not *that* bitch. Clothes, money, fucking jewelry. Your Jag. This apartment. Your promises? All that shit means nothing to me compared to loyalty. See, I'm *that* bitch. The one you can trust. The one you can depend on. The one you rely on. That's me, motherfucker . . . and that's why I deserve it in return. Fuck materialistic shit."

The truth of my own words did me in. My shoulders slumped as my heart finished crumbling. The tears flowed. It was like a broken faucet I couldn't turn off. With my free hand I tried to wipe them away. Nothing. More fell in their place.

I cried out when suddenly one of his arms was around me as

he wrestled the gun from my hand and then tossed it onto the sofa away from us. I caved and cried like a baby. My knees gave out, but his arms held me up. I didn't have no more fight in me. Not in that moment.

I let him check the back of my head as I cried from a hole deep in my soul that he created. I'm talking snot running. Eyes hurting. Mouth wide open. Head flung back. Straight wailing.

"You might need stitches," Make$ said. "I'm taking you to the ER."

I hated how much his touch still felt good to me. Hated myself for wanting to know this nigga cared about me. Hated that I was hoping he was telling the truth about having the STD before we met. Hated that I didn't want to lose him.

I'm weak.

Love got me fucked up all the way up.

$\mathscr{I}$ opened my compact and double-checked my makeup as we pulled up to Club 973 in Newark. My makeup was a little over the top but it matched the deep purple Gucci dress that clung to my curves like a second skin. Michel had styled my long ebony weave until it was nothing but loose and airy curls surrounding my face and cascading down to the middle of my back. Twenty-inch Indian remy. Goldie put me down on the good shit. Fuck yaki. Give that shit a good two weeks and it was shedding like cat hairs.

There were cars lined up and down the blocks surrounding the club. The line to get in, for the non-VIPs, was around the corner. Goldie said she wanted a big blowout for her belated birthday party and the proof was in the pudding, because everybody was talking about it. I'd seen more club flyers floating around Newark and New York in the last two weeks than a little bit. All the local radio station DJs were planning to be in attendance. East Coast celebs and athletes were supposed to make appearances. Shit was *bananas*.

"Looks like Goldie's party is going to be the shit," I said to Make$, excited to get in, get me a cocktail, and enjoy myself.

Make$ leaned forward in the seat of the Jag. "That must be her new Benz," he said, tilting his chin toward the silver SLK 500 parked—and definitely posed up—in front of the club like she wanted it seen.

"Missy told me how she embarrassed some white dude at the car lot who thought she was broke. She bought it cash," I said, as he parked at the corner in front of a hydrant and a handicap access.

His security parked their blacked-out SUV in front of us damn near on the curb.

I couldn't do anything but shake my head as we climbed out the car. "I hope *my* Jag doesn't get towed," I said with a smile as he came around to step up on the curb and press a hand to my back as we walked up the street with the two security guards behind us.

"Oh, you got jokes," he said, fitting his oversize shades on his slender face.

"No, I got the title," I shot back, holding out my hand for the keys with one of my eyebrows arched.

He slapped my ass as he dropped them into my hand.

Make$ did everything in the last two weeks to get back in good with me. He was mad attentive. Flowers. Romantic dinners. Surprise gifts. QT out the ass. That nigga even made a song about me, begging my forgiveness and proclaiming his love. We just got back from a weekend trip to Antigua where he surprised me with the title to the Jag all signed, sealed, and delivered to me in a box with a new Tiffany diamond key chain.

My wish was his command.

I looked over at him as the entire line of clubgoers began to holler, reach for him, and snap pictures with their camera phones as we all entered the club. Did I still have my doubts? Damn straight. Was it possible that he caught the STD before me and didn't know? My doctor said he could've been asymptomatic just like me and that it was possible. Did I love him? No question.

We made our way to the VIP lounge upstairs. It took about ten minutes as he stopped to politic with everybody, my hand in his, right at his side. I spotted Goldie making her rounds looking hella cute in a bustier and ruffled ballerina skirt with sequined booties. We waved across the room and she motioned she would make her way to us soon.

In the VIP, I was sipping on Goldie's signature drink and

dancing in front of where Make$ sat, knowing my ass was look-
ing good. He stood up and pressed his body close to mine, bringing his tattooed hands up to press against my stomach. I felt his
hard dick against my ass.

"When you gone take that pussy off lockdown?" he asked in
my ear as I continued to sip my drink and dip my ass against
him.

We hadn't fucked since the STD bullshit came to light. Even
after I finished my meds and the doctor gave me the all clear—
along with a handful of condoms—I still didn't give it up. The
best he got was eating my pussy even though I made sure his
ass went to the doctor and took his meds to clear his shit up too.
Still, no haps on the sex . . . yet.

I leaned my head back against his shoulder and brought my
arms up to cup the back of his head. "Maybe tonight," I said.

"Maybe." He balked.

I laughed, enjoying teasing him as I stepped away from him
and danced some more to some Rick Ross song that was playing. I looked down and spotted Goldie hugging a dude close, her
body pressed to his like she was trying to blend into him. I eyed
the tall fine dude. He had one of those athletic builds that made
you think he could tear a pussy up. I did a little clap when I saw
Goldie take his hand and lead him through the club and down the
hall leading to the bathroom. She needed a man, because as far I
knew, she wasn't giving up the goodies. *Fucking coochie cobwebs
and shit. I hope he knocks the dust off it.*

"I'm going to the bathroom," Make$ told me.

I nodded and kept doing my thing, just enjoying the drinks,
the music, and even Goldie having some of her best dancers performing in different spots around the club. I spotted Missy. I
hadn't really seen her since I stopped dancing. She looked the
same with all her caramel cuteness, partying it up in a short
sequined dress with a light-skinned girl with long reddish-brown
hair and more hips than anything else on her body. I didn't know

the other chick, but I knew she was one of Goldie's dancers. She had the look.

Missy was so busy partying that she didn't even see me motion to get her attention.

"Motivation" by Kelly Rowland came on and I raised my hand to the air and worked my hips like I was still making money on the pole. I loved that song. It made me feel all sexy and shit. I loved it even more after she tore that shit up performing on the BET Awards last year.

"I just want to feel your hands all over me ba-by," I sang, rocking my wide hips back and forth in my Gucci heels just like she did on that stage.

I looked down just as I spotted the tall sexy dude making his way through the club to post up at the bar. Shit. I shifted my eyes back to where he and Goldie had disappeared. I didn't see her. Nosy as hell, I shifted my eyes back to the bar. My eyes widened to see Make$ brush the tall dude *hard* with his shoulder as he passed, and then he turned to mean-mug Old Boy over his shoulder. *Huh?*

Make$ disappeared down the hall.

Goldie never reappeared.

Huh? Something ain't right.

I sat my drink down and made my way down the stairs quick as fuck. My mind was working overtime even as I pushed my way through the crowd. I finally made it to the hall. I looked and saw the signs for the restrooms.

I paused.

He did say he was going to the bathroom.

I kept it moving and stormed into the men's bathroom. There were plenty of men lined up at the urinals on the wall . . . but no Make$.

"What you looking for . . . this?" a cute Puerto Rican man asked, turning with pee still dripping from the tip of his thick and long brown dick.

I can't front. That sight of that snake made me pause.

He laughed.

I left the men's room, the door swinging closed behind me and causing air to breeze against the back of my legs. I looked up and down the hall. There wasn't shit else back there but the ladies' room and an emergency exit with a sign above it saying an alarm would ring if it was opened.

I didn't hear no fucking alarms.

Not that kind anyway. These alarms sounding off were inside me and all about my woman's intuition.

I stepped over to the ladies' room door and pushed it. It was locked. That shit made my heart race more. Something wasn't right. Fuck the dumb shit.

I walked back out the hall and snatched up the first waitress I saw. "Excuse me, do you have the key to the ladies' room?" I asked, even as all my nerves were firing up until I felt like I could shit up my damn self. For real.

"The manager has the key. It's locked?" the woman asked, looking over my shoulder with a frown before she made a move to walk past me.

I stepped in her path knowing she was gonna knock. I didn't want that. I wanted that fucking door unlocked. ASAP. "I knocked already," I lied. "I have to pee so bad, girl."

This bitch didn't have no key, and all I needed was for her to get the motherfucker who did.

"A'ight, I'll be right back," she said.

Bitch, boo-bye. No offense to her but I was on a mission.

Thankfully the club manager came just a few minutes later, keys in hand. "Sorry about this," he said, his silk shirt soaked down in sweat under the arms.

Whatever. OPEN THE DOOR!

I gave him a tight smile as I bit the gloss from my lips as he slid the key in the lock. As soon as he pushed the door open I stepped up so close to him that my titties pressed against his sweaty back.

My eyes got big as shit as I saw *my* man squatted down between Goldie's legs eating her the fuck out while her scandalous ass was posted up on the nasty wet counter playing with her nipples and shit. Her skirt was up around her waist and her bustier down below her breasts. She grabbed the back of his head and worked her hips as THIS NIGGA started moaning.

Shock and disbelief had me for a hot second. My friend and my man.

"WHATTHEFUCK?" I shouted, seeing shades of red. Blood red. I felt nauseous.

I pushed past the club manager and ran straight at the treacherous two with my fists already balled up and ready for some head action.

"Oh shit," Make$ swore. He jumped up and turned.

I barely had time to take in his dick hard and pressing against his jeans. Ready to fuck. His chin and fucking mouth was still wet with her skanky pussy juices.

Goldie tried to cover her exposed titties with her hands. I felt so much hate for this bitch. Even more than I had for Make$. I trusted this bitch. I TRUSTED this bitch!

"You nasty, no-good bitch!" I screamed, my eyes taking in the money all over the floor and her thong bikini lying on top of it. What?! *He was paying for the pussy?*

Goldie hopped off the counter, pulling up her bustier, just as I reached past Make$ and straight swung on that bitch hard as I could. My fist landed against her chin, knocking her head back, and I hoped I dislodged her dick-sucking jaw. Fucking bird-ass bitch. I'm calling this bitch to get the scoop on my nigga and *she* fucking him. SCANDALOUS!

"And you's a nasty *lying*-ass bitch," Goldie screamed back before she swung back at me.

Fuck it. We went at it with Make$ dead in the middle. Blow for blow. This bitch deserved to get her ass beat.

WHAP. BA-DHAP. POW.

Make$ put his hands up trying to stop us and blocked my blows, leaving me open for that bitch to slap and uppercut me. My face stung from her blows and I tried to jump over his short ass to straight deaden that bitch for putting her hands in my face like she was my pimp. Humph, *she* was the fucking whore.

Make$ grabbed me around my waist and pushed me back as I wiped the little bit of blood she drew from my bottom lip. I wasn't done with that bitch by any means.

I looked out at the people crowded up outside the open bathroom door. Fucking great. Now the world knew my business. Shit. I could see that shit in all the blogs and press now with a headline just as scandalous as the shit going down. That pissed me off even more.

"You ain't shit, Goldie. I fucking trusted your ass. You knew I loved that nigga. You knew that shit and you steady fucking him behind my back. That's dirty. You dirty."

I pointed my finger at her. Fighting back tears. I couldn't believe this shit. What the fuck was the world coming to? Nobody was to be trusted? People didn't give a shit about loyalty no more?

My eyes shifted between the two of them as I shook my head feeling all kinds of fucked up by these scandalous, no-good trifling motherfuckers. I started pacing, trying to figure out a way to get at that bitch.

Two big bouncers stepped through the crowd to stop into the bathroom.

"This my party. I want her ass out of here," Goldie said.

I locked my eyes on Make$. What lies did he have for what the fuck I saw with my own eyes? What bullshit would he pull to make me feel better about *this* shit?

"And the young lady threw the first punch," the club manager said.

I barely heard or saw anything around me. My focus was on my man. He couldn't even look at me.

One of the bouncers stepped toward me.

"This is between me, the trick, and my no-good man. We got this. We don't need y'all," I said, nowhere near done with these two.

"Come on, Luscious. Go on with that shit, man," Make$ said, looking bored as he called somebody on his BlackBerry.

That shit, that blasé shit from him, stung like a motherfucker. I stepped toward him, ready to slap that BlackBerry out his hand and then make him eat that motherfucker.

One of the bouncers picked me up by my waist, causing my dress to rise up around my ass as he carried me out the bathroom leaving my man with his ho.

Shit in my world changed in just that instant. Everything. These two motherfuckers were dead to me and I knew I was going to make them pay for this shit.

"Fuck you, Goldie. Fuck both y'all scandalous-ass trife-life bitches," I screamed over the bouncer's shoulder. "The unjust don't prosper, bitch."

The club manager closed the bathroom door, following the bouncers through the crowd as they carried me straight out that motherfucker like I wasn't shit but a nuisance. Just as I saw Make$'s two bodyguards headed toward the bathroom.

Fuck it.

I pushed the bouncer off me as soon as he set me down on my Gucci feet outside the club. I stalked up the street, vaguely acknowledging that this was my second time getting booted out a fucking club. Ugh!

I climbed into the Jag and started it. I couldn't believe not only did Make$ get caught but his punk ass didn't even come after me. That nigga was busted and embarrassed. Couldn't even face me. Fuck him. I leaned back against the butter-soft leather headrest and closed my eyes as I waited for my heart to stop pounding.

Tears welled up in my eyes but I blinked them away. Fuck crying. Fuck pity. Fuck it all.

I started to call Eve, but she never really cared about Goldie and would be full of nothing but "I told you so." Michel was away for the weekend with a part-time boo visiting from out of town. Wasn't no need to ruin his weekend with my bullshit.

I did call Missy though. Just what the fuck did she know and did I need to whup her ass too for not telling me? Her phone rang three times and went to voice mail. I skipped leaving a message and dialed her number again. And again.

Maybe she couldn't hear it ringing in the club.

Maybe she didn't have her phone on her.

Maybe she was avoiding my call.

I was about to call the bitch again when she called me.

"Luscious! Oh my God, you and Goldie is wildin' the fuck out," she said, the sound of the party still going strong in the background.

"No, that no-good, backstabbing bitch wildin' out and she lucky her ass ain't being carried out on a coroner's stretcher," I snapped back.

"Damn, what happened?"

I squinted my eyes as I held the BlackBerry with a death grip. "I caught her trifling ass in the bathroom with Make$—"

"Oooh. So that shit is true?"

"So I guess you didn't know they was fucking. Right?" I asked, my heart pounding with adrenaline.

"No I didn't. For real. That's pretty fucked up."

I closed my eyes and rubbed my forehead. "Ain't shit pretty about it," I said, not even sure I believed her.

"Well, she just hired me to go on tour with them. . . . I guess she's fucked that up."

I rolled my eyes. "Missy, no offense, but I really don't give a fuck," I snapped.

"I'm just being honest, Luscious. Shit. That was good money I could use," Missy shot right back at me. "Plus I didn't even think Goldie would ever pull no shit like this. She's always about her business."

"I know what I saw."

"So I heard."

Embarrassing. "Missy. Let me call you back."

I hung up before she could say another word. She wasn't offering me any new info. Either she was blind to the fact or keeping herself out of the bullshit.

My BlackBerry sounded again. I looked at it. Make$. I sent his ass straight to voice mail and wished I could send him straight to hell. Turning the phone off I tossed it onto the passenger seat and steered the Jag away from the curb. I had just pulled to a red light at the corner when I spotted the tall dude from the club. The one I saw Goldie hugging. He was walking up the street with his hands pushed deep inside the pockets of his jeans and his head down. He looked over at my vehicle as he continued up the street.

Whoa.

He was fine. That tall, dark and fine swagger with the lean features, high cheekbones, and slanted eyes. Dressed casual but stylish. None of that metallic eagle bullshit on the front of his tee or overembellished designs on the pockets of his jeans. He was young and fine, with that hip-hop swagger but grown-man style. The combo was good. Damn good.

I squinted my eyes as I watched him. Something was nipping at me. Add some dreads and was this . . .

I eased from the light and lowered the passenger window as I slowed down to turn the corner behind him. "Has?" I called out, taking a chance.

He made a face as he stopped to bend down to look inside my car. "I know you?" he asked, his voice deep with that East Coast inflection.

I stopped the car in the middle of the street and put it in park before I climbed out and smoothed my dress over my hips as I made my way around the car and up on the sidewalk. His eyes took me all in as Goldie's words about him came back to me.

"I just know that nigga can do a serious fuckdown. He walk like he gotta keep his thighs open 'cause his dick swinging. You know? One of them dangerous dicks."

Just what I needed to get back at Make$ and Goldie.

"You 'bout to rob me?" Has asked, smiling and showing white, even teeth.

The dumb bitch didn't go for that dangerous dick *but* she fucked my little-dick man. And yes, the dick was little. I didn't give a fuck before. But now? Humph. Hey, love glossed over shit, and hate kept everything real as hell.

"I saw you in the club with Goldie," I said, putting my full flirt on. "Y'all friends?"

Has's face got hard like the mention of her name pissed him off. "Nah, not really," he said.

I nodded, letting my eyes take him all in. Letting my pain guide my actions. I extended my hand to him. "I'm Luscious," I said. "Goldie mentioned you before. I wanted to meet you and introduce myself and bask in all this fineness you got going on."

His licked his lips as he looked down at me, his broad shoulders shadowing me from the street light above. "So you and Goldie friends?" he asked, reaching in his back pocket to pull out a prerolled blunt.

I licked my lips and watched as he lit it and took a big toke. "She was," I said, stepping up to cup my hands over his mouth and then press my mouth to the other ends of my hands, making a tunnel.

His sexy slanted eyes locked with my brown eyes as he followed my lead and blew a stream of thick smoke into my hands for me to inhale into my lungs. I winked at him before I tilted my head and blew the stream of smoke up to the night sky in a rush.

His eyes were locked on my mouth as he pressed the blunt back between his lips. "What happened with you and Goldie?" he asked.

I licked my lips as I took the blunt from him, careful not to burn my acrylic tips. "I walked in the bathroom a few minutes ago and caught her fucking my man," I said, all easy and shit like that shit wasn't totally fucked up. Like it didn't wreck my world and shatter my heart. Like I wasn't ready to crawl into my bed and cry like a hungry baby.

"Word?" he asked, his eyes filled with surprise.

I nodded before I walked back over to my car. I searched the case for the CD I was looking for and slid it into the player. Soon the sound of "Motivation" filled the air. Thankfully there was nothing but abandoned houses and the parked cars of all the partygoers in there kissing Goldie's ass. *All hail the queen.* What the fuck ever. Tricky bitch.

I smoked the blunt as I pulled from my stripper moves and danced under the circle of light created in the darkness by the streetlight. That scandalous bitch actually taught me that a woman didn't have to be naked to be sexy. It was all in the moves and the eye contact. Make that man feel like he is the only one who exists.

Has posted up against the building, pressing the sole of one of his black Jordans against the brick as he tilted his head to the side and watched me. Close. "So what's this all about . . . Luscious?" he asked.

Betrayal. Heartache. Revenge.

I just shrugged as I clamped the blunt with my teeth and used both my hands to ease the skirt of my dress up around my hips. "Why you cut your dreads?" I asked.

Has smiled a little and mimicked my shrug.

This nigga was cool as fuck. Laid-back. He was the shit and he knew it. And it wasn't because he was rich or famous. It was just him. All him.

I walked over to stand before him, placing the blunt in his mouth before I turned and pressed my soft ass back against him. His hands came out to touch my waist, but I was surprised when he gently pushed me off him. I turned and looked up at him.

"So this some revenge shit?" Has asked, smoking the blunt. "You using me to get back at your boy and Goldie?"

An image of Make$ eating Goldie out flashed like a bolt of lightning or some shit. I blinked and looked down at my heels to keep from crying.

"So it don't bother you that she let my man—no, no, let me fix that—she let *a* man eat her out in the bathroom a minute after you walked out?" I asked, looking up at him as I motioned my hands with attitude. "The same dude that flexed on you in the club with the little shoulder check."

Has's eyes squinted more. "Make$? That's your man? He said some dumb shit to me, but I waved that little nigga off. He's nonsense to me, with that one whack-ass song," he said.

"Exactly," I agreed. Like I said, love glosses over things and hate keeps shit forever real as hell.

He frowned deeply. "That's some foul shit they did. Matter of fact, a lot of foul shit went down tonight."

I reached up and took the blunt from his hand, dropping it to the street to crush beneath my stiletto. I closed my eyes as I stepped to this fine nigga, grabbed his shirt tight, and raised up on my toes to press a kiss to the corner of his mouth. He smelled like some sexy-ass cologne, and I let myself get lost in his scent. Get lost in him. Forget Make$ and Goldie's tricking ass.

His body went stiff, like he wasn't fucking with it. "We can't—"

I moved his arms and pressed my body against his. Curves for days. I knew that, and now he felt it. I couldn't bring myself to kiss him on the mouth but I licked a trail from his strong, square jaw down his neck. His skin was fresh and clean beneath my tongue.

He was different from Make$, and in that moment I felt like it was just what I needed.

I leaned back and looked up at him as I felt his dick get hard against my stomach. *Damn.*

"I just know that nigga can do a serious fuckdown. He walk like he gotta keep his thighs open 'cause his dick swinging. You know? One of them dangerous dicks."

Since I locked my heart on Make$, I hadn't wanted to fuck anybody else. It had been a damn year since I even thought about another dude like that. Like I said, I'm loyal. But straight up? After the STD bullshit, catching him with Goldie, remembering all the nights I was lonely while he was out doing him, and knowing this big-dick dude was the one Goldie wanted bad as hell . . .

Well, Goldie can't have everything she want.

I turned and walked to my car. "You coming?" I asked over my shoulder before I slipped into the driver's seat. I turned and stared at him through the open passenger window, hoping he would give me the chance to get back at Make$ and Goldie with one good fuck.

He didn't do shit but stare back at me for a few moments before he turned and walked to a black Ford pickup.

Damn, ain't this some shit.

I wrapped my silk robe around me tighter as I stood in the living room looking out the window at the lit skyline. My eyes were swollen from crying. My heart was hardened with hate for Make$ and Goldie. No matter what I did, I couldn't chase the thought of them fucking around behind my back. I hoped like hell he gave her ass the STD or, better yet, she gave it to him. Couple of crabs fucking burning people.

No-good cokehead ass. And I was dumb enough to do that shit with him, trying to please him and keep him. Losing myself so that I could win him.

Still, I hated that it was two in the morning and I wondered where he was. With Goldie? Still at the club?

I walked barefoot into the kitchen and opened my pocketbook sitting on the counter. I pulled out my BlackBerry and powered it on, tapping my nails against the countertop while I waited. Tapped and did a mental rewind.

I had looked up to Goldie. Respected her grind. Wanted to emulate her hustle. I thought she was a friend. I trusted her. I thought she had my back.

I could see them lying up in bed laughing at my dumb ass. My stomach burned and I felt a rage deep in my bones. I made a fist so tight that my tips pressed painfully into the flesh of my palms. Angry tears filled my eyes. Goldie had it all and even that wasn't enough. The money, the business, the respect. She had to have my man too? I hated that bitch with a passion.

The BlackBerry vibrated in my hand. I had like ten voice mail messages. Fuck 'em. About fifty incoming text messages made the phone vibrate constantly. They all were from Make$. Fuck him.

The phone vibrated again and his image filled the screen. I started not to answer but curiosity got the best of my ass. "What?" I snapped, my voice hard and cold and nasty.

"We need to talk. I'm on my way home."

I made a face as I paced the length of the kitchen. "Home? We don't have a home. You fucked that up when you fucked Goldie. Is that who gave you the STD?"

"Man, leave that shit alone, Luscious," he said.

That pissed me off because it felt like he was trying to minimize his bullshit and my pain. "No, you shoulda left Goldie alone, bitch!"

"Man, I was fucked up and Goldie pulled me in that bathroom and locked the door. I just fucked up. That 'caine had me."

"Oh, you trying to say you and Goldie haven't *been* fucking around. Get the fuck out of here. I saw you fucking flex on the dude we both saw her hugging. Negro, please." I felt like throwing my BlackBerry into the unlit fireplace.

He said nothing. Fucking nothing.

"I'll tell you what. I ain't in the mood for you. Go lay up with

Goldie. Don't come here. I got the door padlocked and chained and if you come here acting stupid these white folks will *handle* that shit for me!"

"Man, Luscious, you know I go back on the road in the morning and I need to pack my shit."

I shook my head as I walked over to the front door to make sure the chain was on. "Nah, buy new shit and that includes a new eight ball because I done flush that motherfucker down the toilet, cokehead. Enjoy being on the road. Enjoy Goldie. Enjoy life. Because as far as I'm concerned . . . fuck you!" I sang like I was Cee Lo Green in that motherfucker.

I hung up on his ass and snatched the battery out the phone, tossing it all into the deep stainless steel sink. I gave myself a twenty count to calm down as I breathed deep as hell and massaged my head with my fingertips. I poured myself a glass of wine and drank it back in a rush. It would take a hundred more gallons for me not to feel my pain anymore.

My life was on some real bullshit. And it was just the beginning because I knew that shit might be on all the blogs before end of day tomorrow. *Probably making me look like the crazy jealous wifey or some shit.*

Hmmmm. I arched a brow as I poured another glass of wine. Maybe everybody *needed* to know just how dirty Make$ and Goldie was. Sometimes you just had to shame the devil . . . and his bitch. If I could make a little change off it too, then why the fuck not?

Good girls finished last. I was so done-dada over that shit. I was so busy watching other people backs while they was busier stabbing me in mine. No more.

Finishing the wine, I sat the glass in the sink and made my way back to our bedroom—no, *my* bedroom. I smiled as I closed the door and looked at Has sitting in the middle of the bed with nothing covering his dick but the sheet. I slipped out of my robe and posed with all my dark and delicious sexiness for him.

Has turned the TV off and let them sexy eyes of his take in all my curves. "You finished arguing with Old Boy?" he asked in that deep voice, sounding amused.

"Fuck him. He's not coming here," I said.

"I'm not worried," he said in that blasé, "I don't really give a fuck" way of his.

I believed him.

I turned around in front of the dresser and bent over, making my ass jiggle as I gave him the million-dollar pussy shot from behind. "Look good?" I asked over my shoulder.

"Hell yeah," he said, flinging back the sheet to climb from my bed.

I turned to face them—him and his dick—pressing my ass against the edge of the dresser.

His long, thick dick was already covered by a condom. It hung from his body, looking every bit of eleven or twelve inches. It made two of Make$'s dick. *Shit.*

Has grabbed his dick to tap that thick motherfucker against my thigh. *Pat-pat-pat-pat-pat.* "You got a pretty body," he said.

I spread my legs wide in front of him.

"Damn."

I stroked his dick. "Your dick way bigger than his," I said as it got hotter and harder in my hand.

He laughed a little. "You crazy," Has said, reaching up to massage my full breasts. My skin tingled from his touch. My clit pumped with new life.

Fucking this nigga Goldie wanted in the apartment and bed I shared with my cheating-ass man made my pussy extra wet. Revenge was my motivation. Payback my aphrodisiac. The fact that the nigga lived up to everything Goldie thought he would be was a bingo bonus.

I thought Has was turning me down tonight, but he just wanted to follow me in his own all-black pickup truck. We barely made it through the door of the apartment before he proved that he could give out that serious fuckdown. His dick was swinging long and was dangerously thick.

It was time for round two . . . or was it three?

I cried out when he dipped his head in to lick my hard nipples. I arched my back and squeezed his dick tighter, enjoying the ridges along that motherfucker and feeling like it was damn good to have a grown-man-size dick in my life.

Has lifted me up onto the top of the dresser. I leaned back against the mirror, looking up at him. "Fuck me like you would Goldie," I said, reaching up to stroke the soft hairs on his chest.

He frowned in confusion even as he slid his dick deep inside of my pussy, inch by thick inch until I felt full. I couldn't even take it all. *Shit.*

As he lifted my ass off the dresser, flinging my legs over his arms, I cried out from the smooth feel of his long and hard thrusts as he worked his hips. He bit his bottom lip and watched me fierce as hell, like he wanted to make sure I was pleased.

I was.

No, there was none of the emotions or chemistry I had with Make$, but a sexy man with a big dick who knew how to fuck could not be denied. Especially not tonight.

Plus, I was smiling on the inside even as he made me cum thinking: *Goldie won't have everything she want. Not anymore. I'll make sure of it.*

$\mathcal{T}$he last three weeks had been weird as hell for me. Even with discovering the truth about Goldie and Make$, it felt funny as hell not talking to either one of them clowns. All communication between me and Goldie was dead. Completely done. Fuck that scandalous bitch. I owed her an ass-whupping and plenty more. This shit between us was far from over.

Make$'s trifling ass been touring around the country the last three weeks and we spoke twice since then. I pretended to accept his apology, but told him I needed time to forgive him. So ignored his constant calls—calls I didn't get from him when he was on the road before his ass got caught. Eventually his calls slowed up but the gifts kept coming. In his mind we would deal with everything when he got home. *Negro, please.*

Even though I knew he was lying about firing Goldie, I didn't even give a fuck that she was still touring with him. Let him continue to take his pussy on the road, because all of my goodness was off-limits to him. Has was busy tearing the pussy up anyway. So it was fine by me. I was just playing my position because on the real, this nigga was still paying the bills and putting money in my account. It's the least he owed me. Still, I knew the jig would be up once he was back in town and looking for the old Luscious.

That dumb bitch was gone. Long gone and singing "Deuces."

This Luscious was going to spend his money and keep me some dick on the side. Fuck being a good girl. I was sick of getting fucked—literally and figuratively.

This Luscious went out with Eve and Michel damn near every night. I hadn't partied that hard since before Make$ locked me down and had me stuck on stupid.

This Luscious was sick of coke hard dicks. When I felt like fucking, I called Has and he came through like a champ each and every time. Our shit was strictly no strings and we were cool with that.

This Luscious wasn't putting up with Make$'s family bullshit. One call to the building manager's office and those chicks wasn't even allowed in the building anymore.

This Luscious was on some new shit.

Matter of fact . . .

I picked up my cell, popping away on a piece of gum while I waited. "Hey you. Busy?"

"Nah, not really."

"Good, meet me at the spot?" I asked, already feeling a thrill shoot through my pussy at the sound of Has's voice.

"A'ight. I was just thinking 'bout you anyway," he said.

"I'm going to give you even more to think about," I promised, already stripping off the boy shorts and sports bra I wore around the house. Shower time and then dick time.

He just did that half laugh of his.

I ended the call and hopped my horny ass in the shower. Making sure to clean it up real good because I was going to steer Has right on down to the pussy for him to snack on. If I couldn't get the appetizer, he would miss the main meal.

I rubbed my smooth dark skin down with Vaseline gel before I sprayed my favorite Calvin Klein Euphoria perfume everywhere on my body. My dark skin gleamed in the white strapless peasant dress I wore with matching espadrilles. I didn't bother with any panties. No need. I would just be out of them anyway. Plus it felt good walking when my pussy was clean-shaven.

I had just stepped out the apartment building when Peaches appeared out of nowhere like a police raid and jumped in my face. I thought about that video of the girl she had jumped and stepped way back from this crazy bitch.

Even though I eventually saw the girl one day shopping

downtown, knowing she wasn't dead or injured beyond repair didn't change the role Peaches' shot-out ass played in it all.

"How the fuck you gone ban us from the apartment building where my son pay your fucking rent?" Peaches asked, pointing her finger in my face with acrylic nails that had to be every bit of three inches long. Now what chick can really wash and wipe her ass good with nails that long? Nah, I really didn't want them suspect motherfuckers in my face.

"Peaches, Terrence and I are going though something and I just need my space," I told her, trying to calm her down like white folks do vicious animals about to attack they ass in the wild.

Peaches leaned back and made a dum-dum face. "What the fuck that got to do with me and his sisters?" She waved a hand at a SUV.

That was the first time I noticed the older-model black Tahoe sitting double-parked with the twins in the front seat.

None of them had jobs and I knew Make$ was fronting the bill and the gas. I sighed on the inside.

"Peaches, listen, I'll talk to you later, okay?" I said, trying to step past her to walk to the garage and get *my* Jag.

She stepped in my path. *Uhm. Okay.* I slid my hand right in my straw Coach bag. It slid across my can of dog mace—but I didn't need that . . . yet. I grabbed my BlackBerry and went to the gossip blogsite MediaTakeOut.com, scrolling until I found the entry: "Platinum-Selling Hip-Hop Artist Caught in Club Bathroom with One of His Strippers/Dancers!"

I turned the phone to her, watching as she read the gossip and saw the pictures of Goldie and Make$ in sexy poses together onstage.

Peaches brushed the BlackBerry out of her face, scratching my hand with one of her nails. "I already heard that bullshit. You around here telling anybody with two ears and an ass about it. You probably the one who told MediaTakeOut about it. How the hell they got a picture of you looking sad and posed up. Bitch, please."

The bitch was a little smarter than I thought. I kept my face blank.

"You stressing my son out about that bullshit. Fucking child-ish-ass rumors. Ain't shit you got to complain about with my motherfuckin' son," she said, patting her damn near flat chest with her talons. "You lucky to have him."

Lucky to have a cokehead, slender-dick motherfucker who gave me trich? Yes, Lord, thank you for the blessings.

I released a heavy breath and looked at her with eyes that I hoped were dull enough to let her know her ass was boring me.

"You 'round here not working, living good, driving my son's whip, and spending his gwap on designer clothes to go party and shop for more designer clothes 'cause you don't do shit else."

"Where you working, Miss Peaches?" I asked calmly.

"Oh *NO* the fuck you didn't!!" she screamed, stomping her foot as she jumped around in a full circle. CRAZY.

"Yes, the fuck I did, because I have *earned* every cent your son has spent on me: keeping the house clean, making sure his bills are paid—including every cent you get for doing nothing, washing his dirty drawers, running his errands, holding my chin up when he fuck up, holding him down when he let me down. I *earn* what the fuck your son do for me." I felt the fire in my eyes burn into her as my chest heaved.

I didn't need this shit.

I DID NOT NEED THIS SHIT!

"You know what, Peaches, take it up with your son," I told her as the twins climbed out of the Tahoe. "He was more than satisfied when I told him y'all was banned from the building. So deal with him. Call *him.*"

Completely not in the mood as the twins stepped up behind their mother, I reached in my purse and wrapped my hand around my can of mace. Nobody moved and nobody would get sprayed.

"Is there a problem, Miss Jordan?"

I turned to find the concierge standing in the doorway. I smiled at him before turning back to the crew. "I don't think so. Ladies?"

Peaches looked offended and leaned so far back that I thought she was going to knock one of the twins over. "Well, lah-dee-dah, Miss Bougie, and just ten minutes from the crack of your ass smelling like a stripper pole," she snapped.

"Come on, Ma, we'll just call Terrence," one of the twins said, turning to walk back to the car on her plastic heels.

"Deuces," I sang in my head, posed up as they all shot me glares over their shoulders on their way back to the Tahoe.

And I stood there watching them watching me until they finally pulled off with a screech of their tires.

"Thank you," I said to the concierge, before I turned and walked next door to the parking garage, whose façade matched the regal design of the apartment building.

Eventually I was cruising through the streets of Newark. I pulled to a red light at Broad and Market. As always, it was packed with people moving at a fast pace to cross the busy streets, reach a bus stop, just shop, or rush back to work after lunch.

Seeing the streets crammed like that reminded me of my teenage days with friends just itching to catch the bus downtown on Saturdays. It would be a day filled with cruising the stores, dreaming about the clothes we would buy one day, flirting with boys, and saving up our pennies to buy greasy slices of pizza.

Humph, back then life was simple as hell.

I was just accelerating forward when my BlackBerry sounded from inside my purse on the passenger seat. I dug it out as I steered past Essex County College with my left hand. I glanced down at the phone real quick. Make$.

I knew that shit was about his mama and I politely turned

the volume down and dropped the BlackBerry back into my bag. Fuck her. Definitely fuck him. Triple fuck them both.

The only thing on my mind right then was getting to Has and forgetting all them clown-ass niggas. For now, anyway.

"You really liked Goldie?" I asked Has as I laid stretched out on top of him while he laid on his stomach in the middle of the bed. My breasts were pressed into his back and my knees straddled his hips.

The scent of kush was heavy in the air along with the smell of our sex.

"Has?" I asked him again when he didn't answer me.

He just shrugged.

"When's the last time you spoke to her?" I asked, pushing my hair behind my ear as I kissed him from one broad shoulder to the other.

"I don't have nothing to say to her," Has said, his voice sounding sleepy.

"Damn, a lot of shit went down in that bathroom," I said, pressing my face against his neck and inhaling the warm and spicy scent of this nigga.

"I tried to pay her back some money I had of hers—"

"So that was your money all over the bathroom floor?" I asked, flashing back to the scattered bills that night in Club 973.

"Nah, it was her money I tried to give back to her, and she said some real foul shit to me, like I wasn't on her level."

I pictured that bitch floating around the club that night and my stomach burned with hate. "Humph, she think she better than people. She don't know shit about loyalty."

Has shrugged again with his laid-back self.

I rested my head against his head and looked out the window covered by sheer curtains. "I remember when she was at the strip club she blew the fuck up real quick and all the others dancers hated that bitch. I used to defend her like, don't throw shade 'cause she came and took over. You know? Half the dancers didn't like her ass and thought she was caught up on herself and I would yoke these bitches up for her and come back and tell her which ones was trying to shit her out of money or scandalize her fucking name. Like I was a friend to the bitch. I *never* had no shade. I was applauding her shit, you know?"

"Damn, you tense as hell, Luscious," Has said, laughing.

I got my focus back and he was right. My whole body was tight with anger. I laughed it off, but it was a front because my anger at that bitch was damn near choking me. "That shit got me hot, you know?"

"Yo, don't let what the fuck she did to you . . . destroy you. Nah what I mean?"

"Yeah, you right," I said, even though I didn't agree with his ass *at all*. Goldie played me. Completely unforgivable.

"I'm not thinking about Goldie myself," he said.

"I thought maybe you told her about us aready." I leaned up and moved my shoulders so that my nipples teased the smooth dark skin of his back as I grinded my pussy against his hard ass.

"Why? You gone tell her we messing around?" he asked, lifting his head to look back at me over his shoulder.

I tilted my head and licked my lips as I looked at him. "Nah, it's too much fun doing it behind they back," I said, my voice soft as I felt my clit starting to swell.

"I'm not gonna let you keep using my dick for revenge," Has mumbled into his pillow.

"We using each other," I told him as I stood up on the bed and nudged him with my foot to turn over onto his back.

As soon as he did I saw his long and hard dick fighting its own weight to stand up tall. I stared into them sexy-ass eyes of his as I worked my hips in tight circles until I was easing down and squatting over his dick. "Let us make an Oreo," I whispered to him.

"What?" Has asked, looking confused.

I held his dick straight up like high noon. "A lot of white crème between two dark things," I said, smiling.

I slid down on to his hardness.

"Oh, you got jokes? Huh?" Has thrust his hips up, filling me with pure DICK.

That shit wiped the smile off my face as I hissed and bit my bottom lip from the feel of his dick pressing against my walls. *Dammit.*

His large hands dug into my ass as he slammed my pussy down onto his dick. I cried out at the feel of his hardness stroking against my clit. "You want this dick, then you gone get this dick," Has said, looking up at my twisted face as he continued to power-drive me.

I couldn't say nothing. The dick beat words out of me. And if they did come, I knew I would be stuttering or some shit. My heart was pounding. My breath was lost. Sweat was starting to form on my body.

I sat up, pressing my hands into his chest as I looked down at him. Our eyes locked. "I needed this," I whispered down to him, meeting him stroke for stroke.

His mouth formed a circle as he switched to stroking the soft flesh of my ass as I rode him. But even as we fucked each other on some real porno-type shit and I felt my nut building, I wished I had some feelings for this nigga. I wished I really knew him.

I missed the chemistry—the kind you have when you make love to someone you give a fuck about. Me and Has was cool and the sex was hot. But that was it.

True, his dick was bigger, but I had loved the hell out of Make$ and there was nothing sexier and more exciting to me than to ride his dick and look into his eyes as I kissed him and told him I loved him. That made the fireworks go off. *That* shit made me nut. Little dick or not.

I felt stupid for the faith and love and trust I had in that nigga. He was my world. My everything. But all of it was based on lies. I lost my heart to a fucking fantasy. I saw what he wanted me to see . . . like a damn fool.

Tears welled up. "Oh shit," I cried out, sitting up straight and tilting my head back as I covered my eyes with my forearm. I couldn't believe I was filled to the brim with dick—good, hard, long, thick dick—and my mind was on Make$'s whack ass. Hurting over his bullshit. Remembering the love I had for him.

"Hey, you a'ight?" Has asked, lightly rubbing my hip.

What the fuck is wrong is with me? My shoulders shook with my tears as the bullshit came flooding back at me. All of it.

Has lifted me up and freed his dick before he laid me down on the bed next to him and then pulled my head against his chest and held me. That shit fucked me all the way up even more.

"I'm so fucking stupid," I admitted, covering my face with my hands as his compassion made me bawl even harder.

He didn't say nothing, but he we laid there for a long-ass time in that hotel room and he just held me while I cried.

It felt good to have a man's arms around me . . . even better than it felt to have his dick inside me.

It was almost a week later and that afternoon with Has was still on my mind. We never did finish what I started and only a phone call he got finally made him release me and say he had to leave to handle some business. I never asked him what business he was in and he never offered. I just peeled my messy self from his body and tried not to look at him directly because I felt so embarrassed to have broken down in front of this dude like that. I just knew he was thinking I was one of them psycho chicks acting crazy and reckless . . . like Peaches or some shit.

Me and Has hadn't spoken since, but he did text me that night to ask if I was good. I wasn't but I lied about it.

"Yo, that party last night was crazzzzzzzzzy."

I shifted my eyes over to my cousin Eve sitting on the floor of Michel's studio apartment flipping through a magazine. I shrugged as I kicked off my gold thong sandals and politely tucked my feet beneath me on the couch. "It was decent," I said, my mind on other shit than parties and bullshit.

I spotted a roach crawling on Michel's curtain and I was glad to be up out of the Pavilion. His fuchsia, turquoise, and white–decorated apartment was spotless, but there wasn't shit you could control about your neighbors when you lived in a big-ass apartment building. And we knew for a fact that Michel was triple fucked because his upstairs and downstairs neighbors was straight nasty: leave their stove greasy–, never clean their fridge–, clothes piled up in the corner–, food left for days around the apartment–, trash-overflowing kind of nasty. He was in the middle of two roach motels.

Now roaches were everywhere regardless of the type of hood but thankfully the Twelve50 had freed me from those chasing-after-a-roach-with-a-shoe days. Fuck that shit.

"Sheee-it, I had fuuuuuun," Eve said, playing with the short layers of her hair as she flipped the page.

I blinked away an image of Goldie and Make$ fucking on his tour bus and focused on my cousin. "It needed better drinks, and I would've hired somebody to perform or host, upped the entrance fee, and made more money than I know they did," I said, fingering my blunt bangs. "People pay artists, radio person- alities and all that, to come and get more people through the door. More people, more fun, more money and profits."

Eve looked thoughtful for a minute as she crossed her legs in the ruffled jean romper she wore. "See, I'm thinking fun times and you're thinking money."

"If I take my mind off of money I'll wind up back in this motherfucker . . . no offense," I added, even though I didn't sound like I meant it. Eve had a studio apartment down the hall.

In fact, when I moved into the building last year it was Michel who figured out that his new bosom buddy on the sixth floor and his friend down the hall were related.

The short of it was that my parents were bougie and pretended my mother wasn't one generation out of Newark's low-income projects. That meant Naomi Jordan barely saw, talked to, or acknowledged my aunt Nola and her five kids—Eve being the youngest of them. So my parents hated that Eve and I were close. Like I did with Make$, to avoid the drama, I just avoided taking Eve to my parents', because I liked my crazy cousin. Minus the few faults she had—which I thought were mostly on account of immaturity—Eve was the comic relief of our little group.

"Hot wings and moscato," Michel said, strolling out of the kitchenette holding a bright fuchsia tray and wearing a tight pair of jean shorts and a ruffled strapless shirt. Makeup in place. Lace wig pulled up in a ponytail. Long, shapely legs greased.

Sometimes I forgot he was a dude.

I eyed his crotch as he slid the tray onto the white coffee table. "Where exactly is your dick?" I asked, leaning forward to accept the plastic cup of wine he offered me.

Eve laughed into her own cup.

Michel stepped back and posed like he was at the end of a runway or in a beauty pageant. "Ready to drop down when your man ready for it," he said, playfully sarcastic.

Luscious arched a brow. "You mean Goldie's man," I reminded him, sipping my wine as my left eye jumped.

Michel pouted his glossy lips and shook his head. "We are not going into another long discussion on why Make$ and Goldie need to be fed Ex-Lax brownies—"

"And magnesium-citrate milk shakes," Eve added, leaning over to slap the hell out of Michel's smooth hand.

Okay, *that* made me laugh out loud.

"They gone get theirs; you don't even have to pray or wish on it, baby-boo," Michel said, snapping his slender fingers in a full circle.

"That caramel is a bitch," Eve added before biting into a hot wing.

Michel frowned and looked at me before we both looked at Eve. "What?" we asked.

Eve was busy getting the hot-wing sauce from under her acrylic tips. "That caramel," she repeated. "What goes around comes around."

"Lord, help this dumb bitch," Michel said, falling back against the fuzzy turquoise area rug and fanning himself.

"What?" Eve asked, looking lost as hell.

"You mean karma. It's *karma*," I stressed.

Eve flipped Michel the bird. "Y'all know what the fuck I meant," she said.

"Barely. Shit, I was looking for ice cream, bananas, and whipped cream and shit. I was lost like a motherfucker for a sec," Michel teased.

Bzzzzzz . . . Bzzzzzz . . . Bzzzzzz . . .

I picked up the vibrating BlackBerry just as Michel jumped to his feet and started rapping the hook from Wu-Tang's "Ice Cream." "French vanilla, butter-pecan, chocolate deluxe. Even caramel sundaes is gettin' touched."

Laughing, I answered the call without checking the caller ID. "Hello?"

"Oh, you fucking laughing and my son in fucking jail, bitch!"

My heart dropped into my stomach at Peaches' words. I waved my hand for Michel to be quiet. "What did you say? Make$ locked up?" I asked.

"Yes, he told me to call you. We need to get to Philly ASAP."

I jumped to my feet, already sliding on my shoes. "In Philly? What happened? What's going on?"

"That bitch Goldie said Fiyah and Tank raped her and then

said my mufuckin' son helped cover the shit up. The police locked all three of they asses up."

The strength left my knees and I sat back down. Michel and Eve were looking at me for details, but what the fuck could I say? The same bitch I caught my man eating out in the club just got him locked up in another state and now he want me to come be by his side like one of those wives of a cheating politician or minister or some shit. Looking stupid. Looking played out. Caught up in they bullshit.

I will handle it, Luscious.

All of a sudden, his promise after I saw the DVD of Peaches getting that girl jumped came back to me.

I'll take care of it.

Did him trying to handle or take care of what his crew did to Goldie get his ass in jail? But why would he cover up them raping *his* side-chick? And did he forget that he told me he fired Goldie?

"The twins drove the truck to Maryland, so I need you to come get me, Luscious."

I bit my lip as my thoughts raced just as hard as my heart.

When was enough enough?

"Luscious!"

I wanted to tell her, *Fuck your son, because he's getting what he deserves for even dealing with that ratchet bitch behind my back.* I wanted to hang up the phone in her face. I wanted all those crazy motherfuckers out of my life.

But that would piss him off and my money would be shorted. I wanted no part of a stripper pole again, and Make$ owed me the good life.

"I'm on my way," I said, ending the call.

Damn.

Goldie had been raped.

That's all that kept playing in my head as we drove through

the busy Philly streets to the Curran-Fromhold Correctional Facility.

Not *"My man is locked up."*

Not *"I hope my man is okay."*

Not *"Make$ is already on probation."*

Not *"I can't wait to get to the police station."*

Not *"Has his lawyer gotten to the police station yet?"*

Not even *"I wish Peaches would stop complaining about me bringing Eve and Michel with us."*

Goldie got raped.

Bitch probably lying, I thought as I gripped the steering wheel tighter.

And if she wasn't?

Fuck her. Serve the bitch right.

You lie down with dogs and you get up with fleas.

And I meant that shit. Fuck Goldie. She deserved one of those beat-downs Peaches' ass had put on that girl.

Funny how hate will make you see—and feel—shit differently.

My BlackBerry vibrated in my left hand while I steered with the right. "It's the lawyer," I told Peaches, while I answered the call and pulled over to park in front of a homeless shelter.

"Hurry up and answer," she snapped, sitting tense as hell in the passenger seat decked out in twelve shades of blue.

Shut the fuck up! "Mr. Levitz, I'm putting you on speakerphone."

"Mr. Gardner just had his bail hearing and there was no bail set—"

Peaches cried out and then slumped down in the seat so low that I thought she passed out completely. I ignored the bitch.

"Also he failed a drug test and I already spoke with his Essex County probation officer. She plans to immediately notify the courts that he has violated the conditions set by his probation.

She will be requesting a revocation of his supervised release because of the failed drug charges and the seriousness of the Philadelphia charges—"

Peaches came back to life, sat up straight, and hollered out again.

"Hand me that bottle of water, Eve," Michel mumbled from the backseat.

"Peaches . . . please," I stressed, shooting her a serious hard stare.

"Anyway . . ." He cleared his throat. "As I was saying, there's really no need to come to Philly. You won't be able to see him until he's finished being processed, and depending on what happens in Essex County, he might get shipped there."

Make$ was staying in jail. Humph. *See how much pussy you find up in that bitch,* I thought, even as I turned in my seat to face Peaches. "What do we do?" I asked, forcing my eyes to fill with tears as I pretended to let my hands shake like I was nervous. Like I gave a fuck.

Peaches reached over and grabbed my hand. "Wait to hear from him and do what he say," she said.

I fought not to get her touch off of me. After the shit Make$ did to me—the disease plus fucking Goldie and God know who else—maybe a little time sitting in jail would help him get his mind right about what was important. But it meant more wifey duties for me: weekly visits, care packages, high-ass phone bills, and making sure he got everything he needed in there. But I would do it for him—and continue to do for myself while he was in there. It cost to be a prison wifey. Fuck the dumb shit.

I dropped my BlackBerry in my bag as I turned the car around and headed back to Jersey.

I stayed quiet while Peaches made her phone calls, cussing and carrying on like she had the power to talk him free. My thoughts?

Where was Goldie's snake ass, and what really went down?

I pulled up in front of Michel and Eve's apartment building. I used to live here, but I felt so far from it. This used to be my world when my parents cut the strings and left me on my own. Nothing had changed. There was mad people sitting on the stoop and in metal chairs in front of the building. Music blared from one of the windows. Some had box fans in them; a few were lucky enough to have an air-conditioning unit, but most were just open and letting in the summer heat.

I double-parked the Jag and everyone on the block had eyes on us as I climbed out to let Michel and Eve out of the backseat.

"You cool?" Michel asked, pulling me close for a tight hug.

"I'm good," I assured him.

"Free Make$!" someone screamed from one of the windows above.

I didn't bother to look. I was too busy thinking that Make$'s arrest had already hit the news . . . or the blogs . . . or the streets. Same damn difference.

"I'll call you later," Eve said, squeezing my wrist before she walked away in her heels.

I climbed back into the driver's seat. "You going home, Peaches?" I asked as I checked the mirror for oncoming traffic and checked the street ahead for a child about to dash out before I pulled off.

"If you don't mind," she said politely.

That shit made me raise an eyebrow. That was the most manners she'd ever shown. To top if off, she said absolutely nothing during the whole trip across town to her small brick house—the rent was a gift from her son.

Maybe she's worried about Make$.

I shrugged, just happy as hell for the silence.

Later that night I was lounging in the living room watching a marathon of *The First 48*. My attention wasn't focused on the

TV, though. I was too busy thinking over all of the shit I was discovering about the man I used to hate. I always knew he treated me different when he was on the road, but just what the fuck was really going on during this touring? Just how clueless was I? Did it matter at this point?

I would never love Make$ again. Never. But I needed to know just how dumb I'd been during this relationship.

I picked up my BlackBerry from the end table. I had a bunch of missed calls but I wasn't worried about those. Those calls were all about asking me questions. I needed answers.

I scrolled through my contacts and stopped at Missy's number. I hadn't talked to her since that night at Club 973. Biting my bottom lip, I called her. I took a deep breath that didn't do shit to calm my nerves as the phone rang.

"Luscious. So I only hear from you when you know Make$ fucked up, huh?" Missy asked, answering her phone after the first ring.

Her attitude made me lean back a little bit.

"I ain't surprised at all he got arrested," she said.

That made me lean back a little more. "What happened on the road, Missy? I need to know," I admitted, my voice soft.

"Why are you still with him, Luscious? Seriously?" she asked.

Something in her voice let me know that she felt sorry for me. "What happened?" I asked again.

"I was only on the road with them for like two weeks but, Luscious, that nigga out there living life. Groupies. Threesomes. Partying. Living it up," Missy said. "You deserve better than that. It's too much diseases and shit out there for that nigga to be wildin' out like that."

So all my fears and gut instincts about Make$ were true. I felt my face get hot as fuck as I remembered the STD he gave me and how I actually believed him when he said he must have caught it before he met me.

"So you not with Goldie no more?" I asked, pretending all these emotions wasn't building up in my chest.

"Fuck Goldie's scandalous ass too. She's just as dirty as a motherfuckin' dude," Missy said. "You know what? After the way she stabbed you in the back I shoulda known Goldie was on some selfish bullshit. I knew she loved making money, but I didn't know she'd sell her fucking soul for some cash."

I didn't say a word as she told me in detail about the night in Atlanta when one of Goldie's dancers was assaulted and almost raped by one of Make$'s crew. Make$ paid the dancer off with five thousand dollars . . . and Goldie convinced her to take the money.

I felt a chill to my bones as I flashed back to his crazy-ass mother having that girl beaten and his assuring me that he would "take care" of it.

He was in jail now for trying to help the dude who raped Goldie get off.

And now I'm hearing about this shit.

This was Make$'s M.O. He felt like him, his family, and his friends could float above the law on his dime.

I shook my head at the shame of it all.

"This shit with Goldie is some wicked-ass karma and I hope her ass think about that slick shit she pulled with Kerri."

"Kerri?" I asked, still feeling numb.

"That's the girl that was assaulted. She used to dance as TipDrillz. Matter of fact, she was with me the night of Goldie's party."

I remembered her. "How is she?"

"The same. I don't even know if she really realized what happened to her. You know? She just took the five grand went home and went shopping. She blew the money and now she living with her sister in a run-down apartment on Clinton Avenue."

I shifted my eyes to look out the window at the night sky. It was starting to feel like all this info was more shit dropped on my shoulders that I couldn't hold up under.

"I'm telling you all this, Luscious, for you to know you need to get the fuck away from that nigga. You know what I mean? I feel bad knowing that I know what they did to her and said nothing, but I'm respecting what she wants. He knows the same shit I do and paid to keep his rapist-ass friends free. Like it's okay for them to rape. Shit, who's next? You?"

I didn't say anything else. I didn't have anything else to say. I was too busy swallowing down the truth.

6

*M*y phone was ringing nonstop and I was sick of repeating what little of the story I knew. The news didn't reveal Goldie's identity and neither did I. I couldn't help but wonder what the bitch was feeling after everything Missy told me about Kerri/TipDrillz. And now her ass was dealing with the same shit she fucking minimized for another one. Humph. This bitch didn't deserve no sympathy.

See, the unjust don't prosper, I thought as I began moving all of Make$'s shit into the guest bedroom. I was busy planning how to make the apartment all mine while the diseased cheater was on lock and trying to keep his asshole from getting plugged. *I can use all that closet space.*

Was I wrong for skipping through that bitch without a care in the world? No. Hell to the no. I did all my crying and worrying all those nights his ass was on the road forgetting about me—or saying "fuck me" while he fucked my friend and God knew who else.

Goldie.

I turned with a stack of Make$'s jeans in my arms and looked in the mirror. I was pretty girl. I grew up with the whole "you're pretty for a dark girl" or "you're a pretty black girl." Why the need for pointing out my deep chocolate skin tone? Who the fuck knew? But it was always there, like I accomplished some big-ass thing being dark-skinned *and* pretty. Some of her dancers thought that was the reason Goldie was so popular with all that good "real" hair and light skin bullshit. They thought a dark-skinned chick had to be more freaky, have bigger ass and titties, and wild out to get the same attention as a light-skinned chick with less body.

I never really got caught up in that skin tone bullshit.

But . . .

Goldie and I looked so different. Did Make$ believe that all pussy looked the same in the dark, or was he fulfilling some fantasy having a redbone, half-breed bitch like Goldie in his bed? Was that why he claimed to love me but cheated on me with my friend . . . because fucking Goldie was worth the risk?

My cell phone blasted off from the kitchen counter and I dumped the thirty pairs of jeans in my arms onto the made bed before rushing out the room to snatch up the BlackBerry. It was a number I didn't recognize. The last call I took from an unknown or private number was some asshole saying he didn't want to get like a nigga sitting up in jail because he protected rapists—a joke about Make$'s hit single "Get Like Me."

Humph, I hung up on him even as he laughed like he was watching Kevin Hart do stand-up. I promised myself if I got another prank call I would change my number. To hell with childish shit. I couldn't care less that Make$ let his "relationship" with Goldie get his ass in jail, but if niggas had jokes, they needed to go visit him in county.

I used my thumb to send the call to voice mail. I poured myself a shot of Patrón. Two. Hell with it.

Wincing at the feel of the liquor going down my throat, I picked up the phone, put it on speakerphone, and called my voice mail inbox.

"This is Luscious. Leave a message."

Beep.

"Hi, Luscious, this is Ursula Stevens from—"

I frowned. Ursula Stevens ran one of the most notorious gossip sites ever. She didn't give a damn about what she posted or what she said. She was infamous, and lots of entertainment people hated her snooping ass.

"I have it on good authority that your connection to the arrest of your boyfriend Make$ is something I should look into,

and we wanted to offer you an exclusive interview on the site telling us about your connection to the alleged victim. You used to dance for her, right? Anyway—"

My heart pounded. How this chick know all our business?

"Of course we can offer compensation for your time. Call me back at 1-800—"

I ended the call. I didn't want any part of giving an interview on a gossip site. Nothing. A few other chicks had taken that route. I still gagged at the memory of one ex-chick of a rapper actually allowing the posting of pictures of her miscarried fetus in the toilet. What the fuck? If only curiosity hadn't made me click the link to those photos.

Nah, I'm good. Something *that* obvious would be too big a slap across Make$'s narrow face. I wasn't that bold. Not when he was still paying my bills. The world would see nothing but the perfect wifey holding her man down while he did a bid. That's all.

Bzzzzzz . . . Bzzzzzz . . . Bzzzzzz . . .

I had just set my BlackBerry back down on the counter when it vibrated with a text message. I picked it back up and my heart pounded to see it was from Has.

HEARD ABOUT UR BOY. JUST
CHECKING ON U? U GOOD?

I leaned against the counter as I hit him back:

I'M GOOD . . . BUT I'LL B BETTER IF U
CAN CUM THRU 2DAY.

It was time me and Has got back down to it. Make$ was looking at at least a year if the judge sent him back to jail for his probation violation alone.

Bzzzzzz . . . Bzzzzzz . . . Bzzzzzz . . .

I opened the text:

CUM THRU OR CUM IN U?

I smiled as I texted him back:

ONE LEADS TO THE OTHER.

Bzzzzzz . . . Bzzzzzz . . . Bzzzzzz . . .

SHOW ME SUM'N GOOD.

I hurried out my skintight jean leggings and lace thong biki-nis to squat over my phone, spreading the lips of my hairless fat pussy to make sure the photo captured everything inside and out for his sexy ass. I took the photo and then attached it to a text with the message:

CUM & GET IT!!!!! (OR GET IT & CUM.)

LOL.

Bzzzzzz . . . Bzzzzzz . . . Bzzzzzz . . .

"Whooaaaa," I said, leaning back as a picture of his big dick lying across his lap filled the screen. It wasn't even hard and it made Make$'s shit look like a toddler's dick.

WE'RE ON THE WAY.

I licked the screen, already feeling my pussy warming up for a workout. "Come and get this pussy. Come and get this pussy," I sang like it was a club joint, dancing my way into the master bedroom. "Gimme dat dick. Gimme dat dick. Gimme gimme dat dick."

I brushed my hair up into a cone around my head and tied it with a silk Vuitton scarf before I stripped naked to hop my sexy, ready-to-be-sexed chocolate ass into a bubble bath scented with my favorite L'Occitane Honey and Lemon Bath Bubbles. I loved the French bath and body products ever since Goldie introduced—

I froze at the thought and my mouth twisted in distaste. Goldie gave me the bath set from the French company for my birthday. *The devil is a lie.*

I emptied the tub, rinsing out every honey-and-lemon-scented bubble before I dumped the entire basket of goodies in the trash. *Shit probably rooted or some shit.* I wanted no part of nothing concerning Goldie's conniving ass. Nothing.

Well, except Has, I thought as I poured three capfuls of the Bath & Body Works White Citrus Bubble Bath from the gift basket my moms gave me the same night of my birthday party at the Key Club. I didn't even open it because I was so excited about Goldie's gift basket—stuck all up in her shit like she was my fucking god or idol or some shit. Just being dumb as hell.

That shit made my stomach burn and my heart harden.

I thought back to the night of my party when I walked outside to find her and Make$ chitchatting. My eyes shifted over to the mirror to check my reflection. *Is that when their shit started? At my fucking party?*

I had to give myself a ten count to keep from ramming my fist against the mirror. Even long after I slipped beneath the hot depths of the water, it took a minute for my body to relax, and even longer for my mind to slow down.

In some ways Goldie's betrayal burned my guts hotter than Make$'s. A man was hardly ever to be trusted but you always hoped the chick you called a friend would have your back when the man fucked up . . . and not be the cause of the fuckup. *Lying bitch.* I hate an untrustworthy ho. Bitches like that deserve to get they shit shook.

I was just standing up to rinse the bubbles from my body under the oversize showerhead when the phone rang. I shut the water off and grabbed a plush towel to wrap around my body as I stepped out the tub. I picked up the cordless phone on the wall by the commode.

"Hello."

"You have a collect call from a correctional facility—"

Make$. The collect calls began. I didn't give a fuck as long as he made sure the accountant continued to pay the bill.

I pressed all the right buttons to accept the call.

"Whaddup, Luscious?" Make$ said, his voice sounding like he just woke up.

I rolled my eyes as I grabbed a bottle of shea butter from my tray of toiletries on the counter. "Oh my God. How are you?" I asked, proud of how sincere I sounded. *Maybe I should go into acting?*

"Listen, let's cut through the bullshit, a'ight?"

I sat up straight and stopped smoothing lotion on my legs at his tone.

"My lawyer is telling me this shit ain't looking good for me, Luscious, and I got to look out for myself while I'm in here—"

Okay, I sat up a little straighter until my back was flat as a wall. "So what you saying?" I asked, keeping my voice soft even as I felt my pulse racing so hard that I was light-headed.

"With the year I have to do for my probation violation and then my attorney is pushing a plea deal for at least three years for that rape bullshit . . . I know that's a long time to ask any woman to put the pussy on lock—"

My eyes squinted and my asshole got tight. "Soooo what are you saying, Terrence?" I snapped. Fuck it. I had no time for games.

"I'm not gone pay the bills while some other nigga fucking my chick. Period."

Has. He knew about Has? Did he know about Has?

I thought about leaving Peaches alone in my car with my bag and cell phone when I dropped Michel and Eve off. Did that bitch see the text Has sent me? "What other nigga? What the fuck are you talking about? You cheated! Not me?"

"Yooo, exactly. Before I got caught I wouldn't have had no doubts you would hold me down while I did this bid. But now? You think I don't know you mad at me? You think I'm stupid or some shit, Luscious?"

Did he know about Has? I gripped the lotion bottle so damn hard that the cap blew off and lotion squirted out like cum milked from a dick. "So . . . what are you saying?" I asked again. "You got caught fucking around but now *I'm* not be trusted? What the fuck kind of logic is that? Nigga, make sense!"

"Calm down, Luscious. Damn!" Make$ snapped. "I can't sit in here wondering if you paying me back and on top of it I'm footing all the bills. So I want you to move out the apartment until I get out."

"What?!!" I jumped to my feet and flung the bottle of lotion across the room to crash into the one of the wood-framed mirrors flanking the window. The mirror cracked like a spiderweb.

"Yo, Luscious, like my mother said—"

"Your *mah-fer.*" I mocked his mispronunciation, making a face as I paced so hard that my towel fell from my body. Oh, I was hot.

"I'm just sayin—"

"I'm just sayin', you little *mah-fer*fucker," I snapped sarcastically. "So because you fucked up with Goldie and now she got you deep in some bullshit, I'm being punished like a child for y'all shit. Get the fuck outta here."

Humph, that hood upbringing was coming all out of me.

"I'm not breaking up with you, I'm just sayin'—"

"Nigga, you ain't saying shit," I snapped, waving my hand like he was there for me to nudge him in the forehead. "No, no, my bad. You *are* saying something. You saying, 'Fuck me.'"

This nigga just cut me off because his side-chick sent his ass to prison. Because Goldie sent him to prison I was ass out? No ends? What the fuck?

"What is this really about? Like wh-wh-what the fuck you really tryna say?" I asked, shoving my BlackBerry between my shoulder and ear to clap my hands together so hard that they stung. "I put up with your shit including you getting locked up for being involved in the rape of your ho . . . and you fucking dumping me because you're scared I'll fuck around while you locked up."

"No female is to be trusted but I'm not dumping you, I'm just cutting back on your funds until I get out."

I raised both my eyebrows, not giving a fuck anymore. "No, you lame-ass nigga. The female you trusted got your ass in lockup."

"Lame-ass?"

And I paused. I took a moment to decide just which way to flow with this shit. Go all in? Let a nigga slide? Try to get him back on board with the program later?

Shit flashed back to me like I was watching a picture slideshow.

His neglect when he was on the road.

Click.

Wondering about random chicks hanging around the studio when I popped in.

Click.

Random gossip on the blogs.

Click.

Suffering through his family's crazy drama.

Click.

The STD he gave me.

Click.

Catching him eating Goldie out in the bathroom at Club 973.

Click.

Still working and probably fucking with Goldie even after I caught them.

Click.

Locked up for what the fuck ever went down between him Goldie and his entourage on the road.

Click.

And now . . . *now* this Negro was cutting me off because he had to do a bid behind Goldie turning his ass in.

Click.

Now where they do that dumb shit at?

I'VE. HAD. ENOUGH.

"You damn right, you's a lame-ass nigga," I said. "Fuck you and that bitch for fucking up my life. You got just what your ass deserved for messing with that trick behind my back. The unjust don't ever prosper, and *if* she did get raped, then fucking boo-hoo for her trifling ass too. I'm not shedding two tears in a bucket for neither one of y'all motherfuckers.

"Fuck you, bitch. I'm looking at years in the motherfucker and that's how you coming at me!" Make$ blasted into the phone.

I could practically see the veins bulging in his tattooed neck, but I just shrugged. This nigger had fronted on me for the last time. It was time for shit to get realer than ever.

"I wish I was there right now, I could choke the shit out of you."

I laughed. "Ain't you got enough charges?" I joked.

"*And* you got jokes, Luscious? You fucking joking with your raggedy stripper ass using me to come up."

"Use you? Nigga, you played me, and you was so busy playing out there in them streets, Mr. Platinum, that you didn't even see that bitch revving up to run your ass over." I hustled my butt-naked ass into the kitchen and grabbed the box of garbage bags from the pantry.

"Man, shut up, Luscious. Think you so smart, *college girl.*"

He said that shit like it was an insult.

"College dropout, actually . . . and still smarter than you and Goldie combined." I went to the guest room and started yanking all his shit out the closet with my free hand, shoving it into the garbage bags.

"Since you so smart, then get your almost highly educated ass out my fucking apartment!"

I snatched his fifty pairs or better of boxers from the top drawer of the dresser and then slam-dunked them in the bag. "The only thing getting the fuck out this apartment is *your* shit."

"Bitch, you crazy. I'll call my attorney and have your ass thrown the fuck out."

Next went his dozen Gucci belts.

"No, it's your meth head–looking mama who's a crazy bitch and your attorney who's a dumb bitch if he don't understand that your bad credit–having ass got the apartment in *my* name. Just like the car and the gun."

The line was quiet. I paused. For a second, I let it sink in that this was the man I loved with all my heart just a little over a month ago. And now? Now we were warring like enemies. I didn't want to let it get to me, but it hit that this shit was sad as hell. "I hope that redbone pussy was worth all this shit."

"It was."

Pause.

I hung up the phone. There wasn't shit else to be said.

Love had no guarantees, and when it came to a heart being broken there weren't warranties, either.

I pulled up in front of Peaches' house and popped the trunk of the Jag. It took me every bit of three minutes to dump the six garbage bags from my trunk and backseat onto her porch. As soon as I was done, I hopped back into the driver's seat and laid on the horn.

Peaches' front door opened and she fell her little ass over the bags and face-first onto the brick porch.

"That's all your son's shit for you to keep and worship until his ass get out of jail," I yelled out the window.

I didn't even give her ass a chance to get back to her feet before I pulled off. I didn't have to deal with her anymore. And everything I was allowing Make$ to get from *my* apartment was in those bags. I checked my personal bank account. I had just enough money in it to pay the bills for two months and then I was on my own, or it was back in the roach motel with Michel or back to my family. Shit.

I wondered if Make$ had any money stashed around the apartment . . . or in his safe-deposit box that I had a key to. It was worth a check.

Bzzzzzz . . . Bzzzzzz . . . Bzzzzzz . . .

I picked up my BlackBerry and risked opening the new text message as I shifted my eyes back and forth from the road to the cell. It was Has.

Yo, where u at?

The last thing on my mind was dick, and so I didn't even bother to answer him. I pulled to a stop at a red light and I felt the tension across the back of my neck and my shoulders. I couldn't believe that everything in my life had changed so drastically. From being in love and financially secure to being manless, jobless, and damn near homeless.

Right there at the corner of a busy intersection, I felt the weight of all the betrayals and rejections push my shoulders down. It was almost like something inside me fucking snapped. I covered my face with my hands and cried like a baby. Car horns honked. People cussed me out through their open windows as they pulled from behind me and passed me by.

I sat there and gave myself that one last cry of release to keep crazy from holding me close and not letting me go.

As far as I was concerned, this was all Goldie's fault. Everything in me was locked and loaded on that bitch. If it was the last thing I did, the bitch was going to pay.

Aim

7

One Year Later

POW! POW! POW! POW!

I steadied my hand as I squinted my eyes through the goggles and locked them on the stationary target twenty-five yards away against the far wall of the indoor shooting range. My new .357 felt good in my hands. I still had the nine-millimeter I brought for Make$ in my name, but this baby was my favorite. I couldn't believe I used to be afraid of guns and now . . .

I fired off two more rounds.

POW! POW!

I envisioned Goldie's face on the paper target and damn near snapped my wrist in two firing at the center of her forehead.

POW!

I pretended that her blood and brains splattered out the back of the hole in her head to soak the wall. The thought of that made me smile as I pressed the button to electronically move the target up the lane to my booth. I removed my goggles, earplugs, and earmuffs just as it stopped in front of me.

Every single bullet fired was in one of three areas: the head, the heart, or the crotch.

"Shit, who pissed you off?"

I looked over my shoulder to find two white dudes in tight jeans and foil-covered T-shirts watching me. Lots of white dudes love them some dark meat, and with the short shorts I had on, all of my thick thighs were on display. Back when I was stripping I got more money and attention from them than from most black men. Still, I wasn't into fulfilling any slave fantasies or giving them a chance to get pissed and call me a nigger.

I just curved my glossy lips into a smile and turned and gave them my back as I removed the magazine from the handgun and placed both pieces in its case before closing it securely.

"Y'all have a good day," I said to the men still standing there watching my ass. I started to do one of my ass tricks, but my days of performing were done—especially for free.

"Have a good day, Dirty Harry," Sal, the owner of the shooting range called behind me as I strolled toward the glass door of the building.

I'd been going to the range ever since Make$ got locked up last year, and I even had a club membership. Everyone there knew me by my legal first name, Harriet, and shortened it to Dirty Harry because I was a damn good shot. Fuck with it.

"You too, Sal," I called over my shoulder as I took my shades from the back pocket of my jean shorts and slid them on my face to block the summer sun.

After securing the gun case in the trunk of my Jag, where I kept it, I climbed behind the wheel and soon I was zooming out of the parking lot, ready to hop on Route 1/9 to leave Jersey City behind and head back to Newark.

I let the windows down and enjoyed the feel of the warm air blowing against my face as I shifted my whip like I was a race car driver. I turned up the volume on the radio to hear the last hour of *The Breakfast Club* morning show on Power 105.1 with crazy-ass Angela Yee, Charlamagne Tha God, and DJ Envy. The sounds of my jam from last summer filled the speaker.

"Baby, I can be your motivation—"

I turned the volume all the way down. I couldn't forget that song was playing when I caught Make$ and Goldie in the bathroom at Club 973. Now I hated that song just as much as I hated that bitch.

Fucking slut. I pressed my foot down on the gas pedal,

zooming forward as I picked up my cell phone and hit number two on my speed dial.

"Whassup, Luscious?"

My hand tightened on the cell phone. "What's up with your boss Goldie?" I asked.

"Nothing new to report."

I eased off 1/9 and made the turn onto Market Street. "Well, I pay you good money for information, and it's been a minute since you brought me something different. Get me something. Anything. *Everything.*"

"Got it."

I ended the call and tossed the phone onto the passenger seat.

Let's be clear.

This year had done abso-fucking-lutely nothing about dimming my plans to take Goldie's ass out. Instead, it had fed my hate like a baby. Now my plans for revenge against that bitch had stronger legs. Everybody know revenge is best served up cold. She would never see me coming. And I wanted to be there right at the height of her downfall to remind her of the knife she stabbed into my back.

I turned the volume back upon the radio and 50 Cent's "I Get Money" was playing. It felt like my anthem, because getting money was number two on my mind, behind finishing Goldie's ass.

I was just veering onto Springfield Avenue when I pulled my Jag over and I turned that shit *all* the way up, hopping out the car to party right there on the street like I was in the club. Fuck it. I felt like it. And I was into that shit. Eyes closed. Fingers snapping. Hips gyrating. Weave swaying. All of it.

People blew they horns or hollered out their car windows at me.

I didn't give a fuck.

"Yo, Luscious, you in a good mood, baby!"

I looked over my shoulder at a convertible Bentley double-parked by my Jag. I laughed at one of the biggest dope boys I knew, Killer Cain, sitting there posted up in his shit watching me. I walked over to the car.

"I *stay* in a good mood, Cain. What's up?" I asked, bending down to lean on his doorframe.

Cain was big and black as hell but cute in the face like Cedric the Entertainer. Even when I was with Make$ he would throw out subliminals that he wanted me. I had no doubt that this nigga probably had more dick than Make$ but I never fucked with it. Loyal Luscious had been deep in love. Deep and dumb.

"What's up with you?" he asked, leaning over to eye my thighs and hips in the jean shorts I wore with a striped racer-back tee. I was on my casual steez because I had mad errands to run and no time for heels and total flyness.

I turned and reached down in my car for a glossy club flyer to hand him. "You coming to the comedy show tonight?" I asked, handing him the flyer between my fingers. "You can bring who-ever you planned on fucking tonight."

Cain took the flyer with a laugh. "I would love to be fucking *you* every night, baby," he said.

I reached over and stroked his bearded cheek as I shook my head. "I'd rather have you as my friend, baby," I told him honestly.

He turned his head and licked my palm playfully as he winked at me.

I patted his cheek. "Don't be out here licking every pussy offered up to you. Everything that look good ain't good. Right?"

Cain leaned back in his seat, still eyeing me. "I'd risk it."

I turned and opened my car door. "You coming tonight?" I asked again as I climbed behind the wheel.

"Yup-yup," he said, blowing his horn before he pulled off.

I headed straight to Club Marquee on Clinton Avenue. Before I pulled into the gated parking lot, I looked up at the small marquee over the club and smiled:

CLUB MARQUEE AND YUMMY ENTERTAINMENT
PRESENT
ALL-STAR COMEDY SHOW

I blew the horn as I turned the Jag and pulled through the open gate to park next to Eve's red convertible Miata. Yummy Entertainment was made up of me, Eve, and Michel. And we were running this party-promoting shit. We did it all: parties, fashion shows, hair shows, comedy shows, car shows, boat rides, and holiday balls. Once every other month or better there was a Yummy Entertainment event going on in Newark or one of the surrounding cities.

In the last six or seven months word had hit the street that our events were on point. We worked hard to build our reputation and our plan was to kick things up, pool our money, and get into bringing more big-name talent to the city. We wanted to leave these small venues behind and compete with the promoters packing Symphony Hall–type shit. Hell, NJPAC-type shit. Fuck it. Shoot big. Go hard or go the fuck home. Shit or get off the pot.

I walked into the club with a fuchsia patent leather tote in my hand. I paused to hug the owner, Maria, before I continued in to find Eve and Michel setting up the room. "Morning, y'all," I said, holding up my finger as my cell phone vibrated in my hand.

"Hello."

"Hi, Harriet, this your mother . . . in case you forgot."

I smiled and shook my head. "Hi, Mama, I couldn't ever forget you," I said, reaching in my bag for the envelope I'd slipped inside of it as soon as I left the bank.

"We're having a dinner here for Aunt Mack this Sunday. Your daddy and I want to see you there. Are you coming?" she asked, crossing every t and dotting every i in the way she talked.

"I sent over a couple of tickets to the comedy show tonight," I said lightly, taking the stack of money from the bank envelope. "Are y'all coming?"

"No, I told you we have a church board meeting tonight."

I swallowed my disappointment as I split the nearly five grand in cash into three piles. The weekend-long car show we had last week had did us well. Even after paying for the talent, the venue fee, the cost of advertising, and sticking to our agreement to bank twenty-five percent of our profits, we still had a little over a grand apiece. Good money and a good time. Who could ask for anything more?

I handed Eve and Michel their money and a folded copy of the bank statement. Everything was aboveboard. There wasn't shit one of us knew that the other two didn't know.

"I'll see what can I do, Ma," I said, folding my money and sliding it into my back pocket.

"See you Sunday, Harriet . . . and don't you bring Eve," she stressed before she hung up the phone.

I sat the cell phone onto the table as Michel and Eve shared a long look. I cut my eyes at them as I pulled out my iPad. "What?" I asked.

"Nothing," they both said, turning to finish arranging the chairs and tables.

Whatever was on their mind was their business to tell or keep. Not my problem.

I logged onto the Internet and went straight to Goldie's website . . . just like I did damn near every day. Besides my insider— who didn't give a shit about the bitch anymore than I did—I stayed on top of this bitch's movements like I was the Feds trying to bring down a cartel. Google alerts. A fake user account on her Goldie's Girls website. A full report from one of those online search sites for background checks. I just was waiting for that bitch to slip.

Over the year, I had won little victories against her, but she always bounced back.

I turned her in for stripping in her King's Court projects apartment and got the bitch heave-hoed out onto the street. She just gathered up her loot and whatever shit she wanted from the curb and moved to a New York luxury high-rise apartment. *Ugh!*

I had shit in place to help Rick, the owner of Club Naughty and Goldie's ex, to steal most of her dancers and the bitch stopped fucking with strippers and opened a booking firm for video vixens and full-size models. *Damn!*

I even tried to get the bitch robbed and she ended up tasing the hell out of my boy and had him pissed at me. *That bitch!*

I knew where she lived.

I knew her phone numbers.

I knew where she banked.

I knew her routine for her new life in New York.

I knew who she fucked, when, and for how long.

I knew a lot of her clients.

I was all over that bitch, ready to get her once and for all.

I used my fingertip to open the photo file labeled: PAY-BACK! In it were clear as hell pictures of Goldie's upper-Man-hattan apartment. I had to admit the bitch had that shit laid the fuck out. It made my apartment in Twelve50 look like Section Eight.

I flipped through each photo, taking in everything and knowing I could walk around that bitch's house with my eyes closed and not stub a toe. My insider delivered up the goods and I paid her well.

"Luscious . . . Luscious . . . Luscious!"

I tore my eyes away from a picture of Goldie standing in front of an oversize glass desk looking out at the New York land-scape. "What?" I asked, turning the iPad over to shield it from Eve's snooping eyes as she walked over to stand by where I sat.

"We need your help, boo," Eve said, dressed in a lime-green strapless romper with a colorful silk scarf wrapped around her head.

"Coming," I said, standing up to lock my iPad and slide it back into its case.

It was time to focus on Yummy Entertainment business, because I was determined to make it just as big as Goldie's Girls, Inc. The time for Goldie topping me was over.

The comedy show was sold out between the tickets we presold and the money made at the door. Dressed in black sequined leggings, matching red-bottomed shoes, and a satin tank, I worked the entire club, making sure everyone was having a good time, there were no complaints, the catering was hot, and the drinks were cold. Eve stayed on top of the talent, making sure there were no ghetto-ass late performers or big gaps in the show. Michel handled the door.

The cocktail servers—one male and one female—both wore skintight shirts with our Yummy Entertainment logo on it. We had to make sure everybody had some eye candy, and the miniature cocktails we sold for a dollar kept the crowd good and loose for cheap. Double win.

I spotted Killer Cain at a corner table with a Keyshia Cole knock-off. He looked like he had indeed lined up that ass for the night. They were hugged up even as everyone laughed until they cried at the female comedian on stage.

My mind was already on our next event. I hadn't talked to Michel and Eve about it yet, but I already had a big-name talent in mind. Someone from my past. Would he do it, though? I wanted to run it by him before I got them all excited and shit.

Another quick walk around the room and I made my way to the front of the club. Michel was counting the money in the till, looking Gaga in a blonde and green wig with colorful and glittery eye makeup.

"I'll be outside. I have to make a call," I told him.

Michel nodded, causing one end of his asymmetrical bob to float back and forth as he stayed focused on counting.

As soon as I stepped out the building, the summer heat surrounded me like a blanket. Even though the sun was long gone from the sky, the heat remained. It took about five seconds for me to feel like I was ready for a shower.

I rushed over to my car and unlocked it to grab my old BlackBerry from the glove compartment. After our big argument on the phone and me throwing his shit in Hefty bags onto his mama's porch, Make$ had cut off any and everything in his name, including my cell phone.

The days after our breakup had been hard for me, but I made it through to the other side. My desire was to not fall once Make$ left, because I knew that's what his mama and everyone else expected. I had to watch every fucking cent and even thought about giving up that apartment . . . or selling the Jag . . . or going back to stripping . . . crawling back to my parents . . . or *some* shit. But I didn't.

"Humph . . . look at me now. I'm getting paper." I sang the Chris Brown hook.

I powered on the BlackBerry and scrolled through my contacts to find the number for Tek-9. I knew I was taking a chance calling someone who was cool with Make$, but he had always given me that vibe that he was feeling me. I just never took him up on it. Well, Make$'s ass was busy in jail writing letters and sending pictures of himself in his cell, and in the last year Tek-9 had blew up, got the deal with Platinum, and took on star status. He stepped right in to fill the gap Make$ left.

The phone rang twice. "Yo, who this?" he asked.

There was loud background noise. Music playing. People talking. I knew his ass was in the studio or some club.

I smiled. "This Luscious. What's up, Tek?" I asked, sitting down in the passenger seat.

"Luscious? Sexy black Luscious?" Tek-9 asked.

"There's only one," I teased, my eyes widening as I watched Michel step outside the club talking to a tall and skinny dude.

"You still had my number, huh?" he asked, sounding like he was showing every tooth in his head.

"Yup," I said, watching Michel and the dude share a cigarette.

"So whassup?"

"Well, my friends and I have this party-promoting little hustle going on, and we've been doing good but I'm ready to kick things up and do bigger events with bigger venues and talent . . . like you," I said, swallowing down any nerves I felt.

"I charge a minimum of twenty grand per show, Luscious."

Damn.

"And that's not including travel and hotel and a driver."

"What's your walk-through fee?" I asked, looking on as Michel and the dude started kissing like crazy up against the wall.

"Ten grand and unlimited bar."

"And what's the 'Remember when you slept on my couch before you blew up' discount?" I asked, as I looked down at the diamond tennis bracelet on my wrist. A gift from Make$ back when he gave a fuck.

"Not as high as the 'you shoulda fucked me on that couch' discount," Tek-9 shot back at me, the background noise suddenly gone.

I laughed and shook my head. "You know I don't get down like that. It was all about Make$ back then. And y'all friends so I'm not fucking with that."

"And now? That nigga just copped to two years."

"What?" I rose to my feet, my eyebrows dipping together in surprise.

"Make$ copped a plea deal and took two years for the shit went down after that rape last year," Tek-9 said. "You didn't know?"

My heart pounded like crazy. "No," I admitted.

Make$ had another two years behind bars? He had to be regretting bringing Goldie's ass on the road. He was behind bars and she was living it up in New York. Missy told me she heard

Goldie stole a lot of his jewelry and money after the rape that went down in Make$'s suite. He never got the shit back.

"Well, I got it straight from the horse's mouth, you heard me."

"You saw him in jail?" I asked, trying to pace off the nervous energy I felt all up and through my body.

"Nah, that nigga finished the year he got for fucking up his probation this morning and then had to turn right around and go to court today for the rape shit. He out. He don't go back for official sentencing until next week."

Make$ was out.

I strode around my car on my heels and grabbed my iPad from the trunk. With my neon green fingernails I found an article on Make$:

Today, in entertainment news, platinum recording artist Terrence Gardner, better known as Make$, was spotted leaving a Philadelphia County courthouse in the case against him for aiding and abetting and also trying to bribe the unidentified victim of a sexual assault by two members of his entourage, who have already been found guilty of the assault and are awaiting sentencing. It is rumored that Terrence Gardner will accept a plea deal from the district attorney's office—

"Stop playin'!"

My head whipped around just as Michel tried to push the dude's hands from under his skirt. *Oh, shit!* Michel was laughing it off and steady slapping at the dude's hands, but I knew that shit could get mad serious quick if his snake dropped from wherever Michel tucked it. "Listen I'll call you back, a'ight," I said, my eyes locked on Michel across the parking lot.

"Yo, straight up. Let me get some of that I been sniffing up on for years and I'll do the fucking show for free, you feel me?"

"I'll call you back," I said again before I ended the call.

I dropped my iPad in the trunk.

"What the fuck?" the dude yelled.

"Don't hit me!" Michel begged just before he hollered out in pain.

I just closed my eyes because I knew Michel's "secret" was out. I grabbed my gun from the case and loaded the clip as I raced across the parking lot. My knees got weak to see the dude's hands around Michel's throat as he held his slender body up against the brick side of the building.

Michel's eyes were bulging out of his head as he looked at me and barely got out the words, "Help me."

The man used his hand around Michel's throat to slam his head against the wall. *Hard.*

I raised my gun and worked hard to fight my nerves. Shooting at a firing range and actually putting some heat into a motherfucker was two different things. "Let her down," I said, swallowing over a lump in my throat.

The dude looked at me over his shoulder and I could tell from the crazy look in his eyes that the fact that he was just kissing up on a dude was enough to make him kill. "Her?" he asked, like he didn't even see the gun in my hand or had no respect for it or me. "This look like motherfuckin' pussy to you?"

The dude released one hand from around Michel's throat to jack the hem of his skirt up. Michel's lace bikini was torn and his dick was free and hanging.

I stepped up closer to him and made sure I kept my eyes locked on him. I had to let him know to stop this before I shot him. And I would. I would hurt him before I let him hurt Michel. "Put. Her. Down," I said again, my voice so hard. As hard as I hoped he'd realize I could be.

It was him or Michel. Point-blank.

I took another step and pressed the gun to the back of his head. I didn't want to draw any more attention to this bullshit and that's the only reason I didn't bust one off in the air. "Trust me. I got one with your name on it, motherfucker. Put her down," I told him, my voice cold. My hand was steady. My gun was ready to shoot. My target practice was coming in handy.

Finally, he removed his hand and Michel slumped to the glass-covered blacktop. He coughed and gasped for air as he put one slender hand to his neck and used his other hand to pull his dress down to cover his dick. Even as he struggled to breathe life into his body he wanted to hide from who he really was.

I felt sorry for my friend.

The dude started hawking up spit like he wanted to get rid of any of Michel's DNA he took in when they kissed.

"If I was you, I wouldn't tell anybody. The hood's not going to understand that you didn't know you was fucking with a dude," I told him, my gun at my side but my finger still on the trigger.

He looked up at me and I could see in his eyes that he knew what I said was true. That shit would follow him. I knew he wasn't going to say shit, just like I knew Michel didn't want his secret told. I was glad when he shot Michel one last evil, hate-filled stare before he stalked over to his motorcycle and tore out the parking lot.

I released a heavy-ass breath as I stooped down to help Michel to his feet. He flinched and waved his hand at my gun. "You know I'm scared of those things," he said, his usually soft voice hoarse from being choked out.

He stumbled on his heels and I tried my best to hold the gun from my body and help keep him on his feet. "From what I saw, you're used to packing heat," I said dryly.

Michel just sucked air between his teeth. "Not the time, Luscious."

"Now I really want to know where you tuck *all* of that."

"What part of 'not the time' do you *not* comprehend?" Michel snapped.

I just laughed until I remembered that Make$ was free.

Suddenly, wasn't shit funny.

$\mathscr{F}$ear is an amazing thing.

That shit will have you on your toes, looking around corners before you turn them, and double-checking everything to make sure you're safe. To make sure you're not the latest victim. To make sure you're alive to see another day. In life, especially in the hood, you either get or you get got. Period.

Fear will get you through.

And sometimes it will make a straight ass of you.

Knock-knock.

I screamed out loud as hell, like I was in a horror flick, and rammed my hand in my bag for my gun at the sudden knock on my car window. I relaxed as my mother's face filled with alarm. I released my death grip on my .357. I'd gone from keeping my gun in its case in my trunk to keeping it in my purse—something against my gun permit. "Hey Mama," I said, motioning for her to back up so that I could open the door.

"Did I scare you?" she asked, her eyes shifting all over my face.

Shit, scared been my middle name for two days.

"No, you just surprised me," I said, sliding my bag onto my shoulder and finally climbing out the car. I arranged the peach silk halter jumpsuit I wore.

"You've been sitting out here so long," she said, looking not much different from the woman she was when I was growing up. Average height, pear shape, short natural hair, skin as smooth and dark and flawless as a midnight sky, and eyes and teeth as white and clear as milk.

Naomi Jordan was a beautiful woman.

I got my deep chocolate complexion and sexy pear shape from my moms but my looks? My looks were all Kendrick Jordan.

"You're afraid to come in?" she asked, the bright red wrap dress she wore looking brilliant as hell against her skin.

I hugged her close, hoping to stop all the dang questions. "I was on my phone," I lied, allowing myself to inhale the familiar scent of her Trésor perfume.

Truth? I was sitting in my car trying to prepare myself for the all-out bougie bullshit that was my father's side of the family. I didn't fit . . . and they made sure I knew that shit. Everybody was a teacher, politician, attorney, or doctor. Professional shit. Me dropping out of college . . . to strip . . . and then to stop stripping to be the wifey of a rap star?

Pure shame for the Jordans.

They didn't even like me hanging out with Eve—my mother's own niece. Eve always worked as a cashier, a hotel maid, or some other job they looked down their nose at like she was selling drugs or stealing. My mama forgot that *she* was born and raised in the projects. I loved her to death, but her bougie ways wasn't even authentic. That shit was as fake as counterfeit bags.

It was all those high expectations and bars that were set for me that made me want to be free, and that easy money on the pole was the key to the freedom to rebel against all their plans for me. . . .

2007

Nineteen. One year out of my parents' house. Living on campus with nothing but a phone for them to really see what I was up to. Lying became my best friend. This was the fucking life. And my life was not wrapped up in my prelaw classes.

The shit that is so crazy is my parents keeping me sheltered for eighteen years and then just sending me off to college, where I learned shit neither my parents nor my professors wanted me to fuck with. Partying. Fake IDs. Clubs. Drinking. Popping Ecstasy. Boys. Lots of boys.

And my dorm mate, this cool-ass white girl named Erin, was my tour guide to the world of campus life. The more she showed me, the more I wanted to know. To learn. To do.

And when she said she knew how we could make money and threw a gold bikini in my lap as I sat on my Hello Kitty–covered twin bed, I was down . . . until I got on that stage.

J. Holiday's "Bed" played around me and I stood there look- ing out at the owner, this sexy ex-stripper named Slick Rick, like a deer caught in headlights. Just standing there in my bikini, looking stuck on stupid.

"Yo, you gone dance or what?" Slick Rick asked, leaning his fine ass back in his chair with his muscled arms crossed over his chest like he was bored as fuck. Not a good sign for a stripper whose job it is to keep a man entertained.

I nodded, causing my synthetic wig to shift a little on my head. I fought the urge to scratch my itching scalp.

Pssst.

I turned and Erin was motioning her hips for me to dance. Copying her, I started to sway my hips and my ankle turned in, causing me to stumble across the stage in the heels Erin had loaned me. "Shit," I swore, holding my hands out until I stead- ied myself.

Meanwhile, Slick Rick was laughing his ass off. I'm talking slapping the table, tears in his eyes, laughing his ass off.

I was too shamed.

Erin rushed out onstage and stood before me closely, plac- ing her hands on my hips. "Just relax," she mouthed to me.

My eyes widened and my body got stiff as Erin started dancing on me, her hands rubbing up and down my body. She danced around me and pressed a kiss to my neck before she brought her hands up to press against the sides of my breasts. She thrust one knee between my thighs.

"Grind on it," she whispered up to me.

Okay, listen. I felt awkward as a motherfucker and my mind was spinning like "Erin is gay!"

"Grind!" she said again, raising my arms up to the sky.

I circled my hips as she pressed her fingers against my waist and then down into the front of my bikini.

I swallowed and fought not to make a face.

"Oh shit!" the owner said. He had stopped laughing.

And when I looked out the bartender and DJ were staring at us too.

The music ended and I went weak with relief when Erin stepped back away from me.

"A team? Huh?" the owner asked, rising to his feet slowly.

"That's right," Erin said, motioning with her eyes as she smiled.

Still shell-shocked, I gave him a stiff smile that I knew looked dumb as hell.

"Tomorrow. Noon," he said over his broad shoulder before walking away.

"We're in," she said, giving me her fist to pound.

I eyed her. "Are you gay?" I asked.

Erin made a face. "Hell no. There is nothing a woman can do for me but introduce me to her brother or her man," she said, strutting offstage in boy shorts and a bikini top.

I still stood there.

She stopped and turned, rolled her eyes, and pressed her hands to her thick hips. "You wanna make this money or not?" she asked, arching her brows.

I nodded, but on the real, I was more scared of Erin turning me into a dyke over stripping . . .

It took a while for me to realize that she didn't want me and that everything we did onstage was an act. And we made money together. Slick Rick moved us to the night shift in no time, and the tips was damn good. Dudes was loving the combo of the thick white chick and the cute black girl. Ebony and Ivory. I can't lie that plenty of alcohol and Ecstasy pills got me through pseudo-dyking with my friend onstage.

After a while, the stripping and partying caught up with me and my grades fell. I lost my scholarship and eventually fell out of school. Once my parents cut me off, I kept stripping, but then Erin got lost in a crazy meth addiction and quit. Then it was just me trying to keep going at it.

Humph. Slick Rick put my ass right back on day shift. I was used to Erin doing all the work, and the best I could do was these ass tricks that were good but not good enough to go up against freaky bitches who was selling pussy on the side. I wasn't even fucking around with that tricking shit. I was selling fantasies, not ass.

"I made a pan of my peach cobbler, just for you," my momma was saying as I came back to the present.

"Thanks, Ma," I said.

"Harriet, I haven't seen you in a while. You're all grown up."

I turned just as my parents' next door neighbor Mr. Alvarez came down the steps. He was tall and thin, with more gray hair than I remembered since the last time I saw him years ago.

"Hi Victor," my mother said with a friendly smile.

He reached out to squeeze my shoulder and I fought the urge to flinch or box his hands away. I couldn't stand a touchy-feely person and his hands looked like crow's feet.

"How's Sophie?" I asked, even though I truly didn't give a fuck.

His daughter, Sophie, and I were best friends growing up. We even planned to go to the same college, but once we were on campus, Sophie kept up the good-girl routine and my ass was living *la vida loca*. Eventually we were passing each other in the dorm hallways and barely spoke.

"Here she comes," he said, sliding them skeleton-looking hands in the front pockets of his slacks as he looked over his shoulder at his front porch.

Sure enough, there was Sophie, closing the front door and coming down the steps in a navy blue pant suit and a pair of shoes I remembered seeing in Gucci last week. She didn't look very different from the pretty, long-haired Latina girl that I used to think of as a sister. She still had that whole J.Lo thing going and walked like her shit didn't stink.

"Suga," her father called out to her by her nickname as she continued right on to a pale gold convertible Volvo parked on the street in front of her father's house.

Like she didn't see us standing there.

She threw her hand up and waved briefly before opening her car door.

"Suga!" Mr. Alvarez said again sharply, before turning his head to give us a smile.

I thought I could smell liquor on him, and then I remembered from when we was little that he did used to drink. Once Sophie and I thought his brown liquor was tea and threw up the little bit we swallowed from our teacups.

I hadn't seen him much in the year since I moved, and I hadn't seen my old friend Sophie at all.

Sophie closed the car door and walked over to us. "*Sí*, Papi?"

"It's Harriet, your childhood friend," Mr. Alvarez said.

Sophie looked at me with eyes of a stranger. "That was a long time ago."

I felt my mom stiffen beside me, and I knew I wasn't imagining this bitch's rudeness. "Maybe not long enough," I said, eyeing her like, *Bitch, just blink at me too hard and I will drop-kick you in your throat.*

My mother grasped my wrist hard and pulled me up the

stairs behind her. "It was good seeing you, Victor," she called over her shoulder.

In the few seconds just before my mother pulled me into the house and closed the front door, I turned to see Mr. Alvarez still standing in the street, watching us.

My Rick Ross ringtone sounded off as I drove my Jag toward the Twelve50. I glanced down at the caller ID. My insider.

"Hello," I said.

"I got some info on your girl and for this you owe me big-time."

I turned the car into the parking garage as I gripped my phone tight as hell. "Scale of one to ten?" I asked, my voice not filled with *any* hint of playing as I pulled into my reserved parking spot.

"Oh, this shit is a ten. Trust and believe that."

"Give it to me," I demanded, excited to finally have something to take Goldie's ass down. The thought of that shit had my mouth watering and my clit throbbing like I was 'bout to bust a damn nut.

"Goldie booked me for a photo shoot in Puerto Rico with that rapper Big Gunnaz, and one of 'em came at me 'bout staying in Puerto Rico and spending the weekend with him—"

I rolled my eyes and clenched my fist so tight the skin over my knuckles stretched. "And?" I asked, trying not to sound too much like *Bitch, hurry the fuck up!*

"Damn, Luscious, chill the fuck out and let me tell the fucking story. Dayum!"

"I'm paying for info on Goldie's no-good ass and not to sit here and listen to which whoring rapper wanted to sex you for the weekend," I snapped.

"You really letting this Goldie shit get to you. That bitch ain't even that serious. Straight up."

Frustrated as fuck, I let my head fall back against the headrest as I pounded my fist against the steering wheel. "The money I'm paying you is crucial though, right?"

"Oh, so like I was saying. I turned him down all polite like and shit. So when Goldie called to check on the shoot, I mention that shit to her for giggles and shit, but peep this. The bitch kinda sorta asks me—without really asking me—what I think about escorting with famous dudes—"

I sat up straight in my driver's seat. Escorting?

"Yo, I think that bitch tryna feel me out to trick for her. I'm a find out what it pay."

Well, I'll be damned. "So you think Goldie is a madam?"

"I don't know nothing about her being no madam, but I think the bitch is a female pimp. Hell yeah, I can read between the lines. I don't give a fuck, she was feeling me out . . . seeing where my head at. You know?"

I wanted to have some top-notch shit like this on Goldie's ass . . . but how the fuck can I trust somebody who doesn't know that a female pimp and a madam is the same fucking thing? Still, if my informant was right . . .

"Get me proof. Get me some fucking hard-core proof and I got an extra grand for you on top of what I been paying you," I said, climbing out the car and sidestepping like R. Kelly's "Step in the Name of Love" played around me. If this snitching bitch was right, then Goldie's high yella ass was grass and I was the motherfucking lawn mower.

"That's the problem, Luscious: I'm gonna deliver something that can get Goldie locked the fuck up," said my informant. "This more than 'send me pictures of her house,' and 'tell me do she talk about me,' and 'find out her secrets' type of shit. I did all that . . . but helping you put the bitch behind bars is gone take more money to fill the pillow to make it comfy enough for me to sleep on *that* shit. Straight up."

Bitch, please. She didn't care for Goldie any more than I did.

"Get the proof and we'll talk numbers," I said.

"Done deal."

My snitch ended the call and I dropped my cell into my bag as I beat my heels against the concrete toward the door. Goldie went from being a handler for strippers to pushing pussy? *Slick bitch*.

"What's up, Luscious?"

I froze and looked up from searching in my purse for my crocodile sunglass case. Stepping out of the darkness of the parking garage were two big dudes dressed all in cliché black. I couldn't see their faces because of the ski masks they wore.

I can't front. I felt sick as shit. I had been so caught up in that Goldie bullshit that I slipped the fuck up. That all-important fear had been lost in the heat of my revenge. *Shit. Shit. Shit.* Goldie's tricking ass was *still* causing trouble for me.

"Make$ want the money you stole from him," one of them said.

My eyes darted down to take in the billy club he was holding in his gloved hand. I frowned a little bit. Since I heard Make$'s little ass was out of jail, I knew he would get at me about the cash I took from the safe-deposit box at the bank. I didn't know he would send out goons. *Punk bitch*.

Make$ called me just once about the missing money. Just once. Almost a year ago. I denied taking it. He threatened me. I hung up on his ass. He never called me again . . . but I knew it wasn't over.

There was close to fifty grand in that box. He's lucky I *only* took ten grand.

"I don't know what he's talking about," I lied, my voice low as my eyes shifted between the two of them.

"Shut the fuck up, you lying bitch," one of them said, his voice more irritated than angry. "You thought you was going to get away with thirty grand?"

Thirty grand? Huh? What? Say how much?

One of them bum-rushed me and grabbed me around my arms. My hand was still in my bag and now gripping my gun . . . but I couldn't draw, and that felt like losing a winning lottery ticket. The air left my body as he tightened his arms around me and then pressed my body back against one of the beams of the garage.

I hollered out at the top of my lungs and the other dude slapped me across the mouth. *Hard.* The lower half of my face stung like it was on fire. Tears filled my eyes.

The tears wasn't from the pain. I was scared as fuck wondering what these motherfuckers were going to do to me. How far had Make$'s punk ass told them to go to teach me a lesson? I thought about the video of Peaches getting the girl from the club jumped. I thought about him covering up crimes. I didn't trust him. That's why I put up my guard once I knew he was back on the streets. I figured Missy was right. Anyone willing to cover up major crimes might be willing to commit a few of his own. No, Make$ was not to be trusted. Fuck that.

"Shit, she fine as fuck," the one holding me said, his breath smelling like pure unwashed ass. I almost gagged as I twisted my head to the side.

I felt a hand going under my dress. "HEEELLLLPPP!" I screamed, feeling fear and disgust fill my throat.

WHAP!

Another slap and then a gloved hand covered my mouth tight as hell.

I wasn't no gangsta bitch used to that bang-'em-up, shoot-'em-up type of shit. I'd never really been around any thugs except them clowns Make$ used to hang around—and of course the two holding me hostage at the moment. I could talk shit, but bloody violence wasn't a must in my life like I was trying to be a mafia princess or some shit. But I knew right then it was just me up against two dudes and I would most definitely fuck both their worlds right on up with the gun in my bag.

I relaxed my body, forcing myself to fight my nerves.

The goon loosened his hold on me.

I cocked my gun inside my handbag, ready to shoot through the monogrammed Louis Vuitton leather and into his belly if I had to.

"Where my money, Luscious?"

With the gloved hand still over my mouth, my eyes shot over to see the rear window of a parked Tahoe lower and show the face of Make$ sitting in the back. It had been over a year since I'd laid eyes on the man I'd hoped to love forever. Happily ever after. Forever and a day.

Humph, now this motherfucker sat there and watched his goons handle me? Just another damn slap in the face from this asshole. *Really, Terrence? Really?*

Shaking my head to unsuccessfully free the hand on my mouth, I tried to talk and it came out as mumbling.

Make$ climbed out the Tahoe, his figure slender in a black suit and shirt. His head was clean-shaven, his shades were in place, and there was a new tattoo on his cheek. He slid his tattooed hands into the pockets of his pants as he walked over to where they had my ass hemmed up with my high heels dangling in the air.

"Let her down," Make$ said, looking down at the ground as he licked his lips.

They released me in an instant and I dropped to my feet. *Fucking flunkies.*

"Did you spend my money?" Make$ asked, pulling a toothpick out of his pocket to unwrap and stick in his mouth.

"Listen, I didn't take thirty grand out that safe-deposit box," I said, moving my pocketbook up to my chest and crossing my arms so that it didn't look so suspect with my hand stuck in my purse. There was no way I was letting my grip on this gun go. No way in hell. I didn't think they would kill me, but they wasn't going to beat me up, either.

Make$ shook his head and laughed. "You think I'm stupid? I checked the box as soon as I got out," he said, his voice hard and rising.

"If you checked it yourself, then you would know I didn't take thirty grand of your money. Sure Peaches or one of your flunkies didn't gank your ass?"

He rushed over to me and grabbed me by the neck so hard I couldn't swallow. "Keep my mother's name out your fucking mouth," he bit out, his mouth so thin with anger that it looked white around the edges.

Enough was enough of this bullshit.

I undid my arms and used my left hand to push him hard as I held my bag against my chest. I must have surprised his little ass because he stumbled back, freeing my throat. I stepped back and pulled my gun, pointing it at him and then at Goon One and Goon Two. "Let me see some armpits. Hands up," I said, eyeing all three of them.

Make$ chuckled as he barely raised his hands above his shoulders.

"Higher, please," I said sarcastically.

He barely obliged.

"Okay, I'll tell you what," I said. "How about you three hold hands."

They all started complaining in unison and it was hard to tell who said what.

"What?"

"I'm not holding no dude's hands."

"You out your ass."

I lowered the gun to Make$'s crotch with a lift of my brow. "Do it," I said simply. There was no need to yell; the power was in my hand and not in my voice.

I giggled as Make$ reached out and grabbed each of them nigga's hands. "Don't worry, I'm not going to make you play ring-around-the-rosy or some shit like that. But I think it's time you and I discussed real business, Terrence," I told him, steadily backing up toward my car.

"You know I was good to you," I said with a shrug. "Even after your cheating ass fucked me over I still didn't try and take you out. I went in your safety-deposit box, but I only took ten grand."

He tilted his head back and flexed his shoulders.

"See, I felt like the least you owed me was six months rent to get back on my feet," I told him, my gun targeted to burn one in his heart even though I knew I could never shoot this motherfucker. "I damn sure didn't deserve you wanting to dump my ass on the street because you got locked up behind your side-ho."

Make$ looked over at me. "Nobody dumped you—"

"Shut your ass up," I snapped, feeling my anger rising and reaching for it. Welcoming it. "You wanna play hardball, send goons for me, threaten me? You on some fake-ass mafioso-type shit? Then watch how gutter *I* get."

"What you got, Luscious?" he asked.

I sat my bag on the trunk of my car and then dug in it with my free hand to finally grasp my keys. "I'll tell you what I got. A little DVD showing this certain little big-mouth fool popping off just before showing the evidence of a brutal beating that will send her right where you going."

I saw him stiffen.

"So now, motherfucker, I want fifty thousand deposited in my account—all the info is the same—or that DVD will be hand-delivered to the Newark Police Department," I told him, popping the trunk and dropping my pocketbook inside before I unlocked the door.

"Where the fuck I'ma get fifty thousand to just give you?" Make$ asked, breaking his hold of the goons' hands.

Just five feet separated us.

I raised the gun and leveled it at his head. "I don't give a *fuck.* Just get it," I told him with complete thoroughness as I backed up to the driver's door and opened it from behind.

"Oh, and if you even thinking of sending some goons my way, I have given copies of that DVD to several people and told them to get it to the police ASAP if *anything* happens to me. So fuck with it." I climbed into my car and slammed the door.

As I cranked the car, one of the goons reached behind him under his shirt, but Make$ held his hand up, stopping him. I reversed out the spot, backing up to them before I accelerated forward. I lowered the window. "You got one week to get my money, nigga," I hollered before I sped out the parking garage doing about a hundred.

I finally dropped the gun to the passenger seat and said a silent prayer of thanks that I lied my ass off so well.

The last week of my life had been hectic. Twice I had to pull a gun on a nigga. Make$ was free for a little bit before his sentencing. And my archnemesis might be running a high-priced prostitution ring under the cover of her booking agency.

It was a mix of crazy and crazier. My plate was mad full. And even though I was coming out on top of every situation, I felt like my mind was constantly on the brink of slipping. Like at any second I would flip the fuck out and go crazy. Do something crazy.

During my whole drive from Jersey to New York, my hands shook so bad and my heart beat so hard from the scene with Make$. It had my nerves still all fucked up, but I didn't stop zooming through the streets until I eventually steered my Jag onto the New Jersey Turnpike and then through the Lincoln Tunnel until I reached Manhattan.

I looked up at the towering Upper East Side apartment building. Goldie had one of the penthouse apartments. Sitting high looking down over the city of New York. It was an upgrade from Twleve50.

A huge upgrade. When my snitch first told me where she lived, I jumped right on the Internet and looked up the apartment building. I knew she was looking at five figures every fucking month and now I knew just how she was able to afford it. Pushing pussy.

Business had to be booming.

I slowed down as I passed the front of the building. I almost hit the brakes at the sight of Goldie strutting out the door held open by the doorman. Her hair was pulled back into a sleek ponytail. Her shades were in place. The white dress she wore clung to every curve of her body.

"I wonder where the fuck she going," I said aloud even as my lips curled in anger as she stood there waiting.

My right hand released its tight grip of the steering wheel and shifted down to stroke my .357 still sitting on the passenger seat.

No, I didn't want to kill the bitch. She wasn't worth a murder charge . . . but I would have loved to jump out my car, race across the street, and pistol-whip her no-good ass until her pretty white dress was ruined with her own blood.

A white convertible Bentley pulled up to the front of the building and the valet hopped out to race around the car. I watched Goldie slide something into his hand before she came around the car and climbed into the driver's seat.

"That bitch got a *Bentley*. What the fuck?!" I watched my rearview mirror until the Bentley was out of sight, fighting the urge to follow the bitch—only because I didn't want her to spot me and know I was gunning for her.

$\mathcal{B}$ack when me and Has was messing around and taking our anger at Goldie out in the sheets, he used to stand behind me in the mirror and caress everything he loved about my body. My wide hips. My thick thighs. My bald pussy. But beyond the physical, Has was the type of dude who did more than sex the hell out of you. He could lay down a serious mind-fuck. Give you shit to think about. He was a deep thug like Pac or some shit.

I stood in front of the full-length mirror on my closet door. Naked. Exposed. I thought of him. Missed him. Maybe because I liked that he was more than just some weed-smoking hustler. Or because he made me feel sexy as fuck. Or because he just had a good dick.

Or because I was horny as fuck. A year was a long time.

It's just that, as good as Has's dick was, I didn't love him. When we wasn't fucking, he felt like my homeboy. Once I set my eyes on bigger revenge beyond fucking some dude Goldie wanted—like a lame—I knew I had to just let it go. Did I miss the dick? All the dick? All the good dick? Hell yeah. *Shit.*

I walked over to my dresser and pulled a DVD case from the drawer holding all my lacy lingerie. I took out the disc and slid it into the DVD player on the ebony shelf below the flat-screen on the wall. I sat back on the bed. On-screen, I positioned my naked body on the sofa of my living room. Legs wide open. Ass on the edge of the chair. Bald pussy pushed forward.

Soon Has walked through the front door. (I left it open because I knew he was headed up on the elevator.) My eyes took in the sexy sight of him in a wife-beater shirt and oversize cargo shorts. I really didn't need the video I'd secretly taken that day to remember that fuckdown at all. . . .

"Damn, you was ready for this dick, huh?" Has asked as he locked the front door.

I flexed my pussy walls and he laughed as he came over to drop down to his knees and bury his head between my thighs. "Smells good," he whispered against my flesh just before he released his tongue and stroked from the crack of my ass to my clit.

I cried out as I reached for the back of his head. "Oh shit," I swore in a whisper, pressing my feet against the edge of the sofa Make\$ handpicked to circle my hips upward as he sucked my clit between his lips.

Has dipped down to press his tongue deep inside me and then swirl it around before shifting back up to flicker his tongue against my clit. That motherfucker knew exactly what he was doing and he kept up the rotation. Suck. Plunge. Flicker. Suck. Plunge. Flicker. Suck. Plunge. Flicker.

I cried out, feeling my entire body tingle like crazy. I felt my nut about to explode in his mouth. "No, not yet," I begged, pushing his head back to free my clit.

He looked up at me with that square face, his lips and around his mouth still moist from my juices.

"Stand up," I told him, sitting up on the sofa and pressing my feet to the hardwood floor.

As soon as he did, his dick curving out against his zipper damn near struck me in the face. I unzipped his shorts and freed the beast, looking up into his tigerlike eyes as I took the thick and smooth tip between my lips.

His mouth fell open as he thrust his hips forward and twisted his hands in my weave to grip it tightly. "Awww. Suck that motherfucka," he told me, his voice all thick and shit.

It made me suck him harder until the tip damn near touched the back of my throat. His knees buckled as he cried out like he sang soprano. . . .

Watching myself on that big-ass TV sucking Has's dick made my nipples hard. I laid back on the bed and brought my hands up to lightly tease them in between massaging my breasts. "Uhmmm," I moaned, turned on by the feel of my hands and the video, watching as Has tore his T-shirt over his head as I licked his dick like it was ice cream.

"Think Goldie can suck a dick like that?" I asked him, holding his dick like a microphone before I drizzled my spit onto it and massaged it until it looked polished.

"Man, fuck her," he said, tilting his head to the side to watch me.

"Good answer," I told him, lifting his dick so that I could lean down and take his balls into my mouth as I stroked the length of his dick hard.

"Shit!" he swore, damn near tearing out my tracks.

I didn't give a fuck.

He used my hair in his fist to guide my mouth back to his dick and I sucked him until my mouth, his dick, and my hands were wet as hell from my spit.

I freed my mouth and pushed against his stomach. "Take them clothes off," I told him, rising to my feet as I walked around him.

He slapped my ass before he undid his shorts, kicking them and his shoes away to stand there with his dick in his hand.

"Lay down, Has."

He did.

I straddled his face from behind and he got right to it, eat-

ing me out while I bent over to finish the sixty-nine and take his dick into my mouth again. We both went to work like we were on a mission or had something to prove or some shit. It was crazy. On some other level–type shit.

I watched us on the video. On that floor. Licking and sucking each other like we was hungry. My clit felt numb. I spread my knees, feeling the lips of my pussy open wide. I slipped one and then another finger inside as I watched myself sit up and then slide my body across Has's until I was squatting over his dick. . . .

I held Has's dick up as straight as I could with such a deep curve before I slid down onto that motherfucker and felt him fill me. "Bend your legs," I told him. When he did I was glad to have something to hold onto, because the size of him made me feel breathless as he stretched my walls. I pressed my aching titties against his hairy thighs and grabbed each of his ankles as I began to ride him backward.

I gasped at the feel of his hands spreading my ass cheeks to watch the movement of my pussy up and down his dick. When he slipped his thumb into my ass I rode him harder, loving the feel of his dick inside me, his hands on me, and my upper body pressed against his thighs as each back-and-forward rodeolike motion of my hips brought my clit against the concrete-hard base of his dick.

Resting my head against his knees, I licked them nastily, closing my eyes as I let that pleasure course over my body. . . .

My eyes were locked on the screen as I watched my movements get faster and the sweat dampen my body. Has's face looked like he was about to stroke.

"*Oh shit, I'm gone cum,*" he said.

"*Me too. Me too,*" I said.

As the grunts of sex filled the air, I bit my bottom lip and tilted my head backward as I pressed my hand to the clean-shaven mound of my pussy, squeezing it whole before I split my lips and lightly plucked my clit. My hips arched and I cried out with a wince, pressing my legs open wider and arching my hips up as I pressed my first three fingers to my clit in wicked circular motions until I was moaning right along with the video as I came.

I opened my eyes and watched as Has lifted me off his dick to spray his thick white nut all over my ass and back, massaging the tip in the wetness as I continued to shiver.

I lay on the bed trembling, my hand still on my pussy as I watched myself sneak the remote from between the cushions and turn the video recorder off. The screen went black.

With my heart pounding and my clit still throbbing, I felt sleepy and gave in to it. My orgasm had taken the edge off but there was no doubt that my ass really needed to get some. *Quick.*

A couple of hours later, after my nap and a hot bubble bath, I released a heavy breath as I looked at my reflection, forcing myself to focus on my new weave. It was still jet-black but I was trying a loose rod set, and the soft curls surrounded my face before falling down to the middle of my back. It was that messy and tousled look like I just had incredible sex (ironic as fuck, right?), and I liked the change from my bone-straight look.

I pulled on the sheer black lace lingerie sitting atop my dresser. The push-up bra, thong, waist cincher, and garter was sexy as fuck. Just because I wasn't having sex didn't mean I couldn't feel sexy under my clothes. I twisted and turned in the mirror because right then, as good as I looked, I should have been taking pics to text to my man or my lover. Not pulling a short tunic dress over all this sexiness for a business dinner.

Hell, Michel got more dick than I did.

The cream tunic looked good against my dark complexion, with an open back and cutout blouson sleeves. A pair of Fendi snake-print platform pumps made me five inches taller.

I was just sliding on some gold accessories when I heard my e-mail go off from my office. We were trying to book music acts for an end-of-summer party. Thinking that might be one of the talent managers getting back to me, I made my way into my second bedroom—the offices of Yummy Entertainment. Sliding into the leopard-print chair behind the black desk, I opened my e-mail.

"Wow. Okay," I said, leaning back as I eyed the screen.

I had alerts on my bank account, and a deposit had just been made for fifty grand. Make$ came through. I knew I blackmailed his ass, but a piece of me thought he would try me and not follow through.

It took my parents a whole year to make just a little over fifty grand apiece, and I just did it in a week. I wasn't crazy, though. Fifty grand wasn't life-saving type of money, and it was nowhere near what I needed to get the same lifestyle as my enemy. It was a big chunk but not enough.

I wanted a penthouse apartment and a Bentley.

I wanted to hang out with celebrities.

I wanted to live an even higher life.

For damn sure, whatever was good enough for Goldie was even better for me, and once I made sure of her downfall, she would have to sit back and watch me living the high life she took for granted.

Pushing aside thoughts of the bitch, I picked up the cordless phone and dialed the number of Make$'s manager, Chill Will. Make$'s old number had been changed, but I knew Chill Will would never change his number and risk missing a business call from an old contact.

Sure enough, he answered.

"Chill Will."

"Will, this Luscious. Make$ with you? I need to holler at him."

He didn't say shit to me and I wondered if he knew that his client just paid me fifty grand and why. I shrugged. Fuck it. I heard low talking in the background before a little bit of rustling on the phone.

"Fuck you want?" Make$ suddenly said into the phone, his voice nasty as hell.

I let myself take a five count because my call wasn't about drama. "Listen, I just wanted to say that it's sad as fuck that everything we had or what I thought we had ended like this," I began, picking up a pen to tap against the top of the desk. "But let's be clear. This is the last time we will speak. Do not call me, contact me, come see me for nothing. And I'll do the same. It's over. All of it. So let's just agree to move the fuck on."

Make$ laughed sarcastically. "Easy for you to say with my fucking money in your pocket," he snapped. "My fucking car. My fucking apartment. You really came out on top in this shit."

Tears filled my eyes and I was mad at myself for the show of weakness even as I blinked them away. "You think having your heart broken by the man you love is easy? You think finding out your friend is a snake in the grass helping to push the blade in your back is easy? You know what, you really are *dumb* as hell."

"Bitch—"

I shook my head. "No, I ain't your bitch. I ain't your trick, your ho, your jump-off, your nothing. Just like you went from being everything to nothing to me. Just stay away from me. Keep your bird-ass mama away from me. Tell her to keep my name out of her mouth up on the radio talking scandalous and wrong as hell . . . or her ass gone be in one jail and you in the other. Now, goodbye forever, *Ter-rence*."

I ended the call, wishing I could slam the phone down in his face instead of hitting a weak-ass button. That bitch needed to hear a ring-a-ling in his ear.

The crazy thing is, before the STDs and before finding out about him and Goldie, I woulda took him over any amount of money without hesitation. But get this. It's even crazier that Goldie sloring ass told me to never put a man before my money. The bitch was right, but she would forever be dead wrong for proving herself right by fucking my man.

Were they messing around behind my back when I met that bitch down in the neck for lunch? Was that why she acted like she knew more about me than me?

"Ugh," I let loose in frustration, balling my hand up so tight that my fingernails dug into my fleshy palm.

I needed that proof on Goldie's prostitution ring. I was damn near drooling waiting on it. Dreaming about what I would do with it. Blackmail the bitch? Send her and her hos to jail? Decisions, decisions, decisions.

I left my office and walked back to my bedroom to finish my makeup. Then I grabbed my keys and a tiny gold clutch and strolled out the door. My steps faltered when I saw a little girl of about six sitting in the windowsill framed by the night sky and the tiny lights of the distant skyline.

She was alone, with her knees pulled to her chest and her arms wrapped around them in her Hello Kitty pajamas. Her face was shielded by her long blonde hair but I recognized her as the daughter of the couple at the end of the hall.

I glanced down at my diamond Cartier watch. It was nearly eleven at night.

Did her parents even know she was out in the hall that time of night?

Didn't they know it wasn't safe?

Yes, we were in a secured building but the weirdos could be neighbors. People you trusted.

She turned her head and looked at me. Her face was solemn. Her eyes were sad.

I felt nauseous all of a sudden. Like I could vomit. Tension filled my neck. I wondered if I ate something that was tearing me up as I walked down the hall to her. "Do your parents know you're out here?" I asked her the same question I asked myself.

She shook her head. "They're sleeping," she said in a soft voice.

"I don't think you should be out here," I told her, holding out my hand as a weird feeling shimmied over my entire body. "It's not safe for little girls all alone. Okay?"

"Okay," she agreed, taking my hand as she hopped down.

I quickly led her to the door of her family's apartment. Even though the door was slightly ajar, I rang the doorbell as I held her hand tightly.

I had to ring the bell twice more before the front door opened wider. A tall white dude with a bald head in nothing but pajamas bottoms and a chest he needed to cover stood there wiping his eyes. "Can I help you? Is the building on fire?" he asked, his voice filled with sleep.

"Daddy, your belly is shaking," the little girl said with a giggle.

He looked down at his daughter, his eyes widening. "Becky," he said in surprise before reaching out to take her hand from mine and then stoop down to her level.

"I was on my way out for the evening and I saw her sitting in the window at the end of the hall, and I thought a little girl her age shouldn't be wandering the hall by herself at night," I said, definitely throwing my proper English at him.

He looked up at me, pausing at the sight of my thighs and longs legs before he looked back at his daughter. "What were you doing out in the hall?" he asked, his hands on her shoulders.

"I like to look at the lights and I can't see them from our apartment," she said simply with a shrug.

"Thank you very much," he said to me, rising to his feet.

I nodded and gave the little girl one last smile before I turned and made my way to the elevator. I didn't look back and I was glad when the elevator doors opened.

I didn't say shit when he thanked me, because I felt like laying into his ass. I wanted to say . . .

How can you not know your six-year-old has left your fucking apartment? How can you sleep that hard with a child? Don't you know little girls need to be protected?

Didn't he know little girls needed to be watched over?

Who didn't know that?

I pulled my cell phone from my purse as the elevator slid to a smooth stop on the lobby floor. I called Tek-9's cell. "I'm on the way," I said, glad that the wave of nausea had passed.

"Damn, Luscious," Tek-9 said as I strolled backstage into his dressing room on the arms of one of his bodyguards. Tek-9 had performed at the NJPAC as part of a four-day hip-hop festival. Backstage was the who's who of East Coast DJs and up-and-coming hip-hop and R&B acts. Between the press, photographers, entourages, and NJPAC staff, the backstage was crowded.

I couldn't lie. This had been my life for almost a year and it felt good to be back in it, even if just for a little bit. Tek-9 invited me to dinner before he went to the after-party—which I declined to attend with him. Dinner only, and *that* was strictly business.

"Looking good, Luscious," Tek-9 said from his seat. He was already shirtless, with three diamond chains around his neck and his pot belly tattooed with his name in large script.

Tattoos was one trend I never fucked with, even though I didn't mind them on Make$. I was afraid of needles, and my mother swore that people with tattoos couldn't give their kids blood in an emergency. Was that shit true? I don't know, but I never fucked with it. Plus I was dark-skinned and scared my shit would keloid. Make$ wanted me to get his name on me. Thank God I didn't fuck with it. Right now I'd be branded by a man who treated me like shit.

Smiling playfully, I spun for him slowly, knowing I looked good and knowing he wanted me. "Thanks for inviting me," I said, walking over to lean against the wall.

"I thought maybe you wanted to go over that deal we talked about on the phone last week," Tek-9 said, eyeing my legs as he motioned for everyone in the room to leave.

"You mean the deal about discounting your rate for Yummy Entertainment," I asked, definitely playing crazy.

He laughed as he stood up to pull on a crisp white oversize T-shirt.

"What?" I asked, looking innocent.

Tek-9 looked at me for a good five or six seconds. "I told you how I'd do it for free," he said, fucking me with his eyes.

I shook my head. "No, not me. Sorry."

He stepped up close to me and I could smell the mix of liquor, cologne, and weed. "You sure?" he asked, pressing his hand to my bare thigh.

"I fuck for free and for pleasure," I said in a whisper, looking up into his eyes as I patted his hand twice before I eased it off my thigh.

Tek-9 was cool, but I wasn't feeling him or his big pot belly at all. I had to want to fuck someone. Feel an attraction. My pussy wasn't a drive-through. Much as I hated Goldie, I couldn't have messed with Has if he wasn't a fine-ass motherfucker. And I definitely wasn't feeling Tek-9 with his Cee Lo Green looks. Plus I didn't want the rep of being that chick—the ex-stripper jumping from one rapper to the next.

"I'm a big dude, Luscious, but don't sleep on my skills," he said, easing his chains from under his shirt.

I held up my hands, my mind focused on convincing him.

"Listen, about the show. How about you lower your fee and take a small percentage of the door instead?"

Tek-9 laughed. "You're strictly business, huh?"

"Nothing but."

He stepped back with a laugh and unzipped his pants, pulling out his dick to hang against his zipper. "Your loss," he said, laughing.

I looked down. My mouth fell open and my eyes got a little bigger. I never seen a dick so big in person before. That shit was damn near offensive. It was halfway down his thigh and thick as the top of a bat—and it wasn't hard. I can't front. I thought about not getting fucked for a year and I started to pounce on that nigga. He had plenty of dick to make up for his big-ass belly. But I couldn't. I wouldn't. A big dick wasn't shit but pain for a pussy that wasn't aroused and wet. Fuck that.

"Let's go get something to eat," Tek-9 said, balling all that dick up in his hand and pushing it back inside his zipper.

"Dayum, Tek," I finally said, definitely feeling some kind of way by his little show as we made our way out the dressing room. His security team, all dressed in black, immediately surrounded us to escort us through the crowd.

When Ursula Stevens stepped in front of us all of a sudden, I slid on my shades. She was the same blogger who called my phone for an exclusive on Make$ after his arrest. I never did call her back. Sometimes Ursula Stevens's ish hit mainstream media. My parents would *really* bug if I sat up on a blog and told ALL my business.

A lot of entertainment folks considered Ursula reckless with her posts, but here she was, brash as hell, floating among them and looking for a scoop.

The bitch was bold, I thought, as I eyed her: tall, skinny, and all fake boobs, with about five packs of curly blonde weave floating down her back. *Looking like the Cowardly Lion or some shit.*

"No interviews, Ursula," one of the bodyguards said.

She leaned back and pressed a hand to her massive chest. "Actually, I wanted to talk to Make$'s ex and get her take on him starting his two-year sentence for his role in trying to help his friends get away with the rape?"

I pressed my lips together and said nothing. I was happy as hell when we finally reached the exit and stepped out into the hot summer night.

"I can't stand that bitch," Tek-9 said once we had climbed into the back of his SUV.

"She serious as hell about her blog," I said, crossing my legs in the huge amount of space since the second row was gone, giving the SUV more of a limo feel on the inside, with its TV and minibar.

"I should slap her across the mouth with my dick," Tek-9 joked.

My eyes darted down to his crotch. "Now that would be a blackout," I shot back at his ass.

Tek-9 blazed a blunt as soon as the door closed behind us. He offered it to me. I shook my head, already planning to put my dress in the dry cleaner's to get rid of the smell of kush.

"You used to smoke with us," he said, releasing enough smoke from his lungs to fog up the interior.

I coughed. "I don't do a lot of shit I used to do," I said honestly, glad to have cocaine out of my life. I couldn't believe I did that shit just to keep Make$ happy. Thank God I didn't become a head.

"Well, if you looking for some new shit . . . I got you," he said, the tip of the blunt turning bright red as he inhaled deeply while he looked down at his dick.

"If you would keep your mind off my pussy . . . I got you too," I said.

Tek-9 laughed so hard he choked on the weed.

I looked out the window as the driver sped us through the streets. In the distance I could see the top of my apartment building. All I could think of was making the money Goldie made so that I could completely annihilate the bitch.

The next morning, I woke up to all hell breaking loose. Kinda.

My house phone was ringing nonstop. My cell phone was lit up with voice mail messages, missed calls, and text messages. E-mail alerts were going off in my office.

"What? Somebody fucking died?" I asked myself as I flung back the silk covers and sat up on the side of the bed, digging under my satin scarf to scratch my scalp.

I was just about to open a text when Eve called. The phone vibrated in my hand. I answered the call and put her on speakerphone. "What's up?"

"Girl, you coulda told me you fucking with Tek-9's big juicy ass," Eve said, her voice hyped over some possible scandal.

I froze.

"What are you talking about?" I asked her.

"Girl, that shit is all over Ursula Stevens. Pictures and all of y'all backstage at that concert and then out eating dinner," Eve said.

In that moment, as I dropped my head in my hand, I wished Tek-9 *had* slapped that bitch with his dick across her mouth. It definitely woulda been lights out for the assuming bitch.

"That ain't all. Peaches made a video going in on your ass, and that shit is all over WorldStarHipHop, Bossip, the YBF, and Necole Bitchie. Shit is crazy!"

"Let me call you back," I said, hanging up on Eve and letting the phone drop on the bed. It started vibrating like a dildo doing overtime.

My house phone kept ringing and I turned off the ringer before I grabbed my iPad from my nightstand drawer.

"That lying bitch," I said, as I read Ursula Stevens's post with a picture of me and Make$ that was so old, next to a picture of me and Tek-9, next to a picture of Make$ and Tek-9 posted up.

EX-WIFEY OF IMPRISONED MAKE$ NOW BOO'ED UP WITH HIS BEST FRIEND, RAPPER TEK-9. ***UPDATE***
Looks like the wifeys of the hip-hop stars aren't sitting back and just taking these fellas dogging them out and making fools out of them. Case in point: Harriet Jordan, better known as Luscious, the ex-stripper turned party promoter whose relationship with rap star Make$ ended when she caught him giving one of his dancers head . . . in the head. (Click here for the original post.) Of course we all remember that Make$ pled out to two years' jail time for assisting members of his entourage in trying to get away with the dancer's rape.
We all know Make$ was well-known for his groupie shenanigans while he was out on the streets—I just hope his sexual appetite has cooled off in prison or he might be tossing some cookies up in there. (Sshhhh!)
Last night I spotted his ex, Luscious, backstage with Tek-9 before they were hustled into a custom Tahoe and taken to New York for a cozy and romantic dinner. . . .

I couldn't even read the rest of her lies, but she had updated her post with Peaches' video. Did I even want to see this shit? I pushed play on the embedded video and Peaches' face filled the screen. She was sitting in her living room with micro braids and her signature, nasty-ass long nails. Her neck was already in action.

"I just read the story on Ursula Stevens about my son's ex and I just want to take a minute and say I knew the bitch wasn't shit. I knew she was just out for money. I knew it wouldn't take long for her to grab another platinum-selling rap artist. But for her to be so scandalous and so low-down and dirty as to

mess with my son's friend, someone he grew up with and made music with, is just disgusting, and I'm glad she is out of my son's life. Now she a problem for Tek-9's mama. I let my son know all about it and he's pissed but I told him, better he know now before he upgraded that trick from wifey to wife. For Luscious, Lame-Ass, Loser—whatever the fuck your name is—deuces, you no-good bitch!"

If I really had kept that damn DVD of her getting that girl jumped I woulda sent it to the police and been done with her ass for a good year or so. *Fuck that crazy bitch.*

I called Tek-9's number but his shit went straight to voice mail. "Tek-9, you need to handle this. Issue a statement. Put out a video. Whatever. But *handle* this. Come on, dude. Back me up on this bullshit," I said, dropping my head into my hand. "Just call me."

I just couldn't believe after all the shit Make$ put me through, now people was side-eyeing me and talking reckless, when I was never anything but loyal to his little whack gherkin-dick ass. Life stayed a bitch. Damn!

10

Over the next two weeks, shit got even crazier with the rumors flying about me and Tek-9. We both released statements that the rumors weren't true, but shit got even more crucial when the bloggers made it seem like Tek-9 and Make$ was getting into a war of words—and maybe more—over me. They were on some re-creation of the whole Biggie, Faith, and Tupac drama.

Bullshit.

These mofos were completely clueless. Regardless of Peaches' lies trying to be relevant, I knew Make$ didn't give a fuck about me, my pussy, or what I did with it. If he did, he wouldn't have risked losing it by fucking around.

It's just that this rumor shit was fucking with my business. I was trying to ride it out and wait for someone else's life to take over the gossip sites, but my plans to keep fucking with Tek-9 until he cut his fee to perform for us was so *dead.* I did not need them saying I was out fucking the talent to perform for Yummy Entertainment.

And Tek-9 still bragging on his gorilla-size dick every time we spoke was getting on my nerves anyway. He *really* wanted this pussy. *Pause.* Double *pause.*

"'Cuse me?"

I turned away from the racks of ribs I was checking out in the Pathmark on Lyons Avenue. Three teenage girls stood there eyeing me. And they missed not one detail. My hair in a side ponytail. My jewelry. My army-green short-sleeve romper with an off-the-shoulder neckline and ruched hem just below my knees. Bronze, copper, and green stilettos. Skin gleaming. Makeup on point. Yes, banging . . . even in the grocery store.

No lie? They made me nervous and I clutched my Gucci signature tote a little tighter. There was plenty of good and some bad in the hood. Sometimes the bad could be male or female. Fuck what you heard, there was little gansta boos out there.

"You Luscious?" the thick one asked, with her medium-length hair up in one of those firecracker ponytails that I hated. Every hair stood on end like someone blew that shit up. The style didn't do shit but showcase split ends.

I eyed each one. "Yes. Why?"

The skinny one with a bob smacked her tongue like she was trying to clean it. "Can we have your autograph?"

I smiled. "Y'all must have heard about Yummy Entertainment parties . . . but you're not old enough to get in," I said, taking the thin notebook the dark-skinned one gave me. She reminded me of myself at that age.

"Your parties?" the mouth smacker asked, looking confused. She made *parties* sound more like "paw-tees."

"No, we want your autograph because you got busy with Make$ *and* Tek-9. Girl, you the shit!"

I paused in signing my name to cut my eyes up to them. "That wasn't true about Tek-9. I was trying to line him up to . . . perform at a event," I told them.

"No, no, uh-uh uh-uh. I read it on Ursula Stevens and there was pictures and everything," the mouth smacker said, like she was referring to a legitimate news source and not a gossip blog.

Okay. Fuck it. I signed their notebook and wished them well, just wanting their young, naïve, and gullible asses out of my face. But then hell, there was grown people—grown, educated people—who took the shit on those blogs for truth like it was the Bible.

Sliding on my shades, I finished getting the rest of the things my moms would need to make two big pans of her honey-and-orange-glazed ribs for the all-female comedy showcase we were having that night. This Pathmark was always crunk—especially the first of the month—but I knew where everything was and I could get in and out quicker.

Soon I was pulling up before my parents' house and my father stepped out onto the porch. I eyed him, tall and slender, with a short salt-and-pepper 'fro that reminded me way too much of that squared-up bullshit the daddy on *Moesha* wore. He looked every bit the nerdy professor, with his Malcom X spectacles and chinos on. "Harriet," he said, his voice deep. "Take the bottles of apple juice and orange juice over to Victor. Your mother wanted those for him. He's not feeling well."

I frowned as I looked over at Mr. Alvarez's white house with red shutters and brick steps. *Fuck I look like?* "Why didn't his perfect daughter go to the store for him?" I snapped.

Umph. Those lines of disapproval deepened across my father's forehead. I just knuckled up and did it because I was not in the mood for an "I have a dream of a perfect daughter" speech. I slammed the juices into their own plastic bag and made my way up onto the lightly cracked sidewalk and the brick steps to Mr. Alvarez's door.

I knocked and the door opened a little bit. This section of Weequahic was filled with working people and all, but who left their door open? This was some shit straight out of a crime scene on *The First 48* or *Law & Order.* What if Mr. Alvarez was stretched out in the motherfucker with a knife in his guts?

"Come in, Naomi," he called out suddenly.

Okay, so he's alive. I stepped inside and closed the front door, but that made me feel claustrophobic as hell. I left the door wide open as I looked around the house. Even though I hadn't been in there for over a decade it looked just the same as it did when me and Sophie were the best of friends growing up. Ain't shit changed at all. Same old floral furniture. Same mismatched rug. Same dust. Same smell of old food and a house that needed its windows opened with a quickness.

Each step that took me closer to Mr. Alvarez sitting in the

same brown recliner in front of his TV made me feel like I was six years old again. I looked down and saw a vision of me and Sophie playing with naked baby dolls. I smiled at my huge Afro puffs and Sophie's lopsided ponytail done by a father without a wife.

"Oh, it's you, Harriet," Mr. Alvarez said, looking over his shoulder as he coughed, hacked, and brought up phlegm in a dingy handkerchief.

Damn, like that? Just, "Fuck it. I'm a hawk spit like it ain't nasty as hell?" I looked away as he opened the rag to study his shit. My eyes landed on a teapot setting on a tray in the center of the coffee table. I noticed the crack along the side. It was glued back together, but the crack was clear as hell.

I heard a loud crash and I thought I could almost see the teapot on the floor, broken in half. I felt loopy, like I had took an E or popped a hydrocodone. I felt nauseous.

"Shit!"

I looked over at Mr. Alvarez reaching over the arm of the chair to pick up the glass that had crashed to the floor.

"My father asked me to bring this juice over here," I said, biting my lip as my head started to pound. I hurried to set the bag on the table by his chair.

His funky house was really getting to me.

He reached out and patted my wrist. "Such a good girl," Mr. Alvarez said, his voice raspy with his sickness.

I jerked away from his touch. Turning to get the fuck out of there. Maybe it was the old smell of the house or his little spit show. What the fuck ever. It was straight deuces for me. I closed the front door behind me.

I looked over to see if my father was waiting on me on his porch. He wasn't. That shit made me feel so sad and so fucking angry. All at once.

I shook my head to clear it of all the emotions fucking with me. Maybe I was PMSing or some shit. I didn't know. I was just glad that by the time I walked over to my parents' I felt a helluva lot better.

That night, I stopped by to pick Michel and Eve up. Michel didn't have a car and Eve let one of her sisters borrow her little convertible. I called Michel's phone. "Hey, bitch, I'm outside," I said, double-parking beside a green Honda Accord.

"I'm almost ready," he said. "Come up and don't bitch. Just park that pretty Jag and drag your black ass up here."

Click.

He hung up on me.

The block was crowded and the front porch of the building was covered with people trying to find some escape from the heat of their brick-encased apartments. I remembered my little AC window unit broke one summer night, and my box fan didn't do shit to keep the sweat from soaking my sheets even as I lay naked in bed.

Humph. Living in the Twleve50 had me all about central air.

I looked up and down the street but the cars were parked bumper to bumper, without a parking spot in sight. I wasn't trying to park around the corner and walk back in my five-inch stilettos. I stayed double-parked and put my flashers on before I shut the car off and locked the doors once I got out.

"Whaddup, Luscious? Let me get tickets to the show?" Millie, a toothless addict with six kids asked, barely sitting up straight on the metal chair she sat in. Her eyes were damn near shut and I was surprised she could see enough of me to even know who I was.

"They'll be at the door, mama," I said, squeezing her shoulder as I passed.

Millie laughed as she scratched at her face with raggedy fingernails. "You full of shit, Luscious, with your bad ass," she said, her words slurring.

I just smiled as I waved at everybody on the stoop and walked into the building. Growing up in the hood, drug abuse was pretty much in your face. The more dealers, the more users, the more shit to see. It wasn't nothing to see a dozen Millies . . . or to hear a dozen stories about how they got to be strung out.

Some man they loved introduced them to the shit and then left them behind with the addiction.

A preteen starting out with weed and beer and then escalating to harder shit because it started to take more weed to feel the high.

A woman who was running from a past of some kind of abuse that she needed the escape of drugs to forget.

Plenty of stories that ended in nightmares.

As I stepped onto the elevator, I realized my ass was lucky I didn't get hooked on coke when I was dating Make$. And I was dumb to have taken the chance. Just as dumb as I was as college kid, popping pills and shit. I could've just as easily been Millie. Or Erin.

I wondered if my old college roommate was somewhere fading in and out of reality on a high. Or worse. Was she dead? The thought of that made me sad.

So I never judged. I just thanked God for the grace he bestowed me.

I smiled at the flyers for our comedy show on the wall of the elevator as I stepped on. All the bright colors stood out against the whitish walls. Eve actually designed the flyers and I must admit she surprised me, because they looked hella good, had plenty of info, and made someone curious to see what was popping off.

The elevator stopped on the third floor and I stepped aside as a tall and muscular dude stepped on. The smell of weed and cheap cologne filled the air, and I was glad when the ele stopped on the eighth floor and I got the fuck off. His shit was about to choke me.

My heels drummed against the tiled floor as I walked the short distance to Michel's apartment. The sounds of the bass of somebody's music was thumping. *Boom-boom-boom.*

Michel had left his door open. *What the fuck is up with people and their doors today?* Either I had to stop watching all those crime shows or people were reckless. I pushed the door open. I jumped as I envisioned my friend lying on the floor covered in blood. So much fucking blood. All of it soaking his turquoise rug from between his thighs. His dick lying on the carpet cut away from his body.

"Luscious, why the fuck are you standing in a daze?"

I blinked and shook my head as the image of Michel's mutilated body disappeared just as quickly as my paranoid-ass brain made it up. *What the fuck? Okay, no more* First 48.

I shifted my eyes up to Michel standing there looking at me like I was crazy. He was in a silk robe without one of his lace-front wigs, but his makeup was just as beautiful as ever. Just as alive as ever. I shook my head as I stepped into the apartment and closed the door behind me. "You shouldn't leave your door open," I said.

"Girl, I am *loved* in this building," he said, strutting across the studio apartment to his white dressing table in the corner. Above the table were two shelves with six wig heads. He reached for the one with the auburn lace-front wig before sitting down on the bench.

"I worry about you," I said, moving to the kitchenette to pour a glass of moscato.

"Why?" Michel said, turning to look at me, his wig still in hand.

"I'm just thinking about the dude from the last comedy show about to fuck you up because he didn't know you was a man under all that pretty." I leaned against the small counter. "What wasn't there that night?"

Michel turned all the way around on the bench and crossed his long, shapely legs. "I'm just being me and I can't change that. I love being a girl. The makeup, the clothes, ooh, baby, the shoes. All of it. *Love it.* And I've loved it since I was a little boy being told, 'You look like a girl,' every day of my life."

"But you're not a girl, Michel, you got a dick big as a bat. You're a boy playing dress-up and not every dude is feeling that," I insisted.

"But a *lot* do," he stressed.

"But how do you know the difference?" I shot back.

He shrugged and waved his wig.

"Would you ever have the surgery?" I asked, finishing my wine and moving around the counter to pour another one. Fuck it. Michel could drive.

"I'm sorry, friend, but there is no surgery to turn me straight," he said, sounding hurt and a little angry as he pulled the wig over his own hair that he kept cut low.

I sat my goblet on the counter and came around to help him put the adhesive on the back of the wig. "No, I mean would you get the titties and a pussy. You know, become a woman."

Michel looked up at me in the mirror. "I do not want a pussy or even want to be anywhere near a motherfuckin' pussy. There is nothing like the taste, the touch, and the feel of a hard dick. I'm gay. I'm not taking hormones or getting THE DICK cut off."

My face screwed up as the bloody image flashed in my head again. I definitely could do without *that* shit.

"Now, if you ready to get up outta my business," Michel said, meeting my eyes in the mirror.

"I just don't want you to get hurt, Michel," I said, turning to pick up my glass of wine to sip.

"I can understand that but I'm good, so don't worry," he said. "Plus you got enough on your plate."

The front door opened and Eve strolled in. Her face was free of makeup. "Whassup," she said, not at all looking or sounding like her usual lively self.

Michel lifted an arched brow as he finished putting on his

wig. "Humph, somebody got drama for days," he muttered under his breath, giving Eve a mean side-eye.

I turned and eyed her. "What's up with you?" I asked, pouring her a glass of wine.

Eve turned and just crossed her arms over her chest.

I leaned back at that. Eve—"I love alcohol whenever I can get it"—turned down moscato. There was one of two things going on. "You pregnant or on antibiotics?" I asked her, sitting the wine on the counter.

"Ding, ding, ding, ding, ding," Michel said in a falsetto.

Eve glared at him. "Shuddafuckup, *Michael*," she snapped.

I sighed, because Eve didn't need a baby or a disease. "So you two keeping secrets now?" I asked.

"You been busy," Eve said, walking the short distance to plop down on the sofa.

"Not that busy," I popped back.

Now Michel gave me a side-eye and a mouth twist that said, "Whatever, bitch," before he dropped his robe and started to get dressed, his padded bra and thong already on. I finished my drink as he dressed in a short black ruffled skirt with a skintight black tee that read YUMMY ENTERTAINMENT in neon colors. Sky-high fuchsia pumps and fingernails were bright enough to glow in the dark. He sprayed his Gucci perfume in the air and then stepped into the mist with a wink.

Ignoring him, I looked back at Eve. "Which one is it?" I asked, feeling more like her older sister than a cousin and friend the same damn age.

Michel mimicked a baby's cry.

Shit!

Eve sat up straight. "I'm not pregnant!"

Michel shrugged. "I know that. I just wanted you to answer the question . . . with your itchy coochie."

No he didn't. I turned my head so Eve wouldn't see me fighting not to laugh.

When Michel pretended to scratch his crotch with a crazy face, even Eve had to laugh as she tossed one of his throw pillows at him.

"Can we go now?" I said, already planning to buy my cousin enough condoms to fill a drawer. Eve didn't believe in relationships and boyfriends. She was a female playa, but I thought she was playing safe.

"Let me beat this bitch face real quick," Michel said, motioning his hand over his dressing chair.

Eve made her way into the chair and I finished sipping my wine while Michel did her makeup and spiked her hair. We were out there in less than ten minutes. Michel locked his apartment and we laughed as we headed downstairs.

I climbed in the driver's seat and closed the door as Michel let Eve climb in the back via the passenger door. A carload of dudes rolled by in an old Chevy Caprice. One of them leaned out the passenger window. "What's up, lovely?" he yelled back at Michel.

Michel blew gloss-covered kisses as he flipped his wig before he finally climbed in my car as the rear lights of the Caprice disappeared around the corner. There is no way he could convince me that every last one of the niggas in that car would wanna fuck him and not beat his ass for being an undercover dude. Michel was flirting with danger.

"You don't judge me. I don't judge you," he said, closing my passenger door.

I pressed my lips together as I checked the rearview mirror and then pulled off to zoom up the street.

The comedy show was another hit for us. Profits all around. As soon as the last people left we settled up with the owner of the venue and headed to Club 973 to party the last few hours of the night away until the club lights came on.

"Let's go to Dino's," Eve said, her legs looking twice as long in the black linen shorts she wore with matching gladiator sandals and her Yummy T-shirt.

My cell phone vibrated in my hand. I looked down at the caller ID as we stood by my Jag in the parking lot. "I gotta take this call," I said, moving away from them as I flipped my hair back and pressed the phone to my ear.

"What's up?"

"Goldie sent me on a job, right?" my snitch said. "A car service picked me up, took me to the motherfucking Plaza, back entrance, penthouse suite."

"And?"

"And nothing. Girl, I just fucked the hell out of a senator. Goldie on some real big-time shit. Like for real. She making money, you hear me?"

No wonder that bitch was living on the Upper East Side and pushing a Bentley. She was on some politician-type shit. Major.

"I got the video of me and the senator for you. If me letting this freak pretend to be a baby, putting baby powder on his saggy nuts, and diapering his old ass ain't enough for you, I don't know what is."

I paced around the parking lot thinking, while Michel and Eve motioned for me to hurry. "Do you got him on video paying you?" I asked, looking up at the full moon in the sky.

"No. Goldie handles the money. We never touch it or see it."

"Then all we have is a political scandal. Some freaky politician getting served up by a young girl. We got *him* by the balls, not Goldie."

My snitch sighed.

"I need paperwork. Can you get into her office?" I asked, starting to walk back over to Michel and Eve.

"I want Goldie just as bad as you, but you asking for the impossible."

When she told me Goldie was pimping bitches out, I never expected her to actually start tricking for Goldie—but it was her pussy to handle. "Just try for me. Okay?"

"A'ight. But the number I had in my head for payment just went up."

I ended the call and looked over at Eve and Michel. "Let's roll—"

They both waved their hand and *sshhed* me. "Girl, Tek-9 and about nine other niggas got arrested in a big drug raid about an hour ago," Eve said.

That shit made my steps pause as Michel turned up the car's radio.

"More news to come later on this just-breaking story."

Damn. "What did it say?" I asked.

"Just that the police had been investigating him and a group of people for over a year and when they raided his house they found guns and a lot of weed," Eve said.

"Damn," I said.

I liked Tek-9 and now his ass was locked up for slanging dope. Like, why rap if you still was going to hustle? When I first met Make$ he was still in the dope game. But he eventually left that shit alone when he got busy touring and making money.

"And the DJs cracked jokes about him and Make$ winding up in the same facility or cell and be up in there fighting butt-naked over you," Eve added, getting a nasty stare from Michel.

"What? They did?" Eve said, defending herself.

Was I ever going to live that lie down?

"Let's go eat," I said, climbing into the driver's seat. I wished Eve drove so that they could ride together. I didn't feel like all they gossiping and shit.

My mind was racing the whole way to Dino's diner. I hated to hear about Tek-9 getting locked up, especially since I couldn't even chance trying to visit him. The rumors would never die after that. And there went my plans to expand Yummy Entertainment. How was he gonna perform in jail? *Goodbye, Bentley. Goodbye, upscale New York apartment.*

Goldie always came out on top even when the bitch wasn't trying.

The parking lot of Dino's was packed as always for a weekend night. After the club, it was the spot to catch a meal before taking it to the crib. In the days after Dyme's wife made him kick Goldie's ass to the far left, the bitch had worked the third shift at the diner. Eventually Slick Rick recruited her ass to dance in the restaurant's private dining room for a grand.

I wished I coulda seen her around that motherfucker, greasy and sweating and smelling like French fries.

Once we walked into the twenty-four-hour diner we waited for a clean booth. A lot of the chatter in the diner was about Tek-9's arrest. I still couldn't believe it. Dudes had to stop being so damn greedy wanting to make legit *and* illegit money.

The hostess finally led us to a booth in the back by the emergency door.

"Yo, Luscious!"

I stopped and stepped back to look through the open doors of one of the private rooms at Slick Rick the Ruler and his crew of dancers. Slick Rick's sexy self made mad money as an exotic dancer in the tristate area before he opened his own strip club on Clinton Avenue. It was a Club Naughty tradition for him to take the nighttime strippers for breakfast after the club closed.

"Whassup, y'all," I said, eyeing Rick's cinnamon-brown complexion with his jet-black hair freshly faded and framing up his handsome round face.

It's funny that as fine as Rick was, especially with a twelve-inch ruler-length dick, he never did anything for me. He had been one of Goldie's exes too, but it never crossed my mind to fuck him out of revenge. Not like Has. Rick couldn't fuck with Has. Not in my book . . . or Goldie's either.

"I ain't seen you in a minute," he said, dropping his napkin onto his unfinished stack of buttermilk pancakes.

I shrugged. "I been busy."

Rick chuckled. "So I hear," he said, running his tongue over his white and even teeth like he was freeing something from them.

"You still mad, Rick?" I asked, frowning at him like I wasn't in the mood for jokes.

"Nah, I ain't mad."

"What the fuck ever," I said. "Enjoy your breakfast."

I turned and left him and his smug-ass expression behind. Rick was pissed off when Goldie dumped his ass, opened her own strip club in her apartment, and then hired me and Missy from his club to dance for her. *He'll be the fuck all right.*

"Excuse me, Miss Jordan."

I turned to find a white dude in a shirt, tie, and slacks standing behind me. My eyes dropped down to the detective's badge hanging on a metal chain around his neck and the gun holster on his hip.

My nerves instantly got shot to hell . . . especially since he knew my name. He came looking for me.

"Yes?" I asked.

"I need to talk to you in private," he said, already lightly grasping my elbow.

"For what?" I asked, my heart pounding and my stomach feeling like that childhood song "Diarrhea" was going to be real appropriate in a minute.

"You want to discuss this here or outside?" he asked, his New York–Italian accent thick as hell.

I looked around. All nearby eyes in the restaurant were on me—including Michel's and Eve's. My friends were already getting to their feet.

I waved them back down. "I'll be right back," I said, turning to follow the detective out of the diner.

He led me to a unmarked car and then pulled a mini DVD

player from the trunk. "This is a series of videos of you and one Terrence Gardner, aka Make$," he began, his coal-black eyes shifting from the screen to look over at me.

My eyes got big at seeing me and Make$ sitting inside his car as he talked to someone. It was obvious whoever it was wore an undercover camera. That shit was clear as HDTV. I remembered those late-night drives into New York when we first started messing around.

The detective turned the volume up.

I recognized the voice of Poppi, Make$'s dope supplier, as Make$ handed him a stack of cash before Poppi passed him the weight. I was sitting back lounging like I wasn't witness to a major drug deal.

I crossed my arms over my chest as the shit continued to hit the fan.

There was three more scenes of me right at Make$'s side as he handled business. In one snapshot I even counted out the money for Make$ to give Poppi.

I felt like falling the fuck out.

The detective pushed his hands into the pockets of his slacks. "This is enough to get you arrested for possession of drugs and conspiracy to traffic drugs across state lines," he said.

BOOM.

Talk about scared? My fucking heart raced and for a second I thought about kicking off my heels and hauling ass. But just for a second.

"Now," the detective said as he closed the DVD player and locked it back in his trunk. "We had Make$ and his crew under surveillance. These little business transactions with your involvement was a little icing on the cupcake . . . for me."

I couldn't believe I was about to get locked the fuck up. Humph. Life was filled with irony. I was just thinking Tek-9 was wrong for being greedy and *bam*, here's Make$'s shit reminding me to sweep at my own damn door.

"So Make$ is being charged too?" I asked, my heart pounding as he stood behind me and handcuffed my wrist before opening the back door to his car and pushing my head down as I climbed into the backseat.

"When we reached out to your boyfriend almost two years ago, he was very important in leading to the incarceration of several of his business partners . . . including the crew we picked up today."

He laughed as he slammed the door shut and then climbed behind the wheel to pull out of the parking lot.

Make$ was a snitch-bitch. That's why he got out of the game. It wasn't for me. It was to keep his slick ass out of jail. He didn't even protect me.

I leaned forward and pressed my head to the back of the seat as tears filled my eyes and my gut felt so twisted the fuck up. The cuffs were pressing into my wrists and all I could think of was jail. Going to jail. Locked up in jail. Not leaving the jail.

"Oh my God," I cried out, feeling like I could pass out in that bitch.

I never had sweat pour off my body so quick before.

The car pulled to a stop and I lifted my head to look out the window. The sight of an empty and dark parking lot confused the hell out of me. And then he got out the car and came around to climb in the back with me. My confusion turned to fear. I pressed my back against the car door when I felt his body heat coming near me.

"When I saw you on that surveillance tape I knew I had to have you," the detective said. "I been waiting damn near two years for the last of these assholes to get arrested. I kept any of the tapes with you in them. Nobody knows about them but me."

The darkness of the car and his presence was fucking creepy.

"Let's make a deal."

I yelled out from the sudden closeness of his mouth near my ear. "Oh my God. Oh my God. Oh my God," I cried, feeling hot tears racing down my cheeks again. I wished I had my gun. But how could I shoot a cop? Especially one on the way to arrest me?

"Calm down. I'm not gone hurt you, baby," he whispered. "I don't want to see you in jail. Now you be good to me and I'll make that video go away. No video. No charges. No jail."

He pressed his hand between my thighs and palmed my pussy. Fear and feeling helpless made me literally pee myself when he licked my inner ear. The hot piss soaked the seat of my pants and his hand.

"What the fuck?" he snapped, jumping out the car to come around and snatch the door open. I fell out and my upper body landed on the glass-strewn asphalt. Pain shot through my body.

He picked me up under my arms and pulled the rest of my body out the car. "I'll be in touch," he said, turning me around to remove the handcuffs. "And don't try to run. I know all about you. Everything. How do you think I knew where you were tonight?"

This had to be a nightmare. This couldn't be real.

He brushed past me to climb in the driver's seat. "Now walk your pissy ass back," he said out the window before he cranked up and left me standing there with nothing but my fear. I started to breathe deeply like I couldn't catch my breath. My chest started to heave. I bent down and let my head hang between my knees as I fought not to hyperventilate and pass the fuck out.

How the fuck did I get into this shit . . . and better yet, how was I going to get out of it?

11

A little girl of about five or six was in her Hello Kitty pajamas, her Afro puffs looking like Mickey Mouse ears, as she played alone in the middle of the park having a tea party with her dolls. It was night time. The park was nearly empty. No place for a child all alone.

But she played like she didn't know any better . . . until a dark figure floated above her like a cloud. It never got any closer to her than a few feet but it was there like it was watching over her. Like it wanted to play but maybe it was afraid she wouldn't let it. Or like it just wanted to observe her.

She shrugged and went back to pretending to pour tea in the cups with her pretty porcelain teapot. Lightning suddenly struck, and the little girl jumped, dropping the teapot to the ground. It cracked in half. She cried as her heart pounded.

The black cloud suddenly swooped down and surrounded her.

She screamed and ran, breaking through the cloud. The park suddenly turned into a hallway of rooms with doors on either side. Lots and lots of doors. She tried her best to open each one. They were locked. All except the door at the end of the hall. The knob turned and she raced inside, closing the door behind her. She tried to lock it but couldn't, and so she raced around the dark room until a bed suddenly appeared.

She scrambled to fit her body beneath it just as the door opened. She prayed. She was afraid. She was alone. She didn't understand why her parents weren't there to protect her. To watch out over her. To fight for her.

"It's okay, Harriet. You didn't mean to break it. Come out

*from under the bed. You're such a good girl, I know you didn't
mean it. Not a good girl like you."*

*The little girl with the Afro puffs and Hello Kitty pajamas
cried out as a hand reached under the bed and pulled her from
safety. . . .*

"No!" I cried out, sitting up straight as I woke my ass up
from the same fucked-up dream I'd been having for the last two
weeks. *Damn.*

I hated to sleep, but my body needed what it needed. I
mean, I'm only human. And when I woke up I was always
drenched in sweat, my heart racing, my guts filled with fear
and this feeling of helplessness that I couldn't explain or shake
for shit.

"Damn, Luscious, you a'ight, cuz?"

I looked over at Eve sitting on the floor of my living room
across from Michel as they both watched me instead of the television. I wiped my face with my trembling hands as I tried to
shake the dream and all the fucked emotions it brought out of
me.

"You was screaming and on your back with your legs up like
you was running and shit," Michel joked, rising from the floor in
his maxi dress to walk into the kitchen. "Girl, sound like Ghost-
face from *Scream 4* had ahold of your ass."

Eve laughed. "O-kay. We was sitting here watching you, talking about how you a good girl," she added on, making a comical
face as she used the remote to flip through the channels.

I accepted the glass of wine Michel brought from the kitchen
for me. "Girl, please rest your nerves. Don't worry me and Eve
here to watch over you, boo," he said, lifting the hem of his dress
to kick his long leg high in the air before bending his body into
this crazy-ass karate stance.

Eve jumped to her feet and air-punched. "Fuck the karate
shit, ain't no fight like a hood fight, bitch," she said, ducking like
she was in the ring.

I sipped my wine and watched these fools try to entertain me, but they didn't even understand the shit I was going through.

I looked over at my cell phone sitting on the end table. That crazy detective hadn't lied. He called my cell phone like two nights after he left me pissed up and scared in that parking lot.

That had been two weeks ago and I never knew when that nut was gone call telling me to meet him at that nasty motel that looked like it probably charged by the hour.

This sick shit with that dirty cop was really messing with me. I didn't even know his real name. He just told me to call him Detective Dick. He got a kick out of that shit when he was making me do all kinds of shit to him I wished I could forget. I didn't know what it had to do with my dreams, but I was sick of all of it. My nerves were shot. I was steady drinking trying to forget. I even had to stop myself from hunting up a bag of coke—just the memory of Millie and so many others beaten down by that shit made me pour another glass of wine instead.

It was like my life was on pause again.

I couldn't remember the last time I'd been to the shooting range. We didn't have an event or nothing lined up for August. I didn't even leave my apartment. It was the only place I felt safe.

Bzzzzzz . . . Bzzzzzz . . . Bzzzzzz . . .

I clenched my jaw as my cell phone vibrated on the sofa next to me. I knew it was him. I. KNEW. IT. Shit had to change. Shit HAD to change.

I might go fucking crazy.

Michel and Eve continued play-fighting while I picked up the phone. PEVERT flashed on the screen along with the number to a cell phone I knew was prepaid and untraceable. I answered the call even as I rose to my feet.

"Meet me in thirty minutes and have that nice fat pussy wet for me."

Click.

He didn't even wait for me to say shit. He knew I didn't have to. He had me by the clit.

I was a fucking mess. I pulled out the soda bottle from my purse and took a deep swig of it. I poured half the Pepsi out the window and added Crown Royal. Even with the chaser the liquor burned my throat going down. The pain felt good, because I was still numb. Lost. Out of body.

I let my head fall back against the headrest as I looked out at the flashing neon lights of the short-stay hotel. It was run-down. Beat-down. Needed to be torn down.

I felt pains in my stomach when the curtain shifted in a first-floor room. Room 12. I saw a flash of overly tanned skin. He was waiting for me. With his nasty requests. His degradation. The thought of the shit he put me through made my skin crawl. It made my eyes fill with water. Before. After. During.

I took another swig of the liquid in the soda bottle before I forced myself to climb out my car and make my way to the door. My feet felt as heavy as lead or some shit. I'd rather have jumped into a pool of broken glass butt-naked than knock on that motherfucking door.

This had to be what slaves felt like when the master came calling late at night. Tugging at their clothes and underwear. Forcing them to lay and take their sex or be punished.

I was his slave.

God, I hated it. I hated it so much. Jail had to be better than this.

I raised my hand to knock and the door opened before I could. The stale smell of mildew choked me as I stepped in. I didn't have to look around to know the room, I knew it well. The hard mattress. The scratchy sheets. The stained covers. Dirty rugs. Dingy walls. Old TV without a remote. A small fridge that smelled like the pussies of the whores who tricked out this same room.

The whole place screamed STD and crabs. It made me itch.

The door swung shut and I knew it was like a director yelling out "Action." His hands squeezed my shoulders before he pressed an overly wet kiss to the back of my neck. The first tear of the night fell as he yanked the tube-top dress I wore down, exposing my naked body to the funky air. He ordered me to never wear underwear.

I jumped when he pressed his small dick to my naked ass and brought his hands around to pinch my nipples hard. I cried out. It hurt. But I stood there. I took it.

Just like I would take everything else he had for me.

Detective Dick suddenly grabbed a handful of my hair into his fist and pushed me down until my knees were pressed into the sticky carpet. He came around to stand in front of me and I caught a glimpse of his short fat dick barely reaching out from under his big belly. Tight black hairs covered him like a forest and ran down his legs.

"Suck my balls," he ordered, his accent making it sound more like "bawls."

I fought the urge to bite them as I bent my head and tried my best not to flinch as I did like he said. I learned early that showing him I didn't like doing what he ordered made him more fucked up in his thinking. Then it was "Oh, okay you don't like *that*, how about *this*?"

This pervert done peed on me. Fucked me in the ass. Cum on my eyelids. Made me suck his asshole . . . his fingers . . . and his toes. Tied me up. Gagged me. Talked shit to me.

No, I couldn't let this sick motherfucker know how much he made me sick to my damn stomach. How much I hated him. How much I wanted to take my .357, lube the barrel, slide it in his ass, and shoot.

I dreamt about that shit.

POW! POW! POW!

"Oooh," he moaned, thrusting his hips forward until his jelly belly kept knocking me against the head. "Suck both of my *baw-wls* in your nasty mouth you black bitch."

I gagged and squeezed my eyes shut as he tapped the top of his dick against my chin—that short motherfucker couldn't reach my cheek if he even fucking tried.

"Suck 'em harder you no-good bitch!"

I did. Oh God, I did. Ugh.

He wrapped his hands around my throat, this thumb pressing on my windpipe. "Suck my dick."

I hated to even swallow. I was taking enough of his shit and I didn't want to feel like I was taking in any more of him. "Put the condom on, you dumb cunt!" he snapped, snatching what little of his dick he had out of my mouth. "I'm not taking your fucking nasty germs home to my fucking wife."

My germs? Motherfucker, *please.*

I at least took some pleasure that he insisted on condoms. Thank God for small favors. I rose to my feet and grabbed the box of condoms sitting at the foot of the bed. He came up behind me and massaged my ass. If my skin could literally crawl it would have. "You sure got a sweet tight ass on you," he said, slapping each of my cheeks, back and forth. Back and forth. Back and forth. Over and over.

The same way I wanted to slap the shit out of him. Across his mouth. Over and over.

This was the sex I was having after going without for a year. This sadistic criminal bullshit? This couldn't be life.

I turned and gave him a fake-ass smile as I sat down on the bed and slid the condom on his dick, the whole while hoping the fucking blanket had been washed recently. I got back on my knees and I took him into my mouth, fighting that desire to vomit.

"Oooh, that's so good. Yes. Suck it tighter. Oh, yes. That's a good girl . . . that's a good girl," he moaned.

That's a good girl . . .

And just like that. In an instant. I remembered. I remembered and everything made sense. Horrible. Disgusting. Fucked-up sense. Tears filled my eyes as I was taken back to a different time and a different place, where another man had used me for sex. For power. For perversion . . .

I was just five or six, sitting on the bed in Mr. Alvarez's extra bedroom in my pajamas. I was over there to spend the night with Sophie, but she was upstairs sleeping. He had come to her room and carried me down the hall to the room Sophie and I played in. He talked softly and brought me a big bowl of ice cream, but I still hated the way he touched my hair, told me I was so pretty, and asked me to keep secrets.

When he whispered softly to me and pulled me onto his lap on the bed, I kicked my foot out at the first feel of his hand on me. It hit the side of the teapot sitting on the small table where we had our pretend parties and knocked it to the floor. It cracked in half.

I jumped off his lap and rushed under the bed to hide because I just knew I was in trouble.

"It's okay, Harriet. You didn't mean to break it. Come out from under the bed. You're such a good girl, I know you didn't mean it. Not a good girl like you," he whispered under the bed as he reached for me.

"That's a good girl. . . ."

One by one, images of that night came flooding back to me from whatever hole in my brain I had locked that bullshit away. But I remembered. I remembered what he did to me that night. That sick son of a bitch took away my innocence that night. He did things to me. And made me do things to him.

No, this shit right here with the dirty cop was not the first time a man made me do things I didn't want to do. I felt like that scared little girl again.

And I know I was injured. That shit fucked me up because I pushed it so deep away that I forgot it. I didn't want to remember. My brain protected me from this shit . . . but then it protected that motherfucker too.

I raced from my knees into the tiny bathroom and threw up into the commode. In the vomit I was purging all the years of keeping that secret. Until I couldn't take anymore.

"What the fuck is wrong with you?" Detective Dick asked, standing at the door of the bathroom.

I thought of that night as a child and then the nights I suffered as an adult under the fucked-up mind of this dirty cop and I threw up some more. Because I couldn't take anymore. NO MORE.

"So fucking me makes you want to throw up?" he barked, snatching my hair into his fist and raising my head, forcing me to look up into his face. "I'll give you a reason to fucking throw up!"

NO MORE.

He dragged me out the bathroom and pushed me rough as hell. I fell onto the middle of the bed. But my emotions flipped like a motherfucker and I didn't feel shit but anger.

In that moment, the weight of it all was on my shoulders.

Being lied on. Cheated on. Betrayed by my friend. Left with a pedophile by my parents. Molested. Blackmailed by this dirty cop.

I didn't want to do shit but shake all of it off.

I hopped to my feet as the detective moved to a bag in the corner and pulled out a whip. Humph. Today was Independence Day, motherfucker. Enough was enough of this shit. *All* of this shit.

I picked up my foot and kicked that bastard dead in his ass, pushing him into the sink that was *outside* the damn bathroom. I grabbed my dress, shoes, and keys. I spotted his badge on top of his clothes and I snatched that motherfucker too before I ran out that bitch butt-naked and hopped into my car. I threw the Jag in reverse, almost running over a trick and her john trying to make it to one of the rooms.

"Hey, watch where the fuck you going?" they yelled.

Fuck 'em.

The motel room door opened and he jumped back inside when he spotted the people still bitching at me.

I pressed my foot to the gas and I didn't stop until I finally got off of Route 22 and made the turn to take me toward Weequahic Park. I pulled over long enough to pull my dress over my head, even as my mind felt like it was completely fucked by everything that happened that night. Everything that surfaced that night.

I knew I was going to jail. I knew it. And that scared the shit out of me. But there was two things I had to do before I got locked up, and it just so happened that I was just two blocks from where it all needed to go the fuck down.

The door opened. He stood there. His face filled with surprise at seeing me. Good.

"How you doing, Mr. Alvarez?" I said, proud of myself for sounding normal. "Sophie isn't here by any chance, is she?"

"No, no she's at her own house," he said, his Spanish accent hardly noticeable.

"You wouldn't have her number? I really wanted to invite her to a party I'm having," I lied, trying to fight the images of his hands on my six-year-old body. Nothing womanly at all about me. Nothing to draw the attention of a normal grown-ass man.

Victor Alvarez was a fucking pedophile.

"Sure, sure, come in and let me get it for you," he said, stepping back to let me in.

I stepped inside and pressed my hands against the gun that I slipped into the pocket of my dress. I made sure that no part of my body touched his as I moved to stand in the middle of the living room. My eyes went to that teapot. It was a reminder that I lost a piece of myself that night. My eyes filled with tears and I clenched my teeth as the memories flooded me again.

"I hope you and Sophie do get back close like you used to," Mr. Alvarez said, as he picked up a notepad from the table next to his chair.

"I bet you do," I said sarcastically, tearing my eyes away from that broken teapot.

He looked up at me. "Of course I want that," he said. "I must have left that notepad in the kitchen. I'll be right back."

I watched him walk out of the room and then I turned and picked up the cracked teapot. *Does he think of what he did to me whenever he looks at this?* I wondered.

Was it his trophy like those other perverted mofos on *Law & Order: Special Victims Unit* kept?

I gripped that teapot so tight, I thought it might crumble in my hands as I walked into the kitchen. Mr. Alvarez turned from where he was standing by the phone still hanging on the wall like it was the eighties. His eyes dropped down to the teapot in my hand.

What is he thinking about right now?

"I'll take that, Harriet," he said, stepping toward me.

"No, no . . . no you won't, motherfucker," I said, holding it high above my head before I used all my strength and anger and resentment to throw that bitch at the linoleum covered floor. It shattered.

Mr. Alvarez stared down at the pieces and then looked up at me. "Why did you do that?" he snapped, his accent coming out of him a little bit more as his eyes filled with anger.

Like I gave a fuck.

I laughed and it was filled with my bitterness. "The same reason you shattered a big piece of me . . . because I *wanted* to. You nasty, disgusting pervert. You sick son of a bitch."

"What are you talking about?" he roared, the veins of his neck bulging.

"Stop playing like your child-molesting ass is stuck on stupid and don't know what this is about. Stop it!" I pulled the gun from my pocket and aimed it at a spot between his eyes. "I was just a little girl and you had no right to do that shit to me. I should blow your fucking head wide open."

He held us his large hands, and I could tell he was nervous as hell and wondering just where this night was going for him. "Harriet—"

I looked into his eyes. "Strip," I ordered. "Like you did that night? *Remember?*"

He opened his mouth and I lowered the gun to his crotch. Never taking his eyes off me, Mr. Alvarez unbuttoned his shirt and unzipped the jeans he wore before he removed everything until he stood naked before me.

I waved the gun at one of the chairs pushed under the kitchen table. "Sit your ass down," I snapped, blinking away tears as the memories continued flooding back to me. I shook my head like I could free the images. Erase the hurt. The fear. The shame. All the feelings of a six-year-old little girl.

It felt as fresh as if I was still in that vulnerable little body.

As he folded his tall and slender frame in the chair, I seriously fought the urge to just shoot his ass. "Do you remember putting your dick in my mouth?" I asked him, moving across the kitchen to rub the barrel of my gun against his lips as I flipped my hair back out of my face.

"Touching my chest?" I asked, using my free hands to pinch his nipples hard as fuck with a curl of my lip filled with every bit of hate I had for him.

He winced.

"Touching my privates, you sick bitch?" I asked, my voice cracking with the emotions I felt as I reached down and grabbed his limp dick and balls in my hand to snatch, digging my nails into his sack and twisting everything until the skin stretched.

He cried out and sweat popped on his forehead. "You're wrong," he whispered, his voice hoarse as he fought the pain.

I grabbed his jank again wishing I could pull the mother-fucker off and throw it outside for dogs or some shit.

"I didn't hurt you!" Mr. Alvarez barked, his face angry.

I let his jank go and stepped back from the audacity of this motherfucker. "You didn't hurt me," I repeated softly, again and again and again like a chant.

"You never cried," he said simply.

"You didn't hurt me," I kept repeating. In disbelief and shock and pain.

"You're not remembering it right," he insisted.

With my gun still leveled at his chest, I used my free hand to turn on the gas stove. The front left burner filled with blue flames.

"I'm sorry that you're not remembering what we shared," he said, like he felt sorry for me.

"You didn't hurt me," I said again with a little laugh that was bitter as hell as I pulled a knife from the dish rack and placed the blade into the flames.

He continued rambling behind me, but I didn't give a fuck about what he was saying.

I turned and pressed the hot knife to his face. The smell of burnt skin and flesh filled the air.

He jumped to his feet, hitting a high note and covering his brand with his hand. "You crazy *bitch!*" he roared as the skin from the burn pulled away, exposing his pinkish flesh.

And I smiled, loving his pain and feeling in that moment that maybe I was crazy. Fuck it. "Sit. Down," I ordered him, stepping up to press the barrel of the gun to his heart.

Something he saw in my face or in my eyes or in the steadiness of my hand around that gun made him ease his ass back down into the chair.

"I didn't hurt you," I said simply with a lift of my shoulders. "That didn't hurt."

"What are you going to do to me?" Mr. Alvarez asked.

"Nothing that will ever affect you the way you affected me," I told him, shaking my head as a vision of him violating me in the ultimate way filled me. I hated my tears but I couldn't deny them. They needed to be released. Right along with the memories of that night, they needed to be free.

I dropped the knife and the tip of the blade accidentally stuck in his thigh. He extended his legs and clenched his teeth.

With a sadistic smile and my eyes filled with many more tears to flow, I balled my free hand into a fist, raised it high and then slammed it down onto the top of the handle, sending the knife deep into his flesh until I felt it hit bone.

"Aaaaarghh!" he cried out, as blood spurted from around the knife.

I didn't give a fuck if he bled to death. Fuck him. The devil was waiting on his ass *anyway*.

"I'm not done with you, Mr. Alvarez, but right now I got another battle to fight," I told him, my gun pointed on him as I backed out of the kitchen.

He fought to work the knife from his body as he cussed in Spanish.

I didn't turn around until I reached the front door. I slammed it behind me and took just a moment to try and get my mind settled. What a crazy fucking night.

I heard the sirens before I saw Detective Dick's unmarked car coming up the street from a few bocks away. I moved to my car and put my gun back in its case in the trunk. I wiped the tears from my eyes before I grabbed his detective's badge and my pocketbook from the passenger seat and then raced up the steps to my parents' house. I laid on the bell.

His unmarked car pulled to a stop in the street in front of my parents' house just as my mother opened the front door.

"What's going on, Harriet?" she asked, looking past me.

I could see the lights of the siren in her eyes as I pressed my keys and the badge into her hands. "I'm about to be arrested—"

"What?!" she gasped, her face filling with alarm.

I heard his feet pounding on the steps.

"Don't move, Harriet!" he said from behind me.

"What the fuck is going on?" my mama snapped, the hood coming from deep within her. And in the middle of all the craziness, as my hands were roughly handcuffed behind me, I laughed. A little.

My father's tall presence filled the doorway. "What's going on?" he said, stepping past my mother to eye the detective and then to look out at his neighbors standing on their porches or looking out their windows at the commotion.

"Your daughter is being arrested for—"

"Daddy, follow us and make sure he takes me to a police station to be booked," I said, cutting him off as he turned me and led me down the steps. "I don't trust him, Daddy. Follow us."

Detective Dick jerked me by the cuffs. "You have the right to remain silent . . ."

"Please, Daddy," I pleaded over my shoulder.

I begged because in that moment a little piece of me was that six-year-old girl who felt like, where was her daddy to protect her that night. *Why wasn't my daddy there for me?*

And maybe now I understood my rebellion and resentment of them all these years came from that one question. *Why wasn't my daddy there for me?*

I was so afraid that his anger and shame about me being

arrested would make him step back in the house and close the door. *Be there for me now.*

I looked over my shoulder. "Daddy, *please.*"

Detective Dick laughed. "Looks like its just you and me, you cunt," he whispered to me.

"They have your badge number, so no stops," was all that I said.

He pushed me inside the back of the car and slammed the door. I looked through the glass at my parents still standing on that porch. Not moving to do as I begged. My heart broke into a million pieces as I dropped my head against the back of the seat as the police car pulled away.

Fire

$\mathscr{I}$ sat in that room with its desk and two empty chairs and smoked the cigarette a female detective gave me. My legs were crossed, my foot swinging, my eyes locked on the mirror across from me. I'd seen enough cop shows to know they were either watching me through a two-way mirror or via a video camera.

I drummed my nails on the table top, pretending I was in total control of being in one of the interview rooms of a New York precinct. But for real, I was trying to wrap my brain around my life. Trying to figure all this shit out. Trying not to be afraid of doing time. Trying not to ache because once again my father wasn't there for me. Trying not to beat myself up for not at least videotaping one of the freak sessions since the man I now knew as Detective Jon Rossi was going to deny the whole thing. Of course. And to top it all, still trying to come to grips with being molested by the father of my childhood best friend/my parents' neighbor and friend.

The one thing I did know for sure, even as I looked around at the walls and the locked door, was that tonight—for the first time in a long time—I was free. I'd rather have sat in jail than let myself be degraded and used by a dirty cop anymore. I'd rather remember my past instead of having it eat away at me and not even know why.

I released a heavy-ass breath. Thank God the sixty grand or better sitting in my bank account meant I could say a big "fuck you" to the overworked and underpaid public defender's office. But I hadn't even asked for an attorney yet.

The door opened. Detective Rossi, aka Detective Dick, and a black female detective entered the room. The sight of him turned my stomach and I let my eyes drift down to his crotch. I lifted my pinkie and wiggled it at him before I laughed. His neck and face turned red beneath his spray tan.

"Something funny about being arrested for drug charges, Miss Jordan?" the female detective asked, her voice sounding like she lived on cigarettes and emphysema medication.

I didn't say shit, but I stopped laughing. It was time for business. "Thank you for speaking with me," I started. "The only thing I have to say is that for the last two weeks, Detective Dick—oops, I mean Detective Rossi—and I have been involved in a sexual relationship—"

He jumped to his feet and slammed his hands against the top of the table. "You liar!"

I rolled my eyes at him and shifted them to the female detective. "As I was saying. We were involved in a perverted, disgusting sexual relationship involving fetishes and foolishness that was completely of his instigation, control, and pleasure because he used his power as a detective for the New York Police Department against me."

"You lying bitch!" The veins in his neck strained and his eyes bugged.

"He has a hairy mole in the crack of his ass," I added, holding up my hands and making a face like "hey."

The female detective jumped up and pressed her hand to his heaving chest. "Calm down, Jon," she said, her voice all strong as she pushed him toward the door.

I eyed him and I let all the disgust I had for him, Mr. Alvarez, my father, Make$, and Goldie burn into him. I was sick of these fools handling me. Hurting me. I didn't deserve this shit. None of it.

"Now, I would like to make that statement and *only* that statement. I have nothing else to say until my attorney arrives," I finished, pressing my lips together and leaning back in my chair.

She pushed him out the door and I was back in that room alone. Locked in. Left with my thoughts. I finished the cigarette and dropped the butt to the floor to crush beneath the toe of my gold wedges. I ran my fingers through my hair and closed my eyes as all that shit came crashing down on me. Weighing my shoulders down. Mind-fucking me.

Would I have enough gwap to make bail *and* get a good attorney?

Would Mr. Alvarez call the police on me and then I'd be facing assault charges, too? Hell, was Mr. Alvarez's no-good ass still alive?

What were my parents thinking?

Why wasn't my daddy there for me?

I pressed my eyes closed with my fingertips to keep the tears from falling. That shit hurt more than anything.

A uniformed cop came into the room to take me back to the holding cell. I took a seat on the bench, not even paying attention to the two other chicks in there with me. I closed my eyes, leaned back against the wall, and crossed my legs at the ankle, wishing like a motherfucker that I was in my apartment minding my own.

I nodded off at some point and didn't wake up until my head fell forward. I woke up with a start and for a second I was home in my bed. But then that second passed and reality struck like a motherfucker. I sat up straight, frowning at the taste of sleep in my mouth.

It was the first night I didn't have that dream. Damn shame when you get the best night of sleep in weeks in a jail cell. Ain't that some shit?

I stood up and tried to shake some of the wrinkles from my dress. I used my fingers to comb the few tangles from my weave before I twisted the long ends into a knot. I licked my fingertips and wiped under my eyes and around my mouth for any makeup that smudged. I hoped I was going for my bail hearing early. I wanted out of this bitch before they sent me to county.

Yes, I went to the shooting range, owned a gun, and even pulled that mug on three men in the last couple of months, but I was no type of hard-nosed gangstress. I wanted out. I didn't have a record. To me, the charges wasn't *that* serious. I had to get a low bail, right?

I wasn't ever somebody to live in church on Sundays. Sometimes I would let the TV sit on Joel Osteen or T. D. Jakes when they came on on Sundays, but right then I knew I needed to get down on my knees and pray.

Hell, I been on them for way worse than a talk with God.

I eyed the dirty floor and sat down instead, knowing the Heavenly One could hear me just as fine on my ass as He could on my knees. I crossed my fingers and bent my head.

"God please get me out of this. You know my heart. You see all. You know what all I been fighting. Please let me carry my black ass home and I swear I—"

"Jordan," someone called out.

My eyes popped open. *Shee-it, God don't play.*

I jumped to my feet. The black female detective from yesterday opened the cell. I couldn't remember her name. "It's time for my bail hearing?" I asked.

"No, you're outta here. The charges were dropped."

PAUSE.

"What?" I asked, rushing to follow behind her.

"You heard me," she said.

I started to dougie in that bitch, but I stopped in the hall leading to another door. "Why? This not no setup because I told on your partner is it?" I asked.

Was they gone set me free and then wait and set me up to be shot or some shit like I was trying to escape? I watched enough TV not to trust a damn thing concerning a lot of cops. Especially a dirty pervert like Detective Dick.

She turned and eyed me like I was crazy. "You're free. Just get the fuck outta here," she snapped, holding the door open.

Did her and Detective Dick make the charges go away to keep me from getting him in trouble for the shit he did to me? Was she helping that fool?

I made my way past her, but I stopped and looked into her eyes. "He really did that to me, you know," I told her, blinking away tears. "Just please believe that you need to be careful with somebody like that watching your back on these streets, mama. For real."

She didn't say nothing else to me and so I just made my way to the desk sergeant to pick up my property and get the fuck out of there just like she suggested.

I didn't even bother to call Eve and Michel to come and pick me up from New York. I called a car service and waited outside the police station for it. I knew I looked a mess in my wrinkled dress and barely combed hair.

As soon as I powered my cell phone on it went to vibrating.

I started answering the calls and ending them quick. No need to lie; I was too ashamed for getting locked up. It was time for some damage control.

Eve.

"Oh shit, you out. Me and Michel were coming to meet the attorney to go to court with you."

"The charges got dropped," I said, actually feeling the urge to hit a blunt. Just a little something to take the edge off—or get me off the edge. What the fuck ever.

"What *was* the charges?"

Nosy ass. "They mistook me for somebody else. No biggie. I'm out and about to take a car service back to Jersey," I told her.

"You should sue. *I* would sue they asses and sit back lovely as hell for making me sit up in jail all damn night," Eve said, taking a deep breath when she got done.

"I'll call you when I get back to Jersey. I got another call, a'ight?" I hung up because that breath she took meant she was getting ready to have a long conversation. Nothing.

Click.

Michel.

"Michel. I'm out. I'm straight. Mistaken identity. Call Eve. She got the details. I got another call. Cool?"

Click.

Missy.

"Hi Luscious. You good?" she asked.

I gave her the same speech I gave the other two and soon it was on to the next call.

Click.

My snitch.

"Girl, you not going to believe this shit," she said.

My words died as I watched Detective Dick/Rossi walking up the street. He spotted me and I saw his hands clench and unclench at his sides.

A Lincoln Town Car pulled up and I rushed to the curb and waved it down. "This for Luscious Jordan?" I asked as soon as the bearded driver lowered the window.

"Yes, ma'am," he said in a Caribbean accent.

I climbed in the back and slammed the door closed, not even looking in Detective Rossi's direction as the car pulled off.

"Luscious, did you hear me?"

"What?" I asked, leaning back against the seat.

"I said I know you gone hate that like you owe Goldie a favor."

I sat up straight. My heart stopped beating all together. "Why?" I snapped, drawing the eyes of the driver in the rear-view mirror.

I forced myself to lean back against the seat and relax.

"Word around the whorehouse is Goldie pulled some connection from her list of clients and got the charges dropped against you," she said.

"Yeah, right," I said, squinting my eyes as my thoughts raced.

"That's what I said," she said. "Goldie got you off those drug charges and that video of you is a done dada."

I ended the call and didn't say goodbye. Shock has a way of snatching away fucking manners.

I frowned as my eyes shifted back and forth. Goldie? I shook my head. "What the fuck is she up to?" I asked myself, hating feeling like I was waiting for the other shoe to drop.

I gave the driver his fee and a tip before he came around to open the rear door for me. "Thank you," I said, looking at both my parents' and Mr. Alvarez's house sitting side by side. I just wanted to get my car and get the fuck away from both of them and everybody in them.

"Have a good one," the driver said, before jogging around to climb into his car and drive away.

I walked over to my car and dug my hand in my pocketbook. It took me a minute to remember I gave the keys to my mother. "Damn," I said, resting my elbow on the hood of the car. The heat of the metal burned and I lifted off it quick, still eyeing my parents' house and hating that I had to get my keys.

Pulling the handles of my pocketbook up on my bare shoulder, I knuckled up to just get the shit over with. I'd rather have dragged my naked ass across dog shit, though. For real.

I rang the doorbell and fidgeted like a kid.

The door opened and my mother stood there. "Harriet," she said, her face filling with surprise.

"I came to get my keys," I said, ignoring her opening arms.

Her smile faded. "Harriet, don't be that way," she said.

I just shook my head and held out my hand. "I just want to go home. Can I have my keys?"

"No, you're going to talk to me. I am your mother and I deserve your respect at all times, Harriet Lee Jordan."

Lord knows it had been a long-ass night between meeting Detective Dick in the motel and getting released from jail this morning. I had touched on every possible emotion a person could deal with. A bitch was tired and on the edge. Not a good combo for peacemaking.

Then again, maybe it was time to do like Martin and pull out my little notebook with the list of people I needed to check and get to getting with my parents.

"You know what I deserved, Ma? I deserved parents who had my back. Who looked out for me. Who protected me," I told her, stabbing a finger at my chest with each point made. I knew my eyes blazed with anger because I felt it burning in my stomach.

"Don't you dare judge us because we chose not to follow you to jail when you know damn well we raised you better than do *anything* to get yourself arrested," my mother fired back. "Just like we raised you not to drop out of college, not to become a stripper, not to shack up with some man who eventually goes to jail for his role in a rape. Don't judge us, Harriet. Don't you do it!"

I looked at her like she was mad crazy and I didn't give a fuck how it looked. "Don't judge!!!! I spent my whole life being judged by you two. You had a child and not a lump of clay that you could mold into whatever you wanted and then toss outside when I didn't turn out to be what you thought was nice and pretty and presentable."

"Calm down, Harriet." I looked up at my father suddenly standing there.

"Calm down. Calm down," I repeated. "You two have no clue what I been through and I really don't think you care."

"Anything that you have been through that is too much for you to bear was of your own doing," my father said.

My fight left me just like that. Like somebody untied a balloon and released the air until it deflated. My soul was deflated.

"I got arrested because that detective was a dirty cop blackmailing me into having sex with him and I put a stop to it. The charges were dropped this morning," I told him, meeting his hard stare. "See, you didn't do a damn thing to protect me last night. I told you I was afraid that he was going to hurt me and not even take me to jail. I begged you . . . *I begged you* to be there for me. And you let me down."

My mother reached for me and I brushed her hands away. "Why didn't you tell us?" she asked.

"What did you do that he was blackmailing you?" my father asked.

I just held out my hand and didn't even look at them. I ain't had shit else to say. Any thoughts I had about sharing my memories of being molested disappeared with a quickness. I was sure my father would find a way to blame it all on me.

"Give her the keys," my father said before turning to walk back into the house.

Boy, that shit right there fucked me up and good. I was relieved when my mother finally pulled my keys from her pocket and pressed them into my hand before she kissed my cheek. I just wanted to get away from there, go home, wash my ass, and climb under the covers for the rest of the day. Fuck it.

I turned and walked down the steps just as Sophie parked her gold Volvo in front of Mr. Alvarez's house. I saw him sitting in the passenger seat. *Well, he ain't dead.* I thought, moving toward my Jag and watching as he used a cane to get out the car.

I was about to climb into my whip but I turned. "Hi Sophie," I said, with a little wave.

She gave me a stiff smile back. *Bitch.*

"Are you okay, Mr. Alvarez?" I called out to him, sounding sweet and fake as hell.

He stopped in his tracks and turned to look over his shoulder at me. "Just an accident while I was cleaning some fish last night," he lied.

"Oh," I said, sounding like I didn't give a fuck and meaning it as I turned and climbed into my car.

Hmm. He didn't tell that I tortured his no-good ass. The same way he knew I had yet to tell the secret of his molestation all them years ago. I knew the secrets Mr. Alvarez and I shared were still just between us.

For now. I was far from done with his ass.

It's amazing how every so often you get tested to just how much shit your plate can hold. And just when I thought mine was already full of enough shit, I walked into the air-conditioned lobby of the Twelve50 and saw Goldie at the concierge's desk.

For one, that bitch was looking like new money in a formfitting stretch denim dress that I recognized from Neiman Marcus. I'd even tried it on and decided against it just last month.

Me? I looked just like I ran for my life, confronted my molester, got arrested, and slept in my clothes all night. Not the way I wanted to confront my enemy that I ain't seen in over a year. I started to back out the door and regroup, but she turned and saw me.

In the moment, I had to decide how this was going to go down. Was I going to cuss her out, beat her ass, reveal my hate and need to make her pay? Fake it? What should I do? Because I knew this one moment would define everything I been gunning for over the last year. Everything I did was with the thought in the back of my mind that this person now walking up to me had to pay. Did I let that shit go now? Did I trust her now? Did I say, *"Thank you for helping me"*? Or did I say, *"You know what, you owe me that and more"*?

What the fuck should I do?

Goldie was a bold bitch to walk up and stand before me like it was nothing, when the last we saw each other we were fighting like cats and dogs. A heated and violent moment after I caught my man eating her out. After I saw my friend and my man stabbing me in the back when I was in the building.

"I thought we needed to talk," she said, removing these bad-ass graduated shades. "But I know the first thing I need say—"

I held up my hand, because I had to remind myself that she didn't know that I know she got the charges against me dropped. I had no need to be grateful and gracious to her ass in that moment. I needed to get on her level. Not be caught off guard and smelling like yesterday. No haps. "If you want to talk, we can. I just want to change and I'll be back down," I said.

And then I moved around her and continued on to the elevator lobby. I didn't look back at her to see if she waited. I got on the elevator and rode up to my floor.

The choice was hers. If she wanted to talk so badly, then thirty minutes sitting her ass in the lobby—because she wasn't being invited into my house—wasn't going to kill her.

I focused on getting dressed. Getting ready. I didn't think about her or what she wanted or what she expected from me. I got just as fly as she was, seeking her level. Letting her know, this wasn't the same old Luscious she "saved" from my days stripping during the early afternoons at Club Naughty. That Luscious—lost and looking up to her like she was Oprah or some shit—was gone. Long fucking gone.

By the time I pulled the handle on the front door and made my way back downstairs, forty-five minutes had passed. Maybe she waited. Maybe she didn't. Whatever. I didn't know. But what I did know was I looked hella good.

I flatironed my hair until it was bone straight and shiny, falling to the middle of my back like black silk. Smoky eyes, contoured cheeks, glossy lips (completely overboard for daytime, but who cared?). Diamond studs, bracelets, dome rings, and cross (all gifts from Make$ that I hadn't even thought twice about giving back). My body was just as tight and banging as hers, and the soft peach strapless dress I wore clung to every curve and pushed my breasts high (plus the color looked good on my dark complexion). I finished it off with a pair of sky-high gold Louboutins and plenty of my favorite perfume.

"Damn," one of my male neighbors said when I stepped off the elevator in the lobby.

I smiled at him over my shoulder, and his blonde head was poking out the elevator and checking my walk-away. "Good?" I asked.

"Hell yeah," he said.

I gave him a wink and continued strutting through the elevator lobby like I owned Twelve50. I saw the top of Goldie's blond-streaked head buried behind a copy of *Essence* magazine as she sat in the lobby. *Wow, the bitch waited.*

She looked up and eyed me from head to toe real quick before I slid into the leather club chair across from her and crossed my gleaming chocolate legs. "Okay, here I am. Talk."

Goldie smiled (or smirked a little) as she closed the magazine and tucked it back into her python Gucci bag. "You know my time is valuable, and I waited an hour for you, because this is convo we really need to have."

I didn't say shit. I just looked at her.

"Messing with Make$ behind your back was fucked up," Goldie started, using her shades to push her hair back off her face. "And I'm woman enough to apologize for that shit. It wasn't worth it."

My lips stayed pressed.

"After the shit that happened to me. . . ." She paused and looked down at her shoes as she pulled her hair from behind her back to over her shoulder.

I saw her shoulders rise with the deep breath she took. "After the rape, I ain't had no choice but to sit the fuck back and see what I did to other people," she admitted, finally looking back up at me.

Tears were in her eyes but she didn't let them fall.

"I don't know if you know, but I used some connections I have to get your charges dropped," Goldie said, twisting the diamond watch on her wrist.

Damn, I should've wore my watch, I thought, even though I kept my face blank.

"I did that because I felt like I owed you that," she said.

I still didn't know what to do with this new twist. My eyes squinted. I wished I knew what the fuck her angle was.

Goldie sat back in her chair and licked her lips, looking at me. Waiting on a reaction. Waiting on a thank-you?

For a year I'd been watching this bitch's every move. I knew a lot about her, maybe even everything about her. Never once did I show my hand. Never once did I reveal that I was gunning for her. The very fact that she sat in the lobby of my apartment building, apologizing and sharing her sadness about her rape, let me know that I was successful in being that covert.

She had no clue I was gunning for her.

I couldn't reveal that now. I couldn't throw away the last year. I couldn't forgive and forget.

"Thank you for getting the charges dropped," I said, feeling the words damn near choke me.

Goldie smiled. "I just want you to know that it's just between me and you. I'm not looking for shit in return. I just felt like it was the least I could do," she said, rising to her feet and pulling her shades down to cover her eyes.

I nodded and forced myself to smile.

"'Bye, Luscious," she said, moving around the chair.

My eyes squinted as I watched her.

Goldie turned suddenly and I quickly made my face blank again. "I know we'll never be friends, but I hope we can get past the bullshit," she said, before she turned back and walked across the lobby and out the door to get back to her Bentley, her Upper East Side penthouse apartment, and her fabulous fucking life.

13

Two Weeks Later

It took me every last second of the last two weeks to come to grips with all the shit that had happened to me. Two weeks of me waiting for Detective Dick to call and say that he still could get me locked up and to meet him to fuck it all away. Two weeks of not being altogether straight about Mr. Alvarez not calling the police on me for holding him hostage in his house, branding his sick ass, and then plunging a knife into his thigh. Two weeks to finally answer my mother's calls.

And two weeks to finally figure out just what I wanted to do about Goldie.

I had just left the shooting range and was zooming toward home on the 1/9 when I picked up my phone and dialed my snitch. Her phone was off. Since the day before, I'd tried calling her and she didn't answer. Now the phone was disconnected. I fought the urge to throw my phone out the car in frustration. "Damn."

My eyes and ears in Goldie's operation was MIA.

Last night I found out her apartment was empty—and had been empty for the last week.

Sighing, I called Missy's number.

"What's up, chick?" she said.

"Nothing much. My mind ran across Kerri and her sister. How they doing?" I asked.

A while back, I asked Missy to take me to meet Kerri and her sister. I surprised them all by pressing a couple grand into

Kerri's hand. It was a little bit of the money I took from Make$'s safe-deposit box, and at the time I wished I had more to give her.

What Missy didn't know was that when Kerri's older sister Shani told me she wanted to make Goldie pay for what she did to her sister, I eventually talked her into using her banging body and good looks to interview to be one of the new Goldie's Girls video vixens . . . my Trojan Horse.

My snitch was the vengeful sister of the young woman Goldie betrayed. That shit made it all the sweeter for me.

But now she was gone.

"I haven't seen her or talked to them in so long," Missy said.

I steered my car onto the next exit ramp and pulled off on the side of the road.

"Once I found out her dumb ass was working for Goldie after what that bitch did to her sister I was too through with her. No way. You feel me? No fuckin' way. Goldie couldn't *give* me money. I'd be like nah, I'm good, bitch. Keep it movin'."

I rolled my eyes. Yes, we all hated Goldie. She wasn't shit. I hoped she ate shit and died. Yadda, yadda, yadda. I wasn't in the mood for an "I hate Goldie" gabfest. My mind was on making moves.

"Hey, Missy, I'm getting pulled over by the cops, let me call you back," I lied, ending the call.

I sat on the exit ramp going over a million and one different scenarios of what Shani's ass was up to. Did she still work for Goldie? Had she crossed over to the other side? Did she clue Goldie's ass in on my mission to destroy her?

Ugh! I pounded my fist on the steering wheel. "Shit. Shit. Shit. Motherfucking. Shit. Dammit. Shit!"

I flexed my shoulders and rolled my neck as I forced myself to calm down.

Bzzzzzz . . . Bzzzzzz . . . Bzzzzzz . . .

I reached for my cell phone. "Hello?"

"Luscious, you got any more of your tickets left?" Eve asked.

We were having a car show/barbecue and after-party later that afternoon, something Eve and Michel rigged up by themselves while my ass was on a mental vacation. Truth? I didn't sell none of them tickets. "I got a few left," I lied. My mind was barely on Yummy Entertainment anymore.

"Save me five if you got them."

"Okay."

"Where you at? Me and Michel need help out at the park," she said.

"I have to get my car serviced and then I'm coming," I told her.

"Okay. Hurry up."

I ended the call, put the car into drive, and made my way to the Jaguar dealer. I drove around to the service department and parked. As soon as I stepped out of the car, a Jag pulled into the spot next to me. I glanced over at the tall dude behind the wheel. I did a double take.

He was fine. That caramel sexy. Bald head. Close-cut beard. Suckable lips. Broad shoulders.

He turned his head and caught me looking at him. His face spread with a smile that let me know he liked what he saw too. I did a little wave and turned away. I wasn't looking for a man.

He climbed out the car and I peeked over my shoulder at him. Every bit of six foot three, and even beneath the suit he wore, I could tell he was built. Ripped. Stacked. Sexy. He made two of Make$'s little ass in height and weight.

Smacking my lips the way people do when they're hungry and food is about to be served, I went back into my car, being sure to take all my personal shit with me. *I hope this don't take all day.*

I walked to the glass door and Mr. Grown and Sexy was

holding the door for me, looking like he stepped off the cover of *GQ*. So different from Make$ and Has. I could tell he was older. Maybe midthirties. But damn, he was one good-looking, good-smelling man. Too old for me, but damn sure good to look at.

"Thank you," I said, as I passed him to enter the building. My head came to his chest and in that moment that my body was near his—dwarfed by his—I felt the safest I ever felt in my whole life.

"How you doing today?" he asked in a low voice that let me know the words were meant just for me.

"I'm good, and you?" I said.

"I'm excellent," he said.

Yes, yes you are, I thought, moving away from his power to stand at the counter.

It wasn't until I checked my car and took a seat that I noticed he didn't come in to the waiting area. I turned in my chair and looked through the glass window. His car was still there, but I didn't see him anywhere. I did see a business card under my windshield wiper.

I knew it was his. Mr. Grown and Sexy. And that made me feel excited, but I didn't get off my ass and go and get that card to see what it said. I had too much shit going in my life to take on anything else. Or anyone else.

And so I turned back around, released a heavy breath, and focused on flipping through one of the magazines lying around the waiting area and pretending like that card wasn't even there.

I thought about his smile and his warm scent. I looked out at the card. Finally, I walked out there to get it. I pressed it to my nose and the scent of his cologne still clung to it.

I licked my lips as I looked down at it.

JAMAL JACOBS
Superior Auto
973-555-2000 x 001

On the back he had written his cell phone number and the words: "Would like to know more about the woman behind the pretty face."

I smiled as I pushed the card into my wallet. *Maybe* I would use it one day.

I didn't even go to the car show, but I helped them set up, paid for every ticket I didn't sell, and told Michel and Eve to split the profits between the two of them. They didn't even ask me why.

Maybe they knew I wasn't into it?

Maybe they knew I had other shit on my mind?

Maybe they didn't need me anymore?

It didn't matter; it all was true.

From the jump, the party promoting had been their idea, and I just hopped on board after Make$ left my ass hanging in the wind.

I reached into my colorful sequined purse and pulled out my Chanel compact to check my makeup as I sat in Fornos of Spain restaurant. It was time to shit or get off the motherfucking pot. I had to finish this dance with Goldie or leave it alone for good.

I couldn't let it go. After a year of plotting, planning, waiting, and watching, I had to finish this. I had to make her pay. I couldn't just waste the last year of my life, and I didn't want to.

I forced a fake-ass smile as the hostess led Goldie to our table.

It was time to kick it up a notch.

"Hey," I said as she slid into the seat across from me.

"You shocked the shit out of me when you called my office," Goldie said.

"You apologized and I didn't know what to think and I realized I didn't even say that I accepted your apology and I think you're right. Make$'s ass is not worth the drama," I lied.

She leaned back in the chair and said nothing.

Oh, so it was her turn to hardball it? Bitch, whatever. "What really got to me was seeing your reaction to remembering the rape. It fucked with me and I could tell you was still affected by it."

Goldie nodded and shifted her eyes out the window. "That shit was crazy, Luscious," she said soft as hell and closed her eyes. "I . . . uhm . . . I . . . can't forget it."

I thought about being molested and then the shit I went through with that dirty cop. I would never forget. A piece of me felt sorry for her. But I shoved that shit away. This wasn't about compassion. No. Goldie was no more important than TipDrillz. The same way she convinced TipDrillz to get the fuck over it, her ass needed to do the same thing.

"I'm sorry you had to go through that," I lied.

"I'm glad I made it out alive."

The waitress came over to our table and it was the same chick from that day Goldie and me had lunch way over a year ago. Full circle. Friends and then enemies.

What were we now?

"I wanted to talk to you, something actually," I said after we ordered our dinner.

She sipped her wine.

"I have to be honest that since Make$ went to jail I'm in a little bit of a money jam. He snatched all his money, wanted to throw me out the apartment, and left me ass out," I said.

"You need to borrow—"

I held up my hands. "No, no borrow. I wondered if you had any spots available at Goldie's Girls?"

Goldie looked surprised. "I don't know if you know, but I'm out the strip game. I own a booking agency for urban models. Videos girls, hip-hop fashion ads. You know, stuff like that."

Humph, I knew *that* and the truth behind it.

I twisted my diamond watch around my arm, wanting her to

see I had one too. "Tek-9 used a couple of your girls in his 'New Reign' video, right?" I asked.

Goldie nodded. "Yeah he used Sparkle and Ilsa," she said. "They're some really good moneymakers for me."

"Yes, yes, I think a lot of little boys around the world enjoyed Tek-9 oiling them down in the middle of the wrestling ring."

Goldie laughed and then got quiet. I could tell she wanted to ask me something. I knew the rumors about Tek-9 and me was hanging in the air. I knew she heard that shit.

"No, I did not bang Tek-9," I said. *Fuck it. Let's get it out the way.* I didn't really give a fuck what she thought, but I was not claiming dicks I never had.

Goldie arched her brow as she took another sip. "Too bad; I heard his shit is *bananas.*"

Was Tek-9 one of Goldie's clients?

I picked up my Nancy Gonzalez dome-top tote in green crocodile and took a portfolio from inside it. I side-eyed her and saw her eye the bag. It retailed for three grand and looked every bit of it. I slid the portfolio toward her.

"Damn, Luscious, what's this, an interview?"

Just open it, bitch, I thought, as I placed my face in my hand and smiled at her.

She did and then closed it. "Whoa. What the fuck?" she said, looking up at me with big eyes.

"What?" I blinked like my ass was innocent. Like I didn't just hand her a portfolio of professional photos of me. But I meant to put the pic of me squatting in a thong from behind in the front. It was a lot of my big, beautiful, black ass. I knew I looked good. Hell, the photographer had a hard-on during the whole shoot. *Take that, bitch.*

Goldie shook her head as she flipped through the rest of the pictures. "I mean, I definitely think we could book you. The only thing is your being Make$'s ex and the rumors about you and Tek-

9. It could go either way. You know? Niggas on the come-up would definitely want you booked to be like 'Fuck that, nigga, I got your girl,' or if they worryin' about pissin' off Make$ or Tek-9 they may not fuck wit you. *But* both them niggas locked up, sooooo . . ."

Oh no, bitch, don't play me.

"All of that is irrelevant because I want in on the *other* business," I said, just as the waitress walked up with our plates.

Goldie cut her golden eyes at me.

Oh yes, bitch. We're going there.

She waited until the waitress walked away before she said, "Right now the booking agency is my only business. I told you I'm not doing the exotic dancing no more."

I nodded as I took a bite of my shrimp, pasta, and garlic dish. "Goldie, listen. Me and you used to be tight and even the shit that went down between us can't change that, you know. I don't play games. I shoot straight from the hip. I know about the other business. I heard about it like last year. I still have contacts in the industry. Dudes talk, Goldie."

She set her fork down on her plate, licked her lips, and sat back to watch me close as hell with a little smile on her face.

I sat back in my own chair and gave her the same smile. I needed her to let me in.

"I've worked hard to build my business. My *legitimate* business. The only thing I can offer you is a chance to get into modeling and some videos," she said.

So this how we gone play it?

"Cool," I said.

"And you can't be out trying to trick on the side. It's not a good look for my business. I'm really trying to keep my shit professional. You know?"

Bitch, please. You just want your cut.

"So they lied?" I asked her, my hand clenching my fork so fucking tight I thought it was going to bend in my hand.

"Oh, most definitely," Goldie said, turning her attention back to her dinner.

You lying, deceitful, two-faced snake in the grass.

I would've loved to take the proof Shani the Snitch was supposed to get for me and slap it across this bitch's face like "Stop lying, ho!"

"The party promoting not working out?" Goldie asked out the blue.

So, this bitch was in *my* business too.

"We have mutual friends, Luscious," she said at my pause. "They said you were doing good with it."

I took a sip of my white sangria filled with chunks of apples, green grapes, pears, and pineapples. "That's really my friends' thing more than mine."

"Oh, okay."

Humph. That shit right there made me feel like me and this bitch was playing chess. I didn't trust her even more. I had to stay on my toes.

I spotted a dude at the next table eyeing her even though he was with a woman already.

That shit reminded me of Make$ side-eyeing her, fucking her, *choosing* her even when I was sitting right there waiting on him. Stuck on stupid. Deep in dumb.

I focused on my food, fighting the urge to fight this bitch right in the middle of the restaurant and just fuck up everybody's damn dinner.

"I'm having a grand opening of my new Jersey City offices tomorrow night. You should come through," she said.

"I will. I will," I said, wondering if I could sneak into her offices during her little party.

Goldie raised her glass. "I'm glad we trying to get past the past," she said.

I gave this bitch a fake-ass smile as I raised my glass and

touched it to hers, fighting the urge to break the glass against her face.

I was just parking my Jag when Eve called my cell phone. I let it go to voice mail. Her and Michel wanted to go to Club Infinite tonight but I ain't had time for that. I was hot on Goldie's fucking trail and ready to finish this bitch.

   I smoothed my Hervé Léger dress over my hips and pulled the wavy ends of my jet-black hair over one shoulder. Her offices were in a converted warehouse. I looked at the red Goldie's Girls logo on the glass with poster-size black-and-white photos of some of the girls and a few dudes on her roster.

   I stepped in the building and a security guard (WTF?) stood there with a clipboard. "How you doing?" I said, attempting to step past him.

   "Yo, yo, lovely. Invite only," he said, holding out his arm.

   My breast hit his arm.

   "Harriet Jordan," I said, stepping back and smoothing my hand over my hair as the door opened and a group of people walked in.

   He checked the list and then lightly grabbed my elbow to steer me out of the way. "If you could hold up for one sec," he said to me, before giving his full attention to the crowd.

   What the hell?

   They all side-eyed me as they gave their names and was verified before they climbed onto the elevator. Someone whispered, "Security, one. Party crasher, zero."

   Party crasher?

   "Excuse me, what's the problem?" I asked.

   "You're not on the list," he said.

   Was Goldie's slick ass trying to be funny? I would kick this nigga in the balls, then go upstairs and wreck her shit *at* her party. "Try Luscious Jordan," I said, trying to keep my tone in check.

He shrugged his shoulders and checked. "Better name. Still not on the list."

"She's gone make me whup her motherfucking ass," I said, feeling myself getting pissed off.

"Not at the party," he said, trying to be funny.

"Don't get slapped," I said.

"Don't get tased," he shot back, holding up his taser and turning it on.

Zzzzzap!

I jumped back.

The door opened and I recognized a popular New York blogger and her crew all glammed up and ready to party.

"Excuse me, the invited guests need to get in, please," he said, overly polite, pulling me out the way.

Oh, this Negro got jokes.

"Hi, Luscious," the blogger said, giving me a little wave.

I smiled and waved back and then watched her and her crew get in and climb onto the elevator. As soon as the elevator closed, I walked out the front door. "You need a bigger suit, clown," I shot over my shoulder before the door closed.

"And you still need an invitation," he sang behind me, poking his head through the door.

I flipped his big-head ass the bird and then made my way to my car. I was so pissed, I was tempted to sit there all night, wait for Goldie, and then beat the light skin off that bitch.

"Excuse me, Miss Jordan?"

I turned. A tall thin dude with a suit on and a colorful bow tie was standing in the doorway. I didn't know him. The jokey bodyguard was standing behind him silently throwing up a deuce to me and mouthing the words to Chris Brown's song "Deuces."

"I'm Goldie's assistant, Ryan, and I forgot to add your name to the list. I am *so* sorry," he said.

I started to tell him fuck him, fuck Goldie, and fuck their

world and everybody in it. But I wanted to get in that office. I wanted the solid proof that my snitch couldn't or wouldn't get. And I needed to see if Shani was still working for Goldie.

Just like how could the bitch miss that Goldie had a separate office and an assistant? Did this all go down after she stopped calling with info, or was she holding back on me the whole time?

I walked back to the door and made a face at the security guard before I chucked up a deuce to his irritating ass as we moved past him and onto the elevator.

"One of the other guests had mentioned you were in the lobby and then I remembered Goldie told me to have your name added to the list. I am so sorry," he kept saying.

"No problem," I told him as the elevator opened and we stepped into a nice-ass loft filled with people. I recognized video directors, some athletes and celebrities, bloggers, and magazine journalists. Kanye West played in the background and everything was casual as hell. A definite hip-hop soiree.

Ryan handed me a cocktail. "This place is nice. Show me around," I told him.

He did. But I didn't hear most of the bullshit details he told me as we walked around the loft. I didn't give a flying fuck in a monkey's ass about who designed what, who made what chair, which model was posing in this or that photo for this or that urban fashion designer.

"Now this is the little studio we have for test shots of wannabes, because you know everybody who think they cute ain't, and sometimes it takes a photo to make shit picture-clear, baby," he said, pulling back a heavy leather curtain.

I looked up at him. He reminded me of Michel. I missed him and Eve; I knew they was having a ball at Club Infinite. I was stuck at this bullshit.

"Y'all have everything here. Even offices? I bet yours is decked out, right?" I asked. *Fuck the dumb shit. Show me what I need.*

"Girl, I don't have an office. My little desk is in the front," he said, leading me back toward the front of the loft, where most of the partygoers were talking and chilling.

"Goldie doesn't have an office here?" I asked.

"No, actually. She will continue to work from home most days, and when she *is* here, she uses the photo studio," he said.

And this booking agency wasn't a fucking front. *Bitch, please.*

"Where you two wandering off to?"

We both turned at Goldie standing at the end of the hall. She leaned against the wall in a white strapless jumpsuit.

"Ryan was giving me a tour," I said, sipping from my drink.

"Well, y'all missing the party out here," she said, pointing her thumb in the direction opposite from us.

We walked back down the hall to join her. "Ryan, the models are posing for group photos for the press. Keep it organized for me. You know they asses is wild," she said before she walked away.

I frowned. I felt fucking dismissed and I didn't know if Ryan's happy ass knew it but he got dismissed too.

I followed him over to the area where the models were trying to outdo each other in the group photo. I didn't spot Shani. "Is this everybody?" I asked.

"Just about, except for the one that just up and quit a few weeks ago," he said.

Shani?

"What lit a fire under her?" I asked, pushing him.

"Lord, she found Oreo jungle love with some old white politician, chile," Ryan said before he moved over closer to watch the models.

I didn't say shit else. I heard enough. I knew enough.

Goldie didn't have files there and Shani hauled ass on me *and* Goldie. I was ready to bounce. Goodbye, corny-ass, bougie-ass industry party. Hello, Club Infinite.

14

*T*he next month flew by. I couldn't lie, but the bitch had me busy as hell working. I did photo shoots for Baby Phat and Apple Bottoms, booked three urban fashion shows, and flew to Puerto Rico for a video shoot as the female lead.

The money was good. And I even liked the work.

But don't get shit twisted. I didn't forget the bull's-eye I had on that bitch's back. I couldn't forget even if I wanted to and I didn't. I remember promising myself that I would make her pay. Not for Make$. It wasn't about that.

It was her disloyalty.

And I admit that because I looked up to that bitch. I admired that ho. I really thought I could count on her. I trusted her to go on the road with Make$. I used to cry and complain and moan and groan to her about the shit he did to me. I used to go to her for advice. I used to call her on the road and ask her to go check on his no-good ass. When I found out she wasn't what I built her ass up to be, it really pissed me off.

Loyalty was everything to me.

I didn't have any choice but to make her pay.

As far as I was concerned, it was out of my hands. She lit the fuse. And there was no going back.

I still didn't know what I would do with the proof once I had it, but I wanted it. It was important to the big plan. I wanted it and I was going to get it.

"Hi stranger."

I looked up as I walked into my apartment, pulling my rolling carry-on behind me. Michel and Eve were sitting on the couch looking at TV. They both had keys to my apartment, but I hadn't seen them in a good month—if not longer.

"Hey y'all," I said, taking off my shades and closing the front door.

"Hey y'all," Michel mimicked, sounding mighty damn testy.

They turned the TV off and stood up.

I screwed up my face and stopped. "Am I about to get jumped?" I joked with a laugh.

"You need your ass beat," Eve said, crossing her arms over her small chest.

"Sure do. You so happy to be sniffing up Goldie's ass that you just fucking threw us away like a bloody tampon," Michel snapped, his voice sounding deeper than I *ever* heard it.

"Yessss," Eve agreed.

"Fuck is this? An intervention?" I snapped, kicking off my shoes and plopping down onto the sofa.

"You cracking jokes and shit and we dead damn serious," Eve snapped.

I looked up at her and her face was pissed off. I shifted my eyes to Michel. These mofos *was* dead damn serious. I covered my eyes with my hands.

"Y'all, I haven't forgotten the two of you. I haven't given up Yummy Entertainment. Trust me. Everything I'm doing is for a reason," I told them. "I don't give a fuck about Goldie. The modeling. The videos. None of that."

"What?" Michel asked, sitting down and crossing his legs in the skinny jeans he wore.

"Listen, you know what she did to me, and it's best to have your friends close and your enemies closer," I told them, leaving it at that.

Eve sucked air between her teeth and grabbed her keys and purse. "Whatever, Luscious. You trippin,'" she said.

I leaned back. "Really? All of that?" I asked, feeling myself get angry.

"Yes? And?" Eve snapped back.

I stood up.

Michel stood between us, his pretty hands up in the air. "Chill, y'all."

"Oh, you flexing at me? You need to whup Goldie's fucking ass instead of fucking working and partying with that ho," Eve yelled.

"Get the fuck out my house yelling like that, Eve," I said, fighting the urge to mush her in her fucking face. "Get the fuck outta here with that all drama. Man, please."

"You ain't said nothing but a motherfuckin' word, *cuz*," Eve said, stalking over to the door to snatch it open.

I closed my eyes when she slammed it.

BAM!

I dropped back down onto the sofa. "Tell your girl to keep that ghetto bullshit out my building."

Michel made a face. "My rent ain't but two fifty, but I don't want nobody slamming doors in my building either, Luscious," he said, sounding offended.

"I didn't mean it like that, Michel," I said.

He relaxed. "I know. Just like I know this and I hope you listen to me because I mean you well. But mind that same hole you digging for Goldie don't be the one you fall in."

I looked over at him, just as beautiful as he could be as if he was born a girl. I shook my head. "Trust me, I got this," I said.

"Okay, if you say so. But you ain't been the same since you got arrested that night, Luscious. You never talk about it. Explain it. Nothing. You just act like it never happened. Like our crazy asses ain't here to listen to you."

I didn't say shit. What could I say? It damn sure wasn't going to be the truth.

He was right that I hadn't been the same since that night, but he was wrong about the reasons why. A lot of shit happened to me the night I got arrested. I didn't tell nobody, on the real. Being caught up in paying Goldie back kept me so busy that I didn't think about being molested or the shit the dirty cop put me through, or having my parents turn they backs on me.

Thinking of it now, I got a headache. It was a lot. Too much. Way too fucking much to share. To talk about. To think about.

"I'm good." I stood up and grabbed my carry-on to unpack.

Michel look disappointed in me as he grabbed his tote. "I'll calm Eve down. We just worried about you," he said.

"Let me get a nap and we can all go eat later. Okay?" I said, getting down on my knees as I unzipped the carry-on.

"You call us," he said and left.

As soon as the door closed behind him, my cell phone rang. I reached for my bag and got it out. It was Goldie. I rolled my eyes. These days I hardly spoke to her unless she was calling me about a booking.

"Hello."

"Hey, Luscious. How was the video shoot?"

"It was good."

"I'm having a quick meeting with everybody at my apartment in an hour. I know you just got off the plane, but can you get here?"

My heart stopped. I was ready to get the fuck out of Goldie's world and back into mine. My friends. Even my family. The sooner I got proof, the sooner I could get back to my life.

"No problem," I said, rising to my feet.

She gave me the address but I didn't need it. After I hung up, I thought about Michel and Eve and I missed my "girls."

Maybe, just maybe, if I didn't get any closer to this shit I would just let it go and beat the bitch's ass real good.

Stepping into Goldie's Upper East Side apartment was like seeing Twelve50 on megasteroids or some shit. There was no denying that everything about the building said money. Major money.

Just how much pussy was that bitch slinging? Damn.

I tried not to look around the place like a crackhead scoping the joint as I stepped on the elevator designated just for the four penthouse apartments. As it rolled to an easy stop, I pressed my hands against the sides of my linen shorts and smoothed the stark white tank I wore over my wide hips. The doors opened and I stepped off, my heels beating against the marble floor as I searched for penthouse apartment P4.

I was just about to use the brass door knocker when the door opened.

"Has?" I said, stepping back at the sight of him. Still tall. Still wild and sexy. Still laidback. Still Has.

What the fuck?

His eyes got big as shit to see me. He stepped out into the hall and closed the door. "What the fuck are you doing here, Luscious?" he asked, touching my elbow.

I jerked away from his touch and looked up at him with eyes filled with all kinds of confusion and questions. "I could ask you the same thing."

He leaned back against the wall and covered his face with his hands. "Listen . . . me and Goldie ran into each other about nine months ago and we talked things out and—"

Boom. He wasn't my man, but damn if it didn't feel like another fucking hard knock for me and another goddamn win for Goldie.

"Yo, me and Goldie live together," he added.

A gut punch on top of the backhand pimp slap. Fuck it.

"Do she know me and you was fucking?" I asked him, crossing my arms over my chest as I forced that motherfucker to meet my eyes and then stared him down. *Hard.*

Has shook his head and licked his mouth. "Yo, look, I knew Goldie first, Luscious. You *know* that."

"But you *fucked* me first." I pointed my finger into his chest.

"And I was wrong. We was wrong, Luscious."

I looked at him, standing there in his cargo shorts and Timbs with a wife-beater. Has looked so out of place on the Upper East Side. But this was his home. His home with Goldie.

"Are you gonna tell her?" he asked.

I shrugged and walked into the apartment, giving him one last resentful look over my shoulder. I barely took in the decoration or the apartment as I made my way toward the voices. I didn't need to, anyway. I had full photo layout of this bitch courtesy of Shani the Snitch.

"Okay, good, Luscious is here," Goldie said.

I gave everybody a fake smile and squeezed onto the leather sofa in between Nivea, a blasian chick who had done videos with everybody from Jay-Z to Aerosmith, and Frenchie, a thick white chick who looked like the twin of Ice T's wife, Coco. I wondered just how many of the twenty or so people spread out over the living room was tricking for Goldie. Shani said not everybody was in on it.

"Okay, I had good news and I wanted to share it with everybody at the same time," Goldie said, looking laid-back in white palazzo pants and an off-the-shoulder peasant top. Her eyes shifted toward the entrance to the living room and I knew without looking around that Has's traitor ass had come back into the apartment. Goldie smiled over our heads at him.

He probably scared as shit that I was gonna put our shit on blast.

Hell, I was the one started it and finished it, but I can't lie. I did not want Goldie and Has together. It was another damn check in the "win" column for this scandalous bitch.

So what, now this nigga was laid-back like the king of dicks comparing our pussies—like Make$. Ugh. I dug my fingers into my own knees.

"Come on, baby," Goldie said, holding out her hand. "I thought you was headed out, but since you here, we can do this together."

I didn't turn around, but when Has came up to stand next to Goldie, I felt one of my acrylic tips break away from the nail bed from me digging in so hard. I bent my head to make the aviator shades I had on top of my head fall down and land on my nose. I locked my eyes on Has and I didn't miss the way his eyes kept shifting to me. All nervous and suspect and shit.

"So, last night Has and I got engaged," Goldie announced.

Everyone screamed out in excitement and jumped up to see the ring she was holding up. I knew I had to get up and fake the funk or that shit would seem like I was hating. I came up and smiled. I couldn't bring myself to hug the bitch. "Congrats, girl," I said.

"That's right, Luscious never met him. This is Has. You know, *that* Has?"

Yes, bitch, I know that *Has. Real well. From the top of his head to the tip of his big dick.*

"Nice to meet you, Has," I said.

He didn't say shit, but give me a homeboy head nod. *What the fuck ever, Has.*

I checked out her ring. Three carats easily. If not four. Has was working at some warehouse last I heard. Almost getting caught up in that counterfeit ring and barely beating Fed charges had him get up on the good foot and get a job. So no shade, baby-boo, but I did not believe he brought that ring. Just like his ass wasn't putting in much on that high-ass Upper East side rent.

Okay, I was hating. But fuck Has. He was supposed to be my ride-or-die in the Fuck Goldie campaign and now he was fucking that bitch *literally*.

While everybody was oohing and aahing over that ring, I

moved close to her assistant Ryan. "Where's the bathroom?" I asked him.

"Right down the hall. Third door on your left."

"Thanks." I headed for the hall. I opened every door in that motherfucker until I found her office. It was the second door on the left.

"What you up to, Luscious?"

I made a face at the sound of Has's deep voice behind me before I turned around. "Looking for the bathroom. Why you watching me so hard? Aren't you engaged?"

He just pointed to third door on the left.

Damn, Has fucked me all up. Goldie had to have some records in that office. Phone numbers. List of clients. Tracking of the money. Billing. Something. Shit.

I mean-mugged his ass before I walked into the guest bathroom. It didn't do shit but piss me off even more since it was as big as my kitchen and decorated nicer than my parents' whole house.

I stayed in there for a minute, hoping Has's ass was gone and I could get in that office. When I finally opened the door the hall was clear but I tried the rest of the doors they all were locked.

Has wasn't stupid. Game always recognize game.

I went back in the living room. Has was standing out on the balcony smoking, and everyone else, including Ryan, was sitting already, still fawning over Goldie. I wanted to leave, but I sat my ass right on down and eased my back against her comfy couch while I listened to her retell about her romantic wedding proposal on the balcony. All the while I got a kick out of reminding myself in vivid detail that I had fucked her fiancé first. And fucked him well, too.

Has sucking my clit.

Has nutting all over my titties and then playing in it with the tip of his dick.

Has sucking my titties while I rode his dick down.

Has telling me how good my pussy was.

Has fucking the valley of my titties while I sucked his dick.

Oh, we used to get stupid. And knowing Goldie and Make$ wouldn't like it made that shit even better.

"We'll probably just elope to the Bahamas or something," Goldie was saying. "Neither one of us got a lot of family, so it will just be the two of us and our best friends."

"You talking about Yummy?" someone asked. "She still in South Carolina?"

Goldie had told me about her best friend, Yummy, getting strung out on drugs by her boyfriend, and then when she had a stroke while getting high, the dude left Yummy alone in their apartment. Her mother eventually moved her and her kids down South. Back when me and Goldie were tight, I knew she always sent them money.

Goldie nodded. "I was just down to see her a couple of weeks ago. She walks with a cane but she can talk a little better now."

"Oh, that's good."

I shoved the rest of their conversation out of my mind. I had other shit to focus on. I looked out at Has on the balcony. That nigga's profile against the New York backdrop looked like a sexy-ass Sean John ad.

Then I remembered I had finally transferred all the contacts of my BlackBerry to my new phone. Smiling, I scrolled through, and sure enough, there it was. Now, did he have the same cell phone number?

I typed away: CONGRATS.

I hit send, my eyes on him the entire time. I smiled when he reached in his pocket and pulled out his cell phone. He looked down at it and then looked over his shoulder at me. He shook his head and then bent over to press his elbows on the wrought iron railing.

Smiling, I typed: I MISS THAT DICK.

I hit send.

He dropped his head before he looked at his cell phone.

Arching my brow, I sent another one: IS HER PUSSY GOOD AS MINE?

He never responded.

Lord, when will these two learn that I ain't the one to play with? I wondered as I put my thumbs to work.

OK, MEET ME IN THE STAIRWELL IN 10 MINUTES OR I'LL FUCK THIS WHOLE PARTY UP!

"I didn't even offer everybody something to drink or eat," Goldie said.

"My stomach *is* growling a little bit, boss lady," Frenchie said.

"Boss lady"? Bitch more of a false lady.

"I'll be right back," Goldie said, walking out the living room. She made it to the door before she turned around and picked up her cell phone off the fireplace mantel, where it had been sitting.

"Damn, Goldie, nobody gonna steal your phone," Kiki, a dark-skinned Dominican said, joking.

"Can't lose this," Goldie said, sliding the BlackBerry into her pocket before she walked out of the room.

"She got her life in that phone," Ryan drawled.

I shook my head as I opened my bag and looked down at my old BlackBerry. Even though it didn't have service, it had so many pictures, contacts, and texts that I didn't want to lose it. I still carried it with me.

I felt so motherfucking stupid. So damn dumb.

All this time I was plit-potting to get in her office when the whole time I bet Goldie had her list of clients and appointments in that BlackBerry. I bet all the evidence I needed was right there in her fucking pocket. If it was with her 24-7, she could do business from anywhere at anytime. *That slick bitch.*

Well, I was slicker. I would wait these other bitches out. If I had to snatch and grab that fucking phone, I was leaving this apartment with it today. Best believe that.

Bzzzzzz . . .

Humph. I opened the incoming text.

GO AHEAD 1ST. I'M COMING.

I stood up. "I gotta get something from my car. I'll be right back," I said to no one in general before I hauled ass out the apartment.

I found the door to the stairwell at the opposite end of the hall. I was in there pacing for a minute. I was still trying to get shit straightened out in my head about Has and Goldie. Humph, niggas just couldn't leave that bitch alone. Who the fuck was she? Damn sure wasn't a supermodel-type chick. Fuck *her.*

I had just sat down on the top step when the door opened. Has eased into the stairwell.

"Yo, Luscious, you trippin'," he said, before he shook his head.

I stood up. My heart was pounding and I felt so anxious as I moved to stand close to him. I smiled and licked my lips as I stroked his dick. "I missed it," I told him, easing forward to snuggle my face against his neck to lick it while I took in the smell of him.

Has stepped back from me but I could see his dick was hard behind his zipper.

"Has, stop frontin', because a hard dick don't like," I told him, unzipping my shorts and letting them fall to my feet before I stepped out of them. "Just like this wet-ass pussy."

"You trying to fuck in the stairwell?" Has asked, frowning.

"Yes, fuck your boring little party. Let's get a quickie for old time's sake." I eased my white top over my head and pushed my breasts high in the sheer bra barely covering my hard nipples. "Hurry up before your girl miss us."

"I'm not fucking you, Luscious," he said.

"I won't tell if you won't tell," I whispered up to him. "It'll be our little secret."

"No, Luscious."

"Scared you gone get hooked again?" I asked him, turning around to bend over and back my thong-covered ass up against his dick. "Trust me, it's still good as ever."

He held me by the waist, unbent my body, and turned me to face him.

The feel of his hands made me moan.

He dropped his hands. "The fact that you trying to fuck me when you working for my girl—"

"Your *fiancée*," I reminded him, reaching up to unsnap my bra and ease it off my body to fall to the floor.

His eyes dipped to take in the twins. I moved my shoulders, making them swing back and forth.

"Man, Goldie. I mean Lusc—"

"Goldie!" I snapped, reaching up to push my finger against his cheek. "My name is Luscious and you know it. You used to scream it to the ceilings."

"Luscious, look, I'm not gone fuck you," Has said, his face serious as hell.

I stepped back and pressed my hands to my hips as I looked at him. I was embarrassed as hell standing there damn naked and begging for dick. And *that* pissed me the fuck off.

This nigga turned down all this good pussy for Goldie.

Like she better than me.

Like she was God's gift to man.

Like she wasn't a nasty, sneaky, no-good, backstabbing, dick-sharing daughter of a bitch. That angry fire had my whole body hot. Fuck Has. *Mother*fuck Has. And triple fuck Goldie.

"So when you was mad at Goldie my pussy was okay to play over, right?"

"What?!"

Both our heads turned to see Goldie coming through the doorway into the stairwell. Her eyes took me in standing there in nothing but my thong bikini with my big and beautiful breasts swinging.

Has held up his hands. "Goldie, this ain't what you think—"
WHAP!

She slapped the shit out of him. I know his face stung like a motherfucka but I ain't had time to worry about that because I was too busy kicking off my heels. It was on. Fuck it. This was an ass-whipping I'd been waiting to deliver for over a year.

"Payback is a bitch, ain't it Goldie," I said, sounding like I was enjoying this shit . . . because I was.

Has looked like he rather be shitted on. "Yo, Luscious. Chill out," he said.

"Payback?" Goldie snapped, her face damn near burgundy with anger as she came from around him.

"Damn right," I said with much attitude and emphasis. "I enjoyed fucking, sucking, and riding that big dick just like you enjoyed fucking my man, bitch."

Goldie swung with a right.

I ducked like Pacquiao in that bitch and delivered a gut punch before I dug my hands in that bitch's hair in a fist and used my other fist to fuck her head right on up as I bit my bottom lip.

She elbowed my stomach hard as fuck, knocking the air out of me before she wrapped her foot around my leg and tried to trip me.

A motherfucking street fight.

"Ow!" I cried out, even as I kept pounding the side of her face. I wanted that no-good bitch good and lumped up in the morning. *She gone remember me.*

"Man, stop, y'all. Shit!" he yelled, trying to get in between us and loosen my grip on her hair.

Goldie swung around his body and landed a blow to my chin; my teeth clamped down on my tongue and I tasted blood. *Bitch!*

I yanked on her hair harder. Suddenly my hand was free and a bunch of hair was still in my fist. I flung that shit into the air like confetti. "Huh, bitch, here go your hair," I teased, as Has stepped all the way between us.

Some of the gold and brown strands landed on his head.

I stepped close to Has and started grinding my titties against his back. "He was loving this pussy," I told her, grabbing his dick from behind.

She reached out quick and slapped me.

WHAP!

I tried to climb over Has's tall body to get at her. I was damn near on his head when I starting swinging. I knew he caught a couple of them blows. Fuck it.

"Tell her, Has. Tell her how you use to eat my pussy," I screamed even as I boxed that bitch dead in the forehead.

She grabbed a handful of my hair and then leaned back, pulling my body over Has's head. That sewn-in weave took a better licking than real hair. "Matter of fact, you ain't got to tell the bitch ,nothing because I got a DVD right to my house and you can see your fiancé get that big dick ridden real well. Real well," I said, reaching down to wrap both my hands around that bitch's neck.

She tugged again, biting her bottom lip just as hard. My legs dropped on either of his shoulders and I felt his face pressed against my ass. Humph.

"Man, y'all acting like gutter rats," he snapped.

He got Goldie's hand out my hair and grabbed me around the waist to sit me on my feet. My chest was heaving and my head ached. I saw one of my tracks with my cornbraid still attached on the floor.

Goldie looked at me like I was shit on her shoe. "And I got your charges dropped, you ungrateful bitch, and gave your black ass a job," she snapped, talking in between gasps for air.

"My *black* ass," I snapped. "Your man was LOVING. THIS. BLACK. ASS. Your fucking half-breed mutt ass."

Goldie reached on either side of Has and pushed me hard against my chest. I cried out when my body fell backward down the stairs. I must have hit every fucking step until I fell on the landing.

I winced and sat up just as Has came down the stairs. "You a'ight?" he asked.

I knocked his hands away.

"I wish you would help that bitch up," Goldie said, her voice hard as she stood on the top step with her arms crossed over her heaving chest.

I looked up at her and I hated her more than ever, because it felt like the bitch was looking down on me, still on top. "I'll mail that DVD to you, bitch," I told her, climbing the stairs. "You gone love how he nutted all over my back."

She jumped and Has caught her around the waist and carried her cussing and fussing through the stairwell door. I was putting my clothes back on when something flashed in the corner of my eyes. I finished pulling my tank over my head and turned to walk over to the pipe in the corner. Thinking it was jewelry or some shit, I stooped and reached for it.

"Well, I'll be damned," I said.

Goldie's BlackBerry. It must have fell out her pocket during the fight. I felt like I hit the jackpot as I pushed it down into my purse and rushed out the stairwell for the elevator. The hallway was clear. I could imagine the scene inside that apartment. That was *they* fucking problem now. Just like it was mine and Make$'s after I caught her with him.

I didn't give a fuck.

The game had changed. Shit was mad serious. I was on a whole 'nother level and steady rising from anger, hate, and the need to obliterate that bitch.

15

I tried my best to get myself straightened out before I walked into the lobby of Goldie's building. I was nervous she would call down to the concierge's desk to grab me until she came down to take her phone back. I had to force myself not to run like a child through that bitch.

My head was still aching from getting a track yanked out and my body was aching from that tumble down the stairs. I still couldn't believe that bitch pushed me downstairs.

What if I had broke my fucking neck and died?

Nah, nah. Uh-huh. It was on and I didn't give a flying fuck what happened to that bitch.

Slipping on my shades, I held my head up high and strutted through the door the doorman held open for me. I hurried my ass to my car parked down the street and slid behind the wheel. It was so stuffy and hot from the summer sun that I let the windows down after I cranked the car. Tossing all my shit onto the passenger seat, my hands were shaking as I scrolled through Goldie's address book.

Jackpot.

Fucking celebrities. Athletes. Politicians. Each entry related to her pussy business had info on each client. A like or dislike. The girl they usually requested. Fetishes. Their sexual orientation.

I was going to destroy that bitch. Her BlackBerry needed to go in a neat little package to the nearest police station. I sat back in the driver's seat and thought it over. Maybe the black female detective would like to be the one to bust this case wide open . . . but then, she was too close to Detective Dick for me, and she might be just as dirty as him.

I remembered Goldie's contacts. They were strong enough to get my charges dropped. They were probably just as strong for her case to go nowhere as well.

I just didn't know what the fuck to do with all the evidence I had in my hand. It was the key to completing wrecking Goldie's world . . . but how?

Blackmail?

Would the bitch be willing to turn over a hundred thousand dollars to shut me up? Maybe even half a million?

The thought of that shit made me smile.

"Guess who, bitch?"

Click.

My smile faded at the feel of the cold metal of a gun pressed into my cheek. I recognized his voice. I knew it was him. I still looked up to see Detective Dick leaning through the open passenger window, pointing a gun into me. My heart pounded like crazy as I closed my eyes.

Where did he come from? Did he follow me here? Was he stalking me?

I was so caught up in dreaming about spending Goldie's money and fucking up her mini empire that I didn't even see the overweight motherfucker walk right up to me.

Michel's words came back to me so fucking clear: *Mind that same hole you digging for Goldie don't be the one you fall in.*

I thought about laying on the horn, but the feel of that gun and being just millimeters away from a bullet blasted into my skull stopped me. "What do you want?" I asked him.

"Payback, bitch," he said, his voice cold and hard. "I could just wring your fucking neck while I shove my dick up your ass. You thought I was done with you?"

My eyes dropped down to my pocketbook on the floor with my gun inside. I couldn't reach it fast enough. *Shit.*

I looked around outside the car, but New Yorkers were busy with their day and not paying me or the car any attention. The door opened and Detective Dick slid in, laying the gun down to point at me while it lay on his lap.

This motherfucker had to be stalking me, because he had my address, all my info, including my parents' address, since that was where he locked me up. Why pull a stunt to get at me in New York?

"I'm going to kill you," he said, as he raised the gun to press it into my side. His eyes were red-rimmed. Liquor and funky breath scorched my cheek.

This was a man with nothing to lose.

A chill sped over my body. My mind raced. I had to get out of this. I had to think of something. Any-motherfucking-thing.

I looked down at the BlackBerry in my lap. Could I get two birds with one stone?

An asshole like Detective Dick's perverted self was just the one to make Goldie's life miserable. Since she liked fucking after me, she was more than welcome to this asshole. Plus I could buy my freedom.

"Listen, I got something for you. I know this chick who is running a big-time prostitution ring," I started. "Celebrities. Politicians. All of that. She's real connected in this town."

"Oh yeah?" he said, sounding interested. "And what did you say her name is?"

"Kaeyla Dennis, but her nickname is Goldie."

He was quiet for a minute. I waited.

"If you let me go, I will give you the proof I have, and you can do with it whatever you want."

"And why you doing this? I ain't your favorite person, just like you ain't mine. I mean, you got some good ass on you and you suck one hell of a dick, but it's basically fuck you as far as I'm concerned. Ya understand that, right?" he asked, squinting as he looked at me.

I tried to shrug like I was nonchalant. Acting was my thing. "I don't want to die and I could care less about her."

He grunted like his ass was thinking about it.

Seeing him with a gun pointed at me made me feel worse than I did when Goldie pushed me down the damn stairs. "*Fuck* that," he said, pressing the gun to my kneecap.

He moved the gun up to press against my ribs again. "You two cunts cost me my job with the police force and now I'm going make sure that you bitches pay for it. You *and* that bitch Goldie."

Oh, shit.

I sat stiff as a mannequin in that car, just trying to blend the fuck in and not draw any extra attention from this crazy motherfucker as we sat parked on the street in front of Goldie's building for the last hour. He was mumbling to his damn self and drinking from a half-pint of brown liquor.

I looked up just as I saw Has leaving the building with a big duffel bag. My eyes stayed locked on him as he walked up the street and turned the corner.

I'd already seen the girls leave the building twenty minutes ago.

Goldie was home alone. Probably crying her eyes out with no clue that a lunatic had followed me to her home to kill us both.

"Fifteen fucking years down the drain," he said.

I sat stiff as hell and just tried to look at him out the side of my eye to make sure the gun wasn't pointed at me again. He had it in his lap with his finger on the trigger. Aimed at me. Ready to fire and take my life.

"Motherfucking Internal Affairs investigation fucking around," he muttered, tapping the gun against his thigh as he looked over at me.

Oh shit! I got even stiffer, wishing like I hell I could disappear. Wishing even more I could lock my hands around my gun and get myself out of this.

"Mind that same hole you digging for Goldie don't be the one you fall in."

I was so busy plotting to take Goldie down that I missed being stalked and hunted down my damn self.

"I just want this shit over with," he said, his funky breath filling up the car with a smell like rotted-ass vegetables.

Did "over with" mean death? My death? Goldie's death? I hated that bitch but I didn't want either one of us to die.

"Mind that same hole you digging for Goldie don't be the one you fall in."

"I wish I never fucked with you," he said. "My life was fine until I fucked with you."

I froze. I didn't move. I didn't fucking breathe.

Suddenly I felt the cold metal of the gun against my temple. My guts twisted like a pretzel.

"Suck my dick," he said, tapping the barrel of the gun lightly against my temple near my eye. I closed my eyes just as a tear raced down my cheek.

"Suck. My. Dick," the dirty cop said again, unzipping his pants with his free hand.

On the real? I thought that was one dick I would never see or feel or taste again.

"The condom," I said softly.

He laughed like a lunatic and I jumped as he dented my cheek with the gun. "My fucking wife threw me out. It don't fucking matter no more," he said in this mad crazy sing-song tone that was straight out of a horror flick.

My eyes darted around. The sun had fallen and it was dark. He was waiting for Goldie to leave the building. We were parked beneath a tree and it shadowed us from the streetlights. With the tint, someone would have to press their face to the window to see in.

I lowered my head to his lap and the smell of unwashed crotch rose, making me gag as I used my hand to guide his dick into my mouth. I frowned at the salty taste of him. There was no way in hell this motherfucker washed in the last few days.

I gagged at the back of my throat.

He pressed the gun to the back of my head. "If you bite me, I will blow your fucking brains out," he said, before he moaned in pleasure.

As I sucked him, I felt like the scared and confused little six-year-old being taught to suck dick before my mouth could even open wide enough to take it. My tears fell blended with my slobber around my hand. I opened my eyes, and through my tears, I could see my handbag sitting there between his feet. My gun was so close and I couldn't get to it.

That shit made me cry even harder.

"Oh shit. Oh yeah," he moaned, pushing down on the back of my head, and he moved his hips back and forth. "Aaaahhhh."

I squeezed my eyes shut as his cum squirted against the back of my throat. I had to swallow it or choke. A little piece of me died on the inside. This could not be my life. NOT. MY. LIFE.

I tried to lift my head, but the pressure of the gun kept it down, my mouth locked around his dick. I moaned at the disgusting taste of his semen and salty, dirty dick as my shoulders shook with my tears.

He grabbed my hair, jerked my head up, and then pushed it against the driver's-side window. *Hard.* "What the fuck are you crying for?" he asked, pressing the gun against my mouth.

"You lost your job? Your reputation? The respect of your partner? Your family? Huh, you black cunt? Answer me?"

I shifted my eyes down at the gun, scared as hell he was going to miss and shoot me while he was carrying on. I shook my head.

He leaned over to press his face against mine. "Then *shut* the *fuck* up!" he screamed into my face before he dropped back in the passenger seat and tapped the gun against the passenger door. *Tap-tap-tap.*

I used my shirt to spit out as much of the sticky cum as I could as quiet as I could. I side-eyed him. His eyes was closed. I shifted my eyes down to that gun.

Tap-tap-tap.

I shifted my eyes back up to him.

If this crazy motherfucka missed and let that nut rock his ass to sleep, I was going to put a bullet through his head with either his gun or mine.

Tap-tap-tap.

I watched him, thinking hard. It was him or me, and I would deal with the consequences later.

Tap-tap-tap.

My eyes went to the driver's-door latch. Or should I just jump out this bitch and run like hell?

Tap-tap.

My heart pounded like crazy as my eyes shot back to him and then down at the gun.

Tap.

I froze.

His eyes were still closed and his mouth open. His breathing was slow as his chest rose and deflated nice and easily. His gun was a little slack in his hand.

Another goddamn "what to do?" moment. I was having way too many of them lately. Run or grab the gun? My eyes shifted from the door handle, to the gun, to his face. Run or grab the gun?

Run, Luscious, and run like hell, I decided.

I eased my heels off as I reached out slowly for the door lock. I wouldn't have long to hit the bitch and grab the handle to open the door wide enough to get out before he had a chance to wake up and fire his gun.

"One, two, three," I mouthed, getting myself ready.

I hit the door lock.

BOOM-BOOM-BOOM!

"What the fuck?" Detective Dick sat up with his gun pointed at me as someone pounded on the door window.

"So now you sitting outside my house stalking me, bitch!"

It felt like my spirit and my shoulders dropped damn near to my knees as I looked up at Goldie banging on the driver's-side window.

"So you want some more, bitch. Get at me," she shouted, her spit spraying the glass.

"Lower the fucking window," he said.

I closed my eyes as Goldie kept carrying on. He pressed the gun to the back of my head. "Lower . . . the . . . window."

I reached out and did as he said, revealing Goldie's angry face inch by inch as the tinted window lowered.

"You dumb—"

Her words froze and her gold eyes got big as shit as he pointed the gun across my face and square on her forehead. "Just the bitch I been waiting for. I'm Detective Jon Rossi. No, nope. My fucking bad. I'm not a detective no more. You made sure of that with your political johns, right?"

I looked up at Goldie's eyes and saw that what he said was true. Goldie had pulled more of her strings to get him fired for what he did to me.

Damn.

"I think it's time the three of us took a little ride."

The whole time I drove the car, Detective Dick drank his liquor with one hand and kept his gun pointed at my head with the other. Talk about a scared bitch? My eyes shifted up to the rear-view mirror to look at Goldie sitting in the backseat with her hands on the headrest the way he told her.

"Too bad you sucked my dick until I came. We coulda had a ménage," he said.

I was too embarrassed that he revealed that. Even in the

face of danger, I was thinking *Now what the fuck is his purpose?*

"I would need a little time to build up the juices to have enough to spread between you two bitches, but you'll probably be dead by then."

Me and Goldie's eyes met in the rearview mirror.

We gonna die.

She squinted her eyes and then shook her head no.

We will not die tonight.

"Turn down this alley," he said, motioning with his bottle of liquor.

I did like he said, but I was looking around for anything in the area that might be open. A store. An apartment building that wasn't abandoned. Cars passing by.

Any fucking thing.

But all I saw was absolutely nothing popping on the whole block.

This shit looked like a mini ghost town.

Perfect place to kill—and then leave—dead bodies.

"Park by that Dumpster," he said, motioning with the gun.

The alley was tight. Not more than fifteen feet across the two abandoned buildings that had been completely destroyed by fire. The darkness was broken up by a flickering streetlight and I could barely make out a fence that dead-ended the alley. A fence that seemed to be a good seven or eight feet high.

My eyes went back to the rearview mirror and Goldie was already looking at me. This shit didn't look good at all.

I slowed the car to a stop. My nerves made me slam on the brakes too hard and our bodies lurched forward.

WHAP!

I didn't even see that backhand coming until just before it landed across my mouth. I cried out even as I tasted the blood. *Son of a bitch.*

"Dumb fucking cunt," he spat, actually spraying my face

with his spit. "Get out the car. Put your hands on your nappy-ass head and stand in front of the car."

I opened the car door, moving slowly, and plit-plotting like a motherfucker. As I stood there, my eyes shifted to look down the alley. Past the car. To the street. To freedom.

All I had to do was run as fast as I could and then scream as soon as I spotted someone.

No . . . no, all I really had to do was run . . . and leave Goldie behind.

But I couldn't do that.

"Move, bitch!" he said, poking the barrel of the gun into my lower back.

I put my hands on my head and walked to the front of the car, the headlights on me like a spotlight on a stage. I watched as he pressed the gun to Goldie's head as she released the lever to move the seat forward. She climbed out and pressed her hands against her hair as he trained the gun on her even through the glass.

"First chance we get, we are going to take this fool out," Goldie said, barely moving her lips.

"I'm ready to fight, because I damn sure ain't ready to die," I whispered as he climbed out the car with the gun in his right hand and already pointed at us through the open door.

"You strapped?" I asked.

"No," she said. "You?"

"No."

"Shuddafuckup!" he shouted.

POW!

I literally heard the bullet whizzing past in the small space between our heads. We both hollered out and ducked down.

He laughed like a maniac. "Don't worry, you ain't dead yet. I got other games for you to play before I make you bitches regret fucking with me," he said, still laughing as he staggered back-ward, pressing his back to the brick wall right below faded graf-

fiti of a gun with "187" in the background. I learned from Snoop
Dogg that 187 was a police code for murder. The irony of that
shit wasn't funny.

"Now beg me not to kill you," he said, all laughter gone as he
tilted his head to the side to look at us.

"I can do better than that," I said, slowly lowering my hands.

He straightened his arm and turned the gun sideways, aimed
at my chest. "Careful, bitch!"

I started to pull my tank over my head. "I can't hide anything
if I'm naked," I said, tossing the shirt onto the hood.

He licked his lip.

My lace bra followed.

His eyes dipped down to take in my breasts.

"I can do just as good," Goldie said beside me, taking off her
top and bra to toss onto the hood.

His eyes went from her body to mine as we undressed for
this fool. "Damn, you black bitches look good. Neither one of ya
like pussy hairs, huh?"

We both stood there in nothing but our heels.

"See, nothing to hide," I said, raising my hands high above
my head as I turned slowly. Goldie also turned.

We eyed each other. *Let's get this motherfucker.*

I faced him and jumped in surprise to see him already sitting
on the hood with his dick out his pants. *What the fuck?* I knew
right then his slick ass wasn't as drunk as I thought.

"Now, we're sorry," I said softly, stepping forward to stroke
his dick. "Right, Goldie?"

She stepped up with a smile I knew was fake as she stroked
his thigh and brought his free hand up to press against her full
ass. "Yes, I am so sorry, Daddy," she said, soft as hell.

His dick got even harder in my hand. "You bitches gone
make me cum all over myself," he said, pressing the gun into the
soft flesh of my gut.

I gasped like it pleasured me instead of scared the shit out of me. I held his dick tighter. "So if we take care good care of you, we can go?" I asked.

"Shut up," he snapped, like *he* had a reason to be irritated. "I'm trying to figure out which one sucks and which one fucks."

Goldie made a face as she eyed his short, fat dick.

My eyes shot to his face. Damn. I knew he saw her. This ass-hole could not take rejection. *At all.*

"You got a problem, bitch?" he asked, backhanding her across the face.

WHAP!

Goldie's body twisted around from the force of his blow.

He twisted the gun to point it at her.

Shit!

"No!" I shouted, punching him in his exposed nuts hard as fuck.

"Fucking no-good, cunt-ass bitch," he roared, bending over in pain.

POW!

The bullet went into the wall, causing chunks of brick to fly.

I grabbed his wrist and fought to push his arm up high in the air. He recovered and grabbed my throat with his free hand.

Goldie stormed over with titties swinging to pummel his face and stomach with blows. "Motherfuckin' dirty-ass-cop," she muttered as she swung out on his ass.

As soon as he freed my throat I turned and lifted my leg to jam my knee down on his hanging nuts again.

"Fucking bitches are jumpin' me," he screamed at the top of his lungs.

POW!

The gun fired up into the air and we both froze to see if one of us got shot. Dumb-ass move with the gun pointed to the sky. Dumb, wrong-ass move.

He rammed his elbow down on the top of my head so hard I

thought he snapped my neck. I stumbled back on my heels and fell against the funky, grimy Dumpster that he probably planned to dump our dead bodies in.

Goldie grabbed his wrist and bit that motherfucker. *Hard.*

The gun fell from his hand and landed between her feet as he used both his hands to box Goldie like she was a man.

"Kick the gun by your foot, Goldie!" I screamed.

He slapped her but she looked down and then kicked the gun toward me.

It spiraled like a top on the ground and I lunged for it, just as he pushed Goldie's naked body out the way and stepped forward to get it. I rolled over onto my side with that bitch in my hands just as Goldie jumped on his back and started punching him all about the head.

"Move, Goldie," I screamed at the top of my lungs, aiming for his head.

He kept coming. "You ain't got the balls, bitch!"

Goldie kept fighting him.

Shit. The bullet could go through both of them.

I lowered the gun and aimed for his dick just as he reared his foot back to kick me.

POW!

Blood and flesh splattered against my face.

"You . . . black . . . bitch . . ."

Goldie finally jumped down off his back.

He took another step and I raised the gun to a spot just between his eyes.

POW!

I closed my eyes as his blood and brains sprayed out the back of his head against the hood of my car, our clothes, the wall, and Goldie's body.

We both screamed as his body slumped to the ground like the deadweight that motherfucker was.

I let the gun and my head fall to the ground as I struggled to get air in my lungs and calm to my nerves.

Detective Dick learned the same lesson about revenge that I had. His dead body was lying in that hole he thought he dug for me and Goldie.

Epilogue

We didn't get charged for the dirty cop's murder. We didn't even know if anybody found his body yet. Never heard a thing about it. Lord knows, I was all over the news waiting for the story to break and for our asses to get locked up. Especially me. *I* shot the gun. *I* killed him.

That night Goldie told me not to worry about it. Maybe it was another one of her favors from her powerful list of clients. Maybe it was karma. I didn't know. I was just grateful because there wasn't a damn thing about me cut out for life behind bars.

But what I did know, what I couldn't deny, was the fact that if we didn't pull together he would've killed both of us instead of it being the other way around. Two enemies had to stick together to make it out alive.

Just like we had to put the body in the Dumpster, burn our clothes, and toss the gun in the river.

It's funny, after all the shooting I did at the range, I still won't ever be ready for blowing a motherfucker's head off. It's been three months and I still have nightmares about it, waking up shaking and shit and thinking I'm covered in his blood.

That thing I had to swallow the most was just how right Michel had been. I never saw my enemy coming because my attention was locked on my own revenge. I was so ashamed that even in the face of danger I was ready to hand Goldie over to the bastard who tormented me. Even after knowing she saved my ass from those drug charges. Damn near got both of us killed. Revenge didn't get me anywhere but damn near in my grave.

I was young and still learning, but I would never forget the lesson of forgiveness.

Me and Goldie, we ain't friends. Too much shit done went down between us. It was fucked up what she did with Make$ but twice she had the chance to completely destroy me and she didn't do it. Not with my arrest for drug charges and not with the murder of that cop. Both times she saved me from jail. How the fuck could I hate her after that? I'd have to be psycho to still hold a grudge. And now I realize I wasn't doing a damn thing but hurting myself. So I gave her the BlackBerry back.

Michel and Eve forgave me for kicking they crazy asses to the curb while I was on Mission: Destroy Goldie. Yummy Entertainment was back as strong as ever, just like our friendship. The Three Musketeers. Fuck with us.

I was working on my issues with my parents, especially my father, but I loved them and I would never turn my back on them completely. I just went back to the way things were. See you when I see you!

I wasn't ready to forgive Mr. Alvarez, but I think anyone could understand *that*.

I didn't work for Goldie anymore on the booking agency side. Didn't have a clue if she was still a madam, but I wouldn't doubt it considering not a damn thing changed about her and Has's lifestyle.

Yep, Goldie and Has was still going strong. I heard they did get married in the Bahamas, with their best friends at they side. I couldn't do shit but wish them the best and leave them to their lives.

Besides, I had my own to live and I felt like I was *finally* ready to stop doing it alone. I was ready to finally try something different.

"Baby, you ready?"

I turned on the balcony of our suite in the Bahamas, knowing I looked good in my bikini, as I looked at Jamal, Mr. Grown and Sexy, standing there in his swim trunks, holding out his hand to me. I smiled as I took it and let him lead me out the suite to finish our weeklong vacation.

Acknowledgments

I have dreamed of being an author since I was a little girl, and to see that dream accomplished took the support, respect, and guidance of many special people in my life. Every day and with every book, I grow as a writer, and I will continue to grow and improve until I type "The End" on my very last book.

To my editor, Allegra Ben-Amotz: Words cannot express how thankful and impressed I am at your hard work, insight, and speed on this project. Thank you times a million to you and the entire Touchstone team.

To my agent, Claudia Menza: Thanks for helping me keep every layer of my hectic writing career in order, and thank you for taking time to answer all of my questions about the business. I adore you.

To my family, friends, associates (and even my enemies)— thank you. I see every experience in life as a learning lesson and you all have taught me something. Ha!

Of course huge thanks to the readers, book clubs, book-stores/vendors, bloggers, and reviewers that support *all* works of fiction.

Lastly, here's to those before me who had dreams that they worked hard to make a reality and inspired me to do the same.

M.M.

Dear Readers,

Two stories down and one to go in the Real Wifeys trilogy about three wifeys who each face their own issues and struggles in three separate hoods in my hometown of Newark, New Jersey.

In Real Wifeys: On the Grind, Goldie, a stripper living in low-rise projects, the long-term girlfriend of an older man, had to learn that her self-respect was more important than money and power.

In Real Wifeys: Get Money, Luscious, an ex-stripper/college dropout living in a luxury apartment in downtown Newark, is the wifey of a platinum selling rap artist. Tormented by her blazing desire for payback, she almost destroys herself in her bitter quest for revenge against Goldie.

Last up in the trilogy is the story of Sophie Alvarez, aka Suga. There's more info to come on this wifey of a man deep into a criminal lifestyle.

Just wait until you read the story of Luscious' ex-childhood friend who adds a twist to the trilogy that brings it full circle and ends it all with a bang.

I can't wait.

MM

About the Author

Meesha Mink is the coauthor of the popular and bestselling Hoodwives series (*Desperate Hoodwives*, *Shameless Hoodwives*, and *The Hood Life*). *Real Wifeys: Get Money* is the second book in her solo Real Wifeys trilogy, preceded by *Real Wifeys: On the Grind*. Mink also is the acclaimed and bestselling author of both Romance fiction and commercial mainstream fiction as Niobia Bryant. The Newark, New Jersey, native currently lives in South Carolina, where she writes fulltime and is busy at work on the final book in the Real Wifeys trilogy.

CONNECT WITH MEESHA:

Websites:	www.meeshamink.com
	www.niobiabryant.com
E-mail:	meeshamink@yahoo.com,
	niobia_bryant@yahoo.com
Twitter:	InfiniteInk
Facebook Fan Page:	Niobia Bryant & Meesha Mink
Shelfari:	Unlimited_Ink (Meesha Mink &
	Niobia Bryant)

And for more on the best-selling Hoodwives trilogy, please visit: www.hoodwives.com